AF661048

AND SO I LIVED

notionpress.com

AND SO I LIVED

MAHESH UBHAYAKAR

notionpress
.com

Notion Press

Old No. 38, New No. 6,

McNichols Road, Chetpet,

Chennai - 600 031

First Published by Notion Press 2015

ISBN: 978-93-52061-60-0

The cover illustration is courtesy of a photograph published of my actual damaged train coach in the FRONTLINE magazine of The HINDU group. The coach was photographed by Shri.V.Sudershan, their official photographer.

To the Indomitable Spirit in the
Diesel Locomotive Sheds of India!

To you, Readers, who will help take this
movement to its logical end!

ACKNOWLEDGEMENTS

1. My Friends, Relatives & Well-wishers (Sri. Anand Kilpady, Late Smt. Sita Baindoor, Late Sri. Ajit Kalyanpur, the Ugrankars…) who stood by me during my crisis hour.
2. Dr K. Mohan Iyer, Dr Aarti Prasad, Dr K.S.Prabhakar, Dr Pramod and Geetha Shanbhag and all who lifted me from the ashes & helped me to recover.
3. To the Late Shri Radhakrishna S. Kalawar, whose initiative put me on this incredible Journey of enlightenment and willpower, turning me into an achiever.
4. My darling cats who bloomed and faded like flowers, in their short lives, delighting and providing much needed succour.
5. To the Jains and all communities from Lalitpur, Jhansi, who rescued us after the train disaster and nourished us till help came over.
6. To the Diesel Locomotive Shed, Krishnarajapuram, Bangalore, for helping me to find my true calling and experiencing the Life's structure.
7. My publishers – Notion Press and my book Editor, for having the patience, and then the swiftness to deliver.
8. The Computer, the Internet, the interface that made my world smaller, better.

And above all, to my family, forced to support me in my endeavour.

A NOTE TO THE READERS

Hi, I am Sachin Khanauji, the fictitious protagonist cum narrator who survived a horrendous train accident, and lived! I am taking a huge, but calculated risk, to tell this story of an incredible journey, which could be dubbed a celebration of life, a second chance at it or was it the third (the Life Insurance Company having declined to insure me)?

This book is PERSPIRED from some true events, genuine problems, real situations and many a rumour. It is INSPIRED by what could actually hold good for India in the future.

I have tried to keep the narration crisp with required detailing at some places, and have also kept the (in) convenience of a glossary for abbreviations. There are technical, medical, grammatical and other inaccuracies, which may please be forgiven, and treated as a part of this fiction. Rather than as a documentary, I have written it like a story, an unbelievably believable story.

The readers are requested to experience and imagine themselves in each situation. Please read it, incident by incident, and do not indulge in any high expectation or speculation. Just go with the flow and you will find it all co-related, intent on laying the foundation for the final mission.

In the Indian Railways, at most times, a crude and holistic (than textbook) approach is required to handle matters. Consequently I have kept the English dialect also intentionally crude, keeping with the story's prevalent atmosphere, to get the right impact. Paragraphing is less and a long sentence is made to combine two or three sentences, for speedy, continuous but understandable reading.

Lastly, I request the connoisseurs of English to take a vacation from high-class hip English and read this as an earthy, middle-class version.

Prepare to learn about, probably, the world's most difficult industrial activity, or how an umbrella can save a woman's modesty or the first rule to stay pretty. Experience the heart-rending to the howlarious or the sublime to the utterly ridiculous! Feel the unique, bizarre, ugly and beautiful world of Diesel Locomotive Sheds of India.

Thanking you all in anticipation,
Yours Truly,

Mahesh G Ubhayakar

CONTENTS

1. The Factual Nightmare – The Accident Rewound! 1
2. The Survival – The Rebound! 6
3. The Homecoming, Bedridden and Aground! 19
4. The Second Operation – The Turnaround! 27
5. The Appointment – The Railways Background! 32
6. The Diesel Shed – I Lived to be Doomed & Hellbound? 39
7. The Train Journey – Medley of Jokes Resound! 43
8. The Shed and its Atmosphere – Spellbound! 50
9. Shed Developments and some Incidents - Expound! 56
10. Computers, Cricket, Scrap & the Sick (Ening) Foreground! 66
11. A.I.O.S – Inbound and Outbound! 73
12. Back in shed – The Battleground! 81
13. The New Office & a Taste of Accounts – Profound! 89
14. Hooked, Booked & My Goose is Cooked? – Life's Newfound! 96
15. Honeymooned - Out of Bound! 114
16. Accounts & Office Problems Rise & Pound! 120

17. Divide and Confound!	132
18. A Beautiful Coincidence, Unbound!	141
19. Contracts & Problems that Hound!	143
20. Workshops Crowned, Sheds Frowned!	157
21. Railway's Problems, Unwound!	169
22. Scams, Problems that Astound!	184
23. History of Diesel Locos, Lost & Found!	193
24. The Shed, as it Blossomed Around!	199
25. Delays in Wage Revision, Problems Compound!	206
26. "Mogri" – Affections & Emotions go Around!	213
27. Myself, Homebound!	223
28. The Book, The Ideas Abound!	230
29. The Goodies, a Merry-Go-Round!	236
30. The Swansong – with full Lights & Surround Sound!	250
Glossary of Abbreviations	*255*

1

THE FACTUAL NIGHTMARE – THE ACCIDENT REWOUND!

"One Ace," I said, removing one of my last three cards, and keeping it face down, 'looking' confidently into the eyes of Mr Nayan, without flinching or blinking.

He reached out, looking at me and the card, overturned it and as it was actually an Ace, he kept it along with his scores of cards.

"Two Jacks," I murmured, sounding less confident and lowering my stare.

Without hesitation, he grabbed them, and found to his dismay, that they were indeed Jacks. Immediately his wife, Bindu, blurted out, "Donkey! Donkey! Donkey!" and hugged him as he broke into a sheepish smile of acknowledgement.

The card game was called "Bluff" and Nayan was very good at it, especially at the end game, and always made a 'Donkey' of all the other players.

Mrs Varalakshmi, sitting to my right near the window, opposite Bindu, and Pratap Singh, a Junior Hockey International player to my left, broke into a smile as Nayan, who had just taught us how to play the game, was left holding the cards for the first time.

-|-|-|-

We were going to Delhi by the K.K Express Train in the IInd Class Ladies compartment (a coupe, next to the entrance with six seats/berths) and had boarded at its starting point – Bangalore City – on the 17th of April, 1989. Five of our tickets got confirmed at the last minute due to cancellation by five ladies, and the first five tickets waiting for berths in RAC (Reservation against Cancellation) were confirmed into the Ladies compartment, regardless of gender.

Varalakshmi was to undergo a Bank Promotional Training at Delhi and I had to report to the Ministry of Defence in Delhi, for my first employment posting at the age of 23. Pratap was returning to Haryana, after a training camp in South India. Opposite to us were newlyweds, Nayan and Bindu, who were going on their honeymoon. Both were happy-go-lucky, quite portly, and seemed to have come from well-off and well-fed families. They still looked like a bride and groom in their designer outfits, with her 'mehendi' still bright. They made no bones about their public display of affection, and were always hugging and talking to each other, while we consciously tried to look elsewhere. But the hugging was discreet in that it was not face to face, but hugs from the sides, as Bindu would occasionally rest her head on Nayan's shoulder and Nayan, on her head.

In that decade, we were not exposed to even subtle displays of affection, and luckily my acting skills came in handy in convincingly 'dodging' the "show" as I slowly became comfortable with the proceedings. Mrs Varalakshmi found succour in a book. Pratap, who was feeling awkward, struck up a conversation with me to offset it. The seat to the right of Nayan was empty as its occupant had vacated it at Bhopal. On the previous night, the bride and groom were awake till 3 a.m, talking in low, unobtrusive tones. Their conversation bordered on light, humorous talk, as Bindu warned Nayan not to disclose his vast properties or else her father would not give them a decent share of his wealth, as he had planned. Thankfully, they only hugged and talked, and went no further.

At Bhopal, around noon, I excused myself, intending to sleep on the upper berth. Mr Nayan stopped me, holding my arm in an affectionate grip, "Arre, what will you do sleeping; the train is five hours late. Let us play cards to pass time and feel better." He rushed out and came back with a new pack within no time.

I was pleasantly surprised as they had hardly slept for three hours on the previous night, and still preferred to play instead of catching up on some sleep. All three of us tried to excuse ourselves as we did not know any card games, to which Nayan told that he would teach us. And that's when we started playing, as Pratap only watched.

-:-:-:-

After Nayan became the 'Donkey' he got ready to deal the cards again, when the otherwise slow moving train started to speed up. At this point of time, around 02:35 p.m, Nayan looked at his new gold-plated watch, remarking that finally the driver seemed to have realized that the train was uncomfortably late.

Two minutes later, we heard a loud sound, followed by some more sounds, and within seconds we felt a jerk as our coach tilted to one side with a hissing sound. Fine dust fumes of crushed jelly stones came in and started engulfing the compartment. I knew the train had derailed and was more excited, than scared. I saw Varalakshmi freeze in panic, as Nayan and Bindu hugged each other out of fear. I was about to get up when I was thrown into the air. My head hit the side of the opposite upper berth and I blacked out, unconscious.

The train had been approaching a bridge in Lalitpur district (in Jhansi Division of Uttar Pradesh) and having speeded up, in conjunction with intense vibrations, had derailed! Twelve coaches had derailed, of which eight fell off the bridge into the dry river bed. Due to the momentum and commuted impact, our coach got uncoupled before the bridge, catapulted and became almost vertical on one side, like a snake's hood, before it tilted and came crashing down on the rocky side slope leading to the bridge. It rolled down the slope and came to a halt, careening to one side on the flat ground! Around 45% of the coach was crushed like a cigarette pack, and later we learnt that our coach had the most fatalities, whereas the coaches on the river bed had more injuries. The pantry car was thrown the farthest on the river bed, its front crushed and bent like an ostrich's head underground. None of its occupants survived and the gas cylinders went up in flames, bursting in turns.

The accident occurred on 18th April, 1989 at 02:37 p.m (Tuesday) in the town of Lalitpur. Fortunately, it was a holiday due to Mahaveer Jayanthi and the locals were taking out celebratory processions. On hearing of the accident, they immediately sprung into action in an organized manner. They broke into smaller groups; one group rushed to get gas cutting and other extricating equipment, while another scampered to mobilize medicines and doctors. A third group, including ladies, hurried to hotels and packed food, water and other refreshments. Yet another group went to arrange for transportation and so on.

If not for the presence of the locals of Lalitpur, and their timely and collective effort, there wouldn't have been that many survivors. There was no term such as 'disaster management' heard, especially in Lalitpur town. But their hearts and minds worked in tandem with their humanitarian acumen, and they managed the situation to a considerable extent, until the nearby Army Battalion deployed their men and doctors with the necessary equipment, including a portable X-Ray Machine, and took over. The Police arrived last to take custody of the personal effects of the passengers. By then the locals had caught/thrashed/chased away some rogues who were trying to loot the jewellery of the injured passengers on the pretext of helping them.

2

THE SURVIVAL – THE REBOUND!

I gained consciousness and slowly opened my eyes, duly remembering the train had derailed. I was sitting on some pile, and my posture made me feel that I was sitting on a slanted throne, my head bent forward, facing the watch on my left hand which rested on my thigh. The glass had broken and the second hand was missing. The hour and minute hand showed 05:40 p.m. which meant the watch was working; otherwise it should have stopped at 02:37 p.m. So, I had been unconscious for almost three hours.

I weakly lifted my head up to see that a dome light glass securing clamp had come off on one side and the dome was dangling in front of my forehead. I recognized it as the lamp in the toilet which I had used in the morning. A small skipped heartbeat and a shiver down the spine made me realize that the ladies' compartment wall had broken, as well as the toilet framework. Having been hurled into the toilet, I was now sitting over debris, luggage and what not. As I looked around for my co-passengers with my limited neck movement, I could not see anything. But as I looked down between my legs, I saw that two children, maybe siblings - an elder sister and her five year old brother - sprawled, stomach down over the slanting debris with their faces looking towards me, but with their eyes closed. Their faces, dress and exposed body parts were white due to the jelly stone dust on them, and the boy was still, as blood had oozed and dried from his nose. The girl had blood splattered teeth and was gasping faintly, her head bobbing up and down slightly, with every gasp. The bobbing slowed after some time, giving an impression that she was on her last few breaths. I tried to reach out to her but found I could not move my body, let alone budge it. Only my head and hands had some limited movement. I was very weak but felt no emotion or pain during this heart-wrenching scenario. Within moments, her head stopped bobbing and she was still. Helplessly, I watched her die.

With some effort, I lifted my head a bit higher and found there was a big crack though which I could see daylight. As it was summer, it wasn't going to get dark early. As I shifted my view beyond the crack, I could see somebody's back with his hands on his hips. He was standing outside and appeared to be overseeing something.

I called out, mustering whatever energy possible, "O, Bhai Saheb!"

He heard something and turned around with a fast, whiplash-like action, wide-eyed, trying to spot the direction of the sound as it was difficult to see anything inside from the bright, sunny outside.

I moved my right hand fingers up and down and called "O, Bhaaai!"

To this, he shouted out five words in Hindi which reverberate in my mind even today – "Idhar Bhi Ek Zinda Hai" which means "There is one more alive here!" He then asked me to hold on for some time since the extrication was going on somewhere else, and carefully lowered a glass bottle of water tied to a string with another's help. I could hold the bottle but not lift it to my mouth.

Shortly, I heard excited voices, scurrying feet as a window grill was cut within seconds, and hands reached out to lift me up. I kept yelling, "Do not straighten my legs; something has happened there!" They gently lifted out my lean, 6 feet 2 inch frame and carried me to an open area with grass, and put me down on my back, with my legs still bent, and went back for more rescues.

The onlookers stood staring at me and I found that my legs had turned weak and were tilting towards the right, and there was a danger of falling and aggravating the injury I was nursing. I could barely hold on, and asked for help. One person held my legs, while a couple of others went towards a tree and cut a branch to a convenient shape, so that I could rest my leg from tilting more on the right and hold it in shape. I was relieved and fell asleep. Sometime later, I woke up to see it was getting dark and an Army doctor was dressing my wounds with several bandages, including a huge one on my left wrist. I could smell the spirit being applied on my wounds, but neither felt the pain, nor the burning of the spirit being applied. Again, I fell asleep as the doctor injected some pain killer or sedative.

Next, I woke up in a Mahaveer Jayanthi Pandal, or a Marquee, which had been turned into a makeshift casualty ward, where the Army Doctors took some X-rays near my hip and knees with their portable machine. Again I fell asleep.

When I woke up, I was in a train, on an upper side berth on my back, with my legs still bent, but resting on the right side wall of the train. I found I could only stretch my left leg. It was dark and the night lamps were on. On some berths, I could faintly see people lying on their backs, fully covered up to their faces with white cloth. As they were still and wobbled along with the coaches, it was obvious that they were corpses! I could see ghostly outlines of soldiers wearing berets and holding rifles, standing guard.

Next, I woke up at Jhansi Railway Hospital – a 13-bed hospital where more than 35 patients with grievous injuries were kept. I was lucky to get a bed and that too next to a wall to rest my bent leg. As I was unattended, a 55 year old Railway peon named Kantilal, recovering from a stomach infection, looked after me and kept my purse safely with him. I came across people asking for my name, address and phone number, and presumed they would contact and inform my family through my neighbour's phone. Kantilal discouraged me from talking to them stating they were advocates wanting to send requests to hire them to seek compensation from the Railways, and least bothered about my family. I again fell asleep before I could explain the details to Kantilal to contact my parents.

-|--|--|-

Back home, my father, who was a heart patient, and my neighbor, Prasanna, had gone twice to Bangalore City Railway Station in vain to get any information about me - whether I was dead or alive, injured or immobile and unable to contact them. My mother maintained her composure, as always, with quiet dignity. Gathering some money, my father flew along with Prasanna to Delhi, where a relative drove them directly to the Railway Station, where they gathered that I was admitted at the Jhansi Railway Hospital. They were given free transit by 1st class by the next available train which reached Jhansi at 02:00 a.m in the wee hours, where some local youths had camped to guide the relatives of patients. The Station Masters were given instructions to stop all trains at Lalitpur for more than three minutes, since the accident victims' relatives could be on board. The on-duty Station Master approached my father on his own, introduced himself pointing to his name badge, only to assure them that the youths camping were reliable, in case they was searching for accident victims. Two youths led them to the Railway Hospital premises, where another group had camped in a makeshift tent to guide relatives, and also take care of patients, until their relatives turned up. They confirmed my presence in the hospital, enquired whether my father and Prasanna had had dinner, and served them hot tea before escorting them to my bed, duly indicating that Kantilal was taking care of me.

The next day, I woke up, pleasantly surprised, and exchanged our ordeals. But I was surprised that no one had contacted them since many people had sought my name and address, even though the Railways didn't bother to. They had brought even spare clothes for me as I was in the same pant, and bare chested, since my blood-soaked shirt and baniyan had to be cut open. Kantilal gave them my purse in which about Rs.400 and my train ticket were intact, as he had been discharged and had to attend duty. And off he went, wishing me an early recovery without a hint of any expectancy of gratitude or gratuity from us for his noble services.

The fact that we were looked after by locals and a sick Railway Peon for needs other than medical, with hardly any involvement by the Railways saddened me. They talk about Disaster Management – is it only about going all out to resurrect trains and services, making pathetic attempts to shift the injured to hospitals, giving free tickets to the relatives or other small mercies, like free medical treatment?

No attempt was made to seek my address or contact my parents. There should have been end-to-end planning. Even any ex-gratia announced by the Government, is received after months, if lucky. What about the immediate basic needs for the badly injured person's survival, or the redressal of emotional problems, till some relatives take over? I later heard that, when a senior Railway Officer's father-in-law was hospitalized, the understaffed and overworked Welfare Inspectors and other staff were sent to the hospital during duty hours, and they even stayed the nights. This means 'disaster management' is existent only to cater to one's personal disasters or 'emergencies'. In such cases, there is end-to-end planning! What a disaster!

-:-:-:-

Prasanna and my father were contemplating breakfast when we saw an army of civilians entering the hospital. Within moments, we realized that we were UNDER ATTACK – an Attack of an unexpected kind – an Attack of hospitality and humanity.

The army, mostly comprising of Jain businessmen, attacked us with boxes of seedless grapes, cans of milk, 'samosas', 'kachoris', 'jalebis', 'idlis' and the like. In fact, the quantities were huge, and they competed with one another to thrust them into the patient/relative's hands or to keep them at their feet, not allowing them to refuse. Prasanna lifted one box of grapes to give it to a nearby patient's relative, but he shook his head with folded hands, pointing at three boxes lying beside him. They came, they gave and they vanished! But they conquered our hearts and taught us the Art of Giving! We were unprepared for this kind of an attack and had no other option but to surrender. My father said that the Jains are known to be shrewd businessmen, but when it came to philanthropic acts during such calamities, they don't hold back and just let go like this. The accident victims didn't need money at that time, as treatment was free by the Railways, but they required these bare necessities to survive and to be presentable. Medicines taken on empty stomachs would have unwanted side effects.

"Well, that takes care not only of breakfast, but also lunch and evening snacks," my father gloated, as he relished all the items in view.

Nuns from a nearby church came over, prayed for us and offered soothing words. They asked us about the nature of our ordeal, and, being in delirium due to pain, I complained that this was paining and that was hurting, and that my right bum had swollen to twice its size! It seems (Prasanna told me later) that I joked that my otherwise small butt had now become sexy!

Another battalion of Jains raided us late in the morning and bombarded us with tea, coffee, clothes, towels, bags, and suitcases.

How I wish battles and wars were like this!

Shortly after they left, a bespectacled 30 year old man, unable to walk, and ready to collapse with grief, was helped by two people to sit at the corner of my bed, near my leg. He could not speak, kept his hands folded, and looked expectantly towards me, trembling and hiccupping due to his continuous sobbing. His calm escort introduced him as Mr Pradhan and himself as his brother. He said that Mr Pradhan was Varalakshmi's husband. It seems they found a statement given by one Pratap Singh, who had survived the accident with a hairline leg fracture and other minor injuries, at the accident help-desk. He had stated that he had been in the ladies' compartment at the time of the accident, and that no one else had survived in that compartment. Nayan and Bindu had perished on the spot. The upper berths had come crashing down on his right, and he saw Varalakshmi getting crushed under them. A blood soaked and unconscious Sachin Khanauji had caught his hand in a vice-like grip while the coach was toppling, and he had somehow wriggled out immediately. When the coach came to a halt after derailing, he had fallen out of the ladies compartment, which was totally smashed along with several other compartments. On getting up, he could spot only the bodies of Nayan and Bindu, still hugging each other, and Varalakshmi's torso below, crushed and twisted. The police authorities had cremated some of the bodies, duly taking their photos in colour. The help-desk had those photos, the faces of some marred beyond recognition. "Both of us could not identify Varalakshmi's photo even after going through it several times. Then we learnt that you had survived and came over, hoping against hope that she could be alive and you may have seen something."

They were crestfallen on learning that I was totally unconscious for three hours from the time the coach derailed. My father asked them whether there were any ornaments like a necklace/earring/nose ring, through which they could identify the body. However, there were no ornaments in any of the photos. Maybe they were all stolen as they were not supposed to remove anything while photographing. However, he mentioned that she had a unique 'mangalsutra' which was recognizable. When I heard this, something flashed in my mind and I told the brother also to sit down as I narrated what I remembered.

As the ladies' compartment was near the door, and Varalakshmi was sitting near the window, next to that door, a thief had made an observation at Itarsi Station. Just when the train started to depart, picking up reasonable speed, this thief, holding the handle bar with his left hand, let his body revolve towards the window, and in one motion, thrust his right hand in and grabbed at her mangalsutra. As she screamed, he pulled his hand out, jumped off the train and ran away. I was talking to Pratap at that time and Nayan saw the hand coming in, but was too late in his attempt to catch the thief's hand. He immediately went for the chain, but didn't pull it as he'd realized it was too late. The train had gathered enough speed for anyone to jump out and chase the thief, and by the time the train came to a halt, there would be no chance.

But something miraculous had happened! Varalakshmi was reading a book at that time, and she had the habit of fiddling with her mangalsutra, while reading. When the thief's hand came through the window, she panicked in reflex, and her hands clutched at the mangalsutra, which broke and stayed in her grasp. As the other passengers rushed towards our compartment on hearing the scream, she said that everything was fine and packed the broken mangalsutra in a Delhi tour pamphlet, placing it at the bottom of her vanity bag.

They left with an inconsolable Mr Pradhan. I felt very bad on learning about Nayan, Bindu and Varalakshmi, and introspected that if Nayan had not called me down to play cards, you would not have been reading this book.

What I learnt months later from my mother, who knew Mr. Pradhan and had seen Varalakshmi once, was heart-rending. I don't know whether to call it cruel fate or destiny. She was due for the training the previous year, but had requested for a postponement as her child was very young, less than two years of age. So she opted for the next year (the ill-fated year), and though she was eligible for first class, she preferred second class as she felt safe in a ladies' compartment. Ironically, in the accident, there was not a scratch on any of the first class coaches. It seems Mr Pradhan went through the photos again and recognized Varalakshmi through the design of her saree, as the saree itself was blood soaked and was no longer its original colour. They found the vanity bag intact, in the police station at Lalitpur, and also the packed, broken mangalsutra, though some cosmetics were missing.

-|-|-|-

Another team of Railway Doctors arrived at the Jhansi hospital, and there were ego problems and other frictional issues with the incumbent doctors. I only hoped that the interests and well-being of the patients were not compromised.

A doctor read out the history sheet clipped to my bed, pausing in between to remove the big bandage on my left wrist, and it turned out that my watch was bandaged at the accident venue lest somebody steal it. He said that apart from the other open wounds, including the large one on my right hip, three nails from a broken wooden structure seemed to have lacerated my right cheek, with the first nail piercing the right side juncture of the right eye, which was blood red though my eye-sight seemed normal. He said that the bones just next to my testicles on either side had cracked, due to the impact of the hit on the hip, and no cast could be put there. They had to set/heal in a lying condition (lying was not at all a problem; the problem was being unable to turn sideways or sit). He also said that the portable X-ray machine was operated in an open air condition, causing more exposure, due to which the big flesh wound on my right hip suggested some internal injury, which was not clear. As the right buttock had swollen, he wanted a proper X-ray to be taken after I reached my hometown. He also said my wounds were healing fast because I was young, only 23, and also because of the hot summer. He said that a deep gash near the right heel would take time to heal as it had an eye-shaped open split. There were holes in my knees which also had to be examined properly. He re-directed me to the Railway Hospital at Demblur Division in my home city.

After he left, I took stock of my condition and found that I could straighten my left leg, and move it fully. While the right leg could move, I could not straighten the knee, as the hip would pain excruciatingly if I tried. I had to keep my right knee to ankle portion perpendicular to the ground. The good thing was that in that position, the eye-shaped gash near the right heel would not touch or rest on the bed, as the slightest touch or pressure, or even cold air, was causing an unbearable, burning pain there.

But I was relieved and happy to count to five on each my hands and legs. Thankfully, my two discharge outlets seemed to be intact, even though some sharp things had 'clawed' onto my behind. I also noticed that, when the pain-killer/sedative effects diminished, my memory, vocabulary and diction, in both English and Hindi, had improved more than normal. It seems that when some instincts are down, the others kind of make up for them by working better than their normal capacity. That is why you see differently-abled persons making remarkable achievements.

-:-:-:-

I told my father that all my original certificates were in a big, thick plastic cover in my suitcase, at which he went to Lalitpur Police Station, where a mountain of luggage was kept, and searched for the cover with the help of the police. He found it by spotting the plastic cover which was lying in the open, with my blood-soaked clothes from which all my hidden money was missing. He grabbed only the cover and returned late in the evening. Though the outside of the cover was blood-soaked, all my certificates were intact and unblemished.

Meanwhile, at the hospital, three dignified looking Railway officials had come to inquire about the accident. I learnt that it was a prelude to the Railway Minister's sister visiting the hospital later in the day, as also the Minister's impending visit the next day. They asked me whether I had seen or felt anything unusual before the accident. They were impressed with my command over English and Hindi. I told them that before Bhopal Station, the train had stopped for several minutes, and I had got down to see that some nine coaches away, people were bending, looking and gesturing at that coach's undercarriage. Some of my curious and adventurous co-passengers had gone to investigate, as they could make their way back through the vestibules, in case the train started. It seems there was some abnormal sound/ vibration felt in that coach and somebody had pulled the chain. On examination, some Railwayman said that it was a minor problem which could be taken care of in Delhi as the train was already five hours late. The officials seemed to have struck gold and were fighting to take notes. Finally they spoke to a doctor in low tones and left. Soon after, I was given an injection, and I fell asleep.

The Railway Minister's sister arrived and Prasanna tried to wake me up, but though I opened my eyes, I could only see a ghost image of a lady in front of me with other ghosts standing around her. I could neither hear, nor see clearly, and nor could I make any movements. My whole body had gone limp and though I could think, I could not talk or act. Somebody lifted my hand and kept a wad of notes on my palm, closing my fingers over it, and they all went to the next bed. This is the price I paid for my big mouth, and for telling the truth, I felt.

In the night, I was discharged, to be taken by a late night train to Demblur, when I wanted to do one important thing – the big job. I learnt, to my shock, that only one bed-pan was available in the whole hospital, as they hardly had immobile patients. It was under use somewhere, and the ward boy told me to hold my horses. The very thought of using that pan stopped my urge for some time. Then I gathered 'courage' and relented. Some huge relief-filled moments later, I was washed up using a hose pipe with some unspeakable arrangement, to avoid splashing water onto the bed. I wondered if the Jain army came to know, it would have rained bed-pans the next day. However, with the help of the locals, my father purchased a urine pot and a bed pan.

3

THE HOMECOMING, BEDRIDDEN AND AGROUND!

I was loaded into the night train, and reached my hometown, where a couple of my friends helped me out even as I got emotional on seeing them. The Railways had sent an ambulance, along with the Chief Medical Superintendent of Demblur Railway Hospital, who was waiting there. On seeing my condition, they recommended that I be admitted to a private hospital immediately, one which was hardly four kms away from home. The Railway hospital had limited facilities, and the Railway referral hospital was far away from my house. It was conveyed that we would have to pay initially, and everything would be reimbursed by the Railways. My father agreed as he had taken voluntary retirement one year early, just five months back, before which I had been eligible for free hospitalization in his office scheme.

While this talk was going on, I was loaded into this old, dilapidated ambulance which vibrated rigorously, when the engine was on and idling. I felt it could have been used like a hearse instead, as the vibrations wouldn't matter to its beneficiary. I begged the driver to put off the engine when stationary, and switch it on only when required to move the vehicle, as, during its movement, the vibrations reduced tolerably.

In the hospital, I was put in a two-bed ward on the first floor, with two benches, so that two patients' attendants could stay overnight. My mother came shortly with clothing and other items, and I extended my hand to her, shedding a tear while she remained rock solid. The other bed was empty.

The orthopaedic doctor came later, saw the Jhansi hospital records and talked politely. He wrote for X-rays and wanted them before he finished his rounds. I was taken by stretcher into the X-ray room, where the radiologist took some X-rays near the hip, knees and crotch, lastly lifted my right leg, which pained unbearably. I was back in the ward when the Doctor saw the X-rays and threw a fit. The Radiologist had taken one angle wrongly. He was supposed to have lifted the left leg, since it was obvious that the problem was in the right leg. I was again being taken to the X-ray room, when the electricity went off, and though there was a generator, it was not enough to power up the X-ray Machine. I was left, deserted in the corridor, near the X-ray room, where I lay bare on the steel stretcher, with a white bed sheet over me. To beat the cold steel, I tucked part of the bed sheet under me to the extent possible. Since mosquitoes were around, I covered my face also and looked like a corpse. After the 45 minute hardship, the power came on.

The Doctor saw the X-ray and said that there was a compound fracture of the right hip joint. There is a socket in the hip joint which holds a ball, and since this socket had broken into two pieces, the ball had come out and was dangling. It had to be operated early while the two fractures near my testicles had to set without a cast, as it could not be put there. There was no bone damage to the knees, and it seemed that the holes were slightly deep wounds which had healed appreciably.

Two days later, I was operated for over two and a half hours, and the anaesthesia was wearing out, as I was wheeled into my ward. My father said that I had shouted, "Doctor, you have cut off my legs," while still on the stretcher, and semi-conscious. When I was quite conscious, I saw that my right leg was hammered down straight and I could not move it at all. There was an 'L' shaped rod, inserted near the operated portion, to hold the structure as, due to my youth, the same pieces were resurrected and no metal rod or artificial material had been used. Next, there was some tube coming out of some hole near my right hip, leading to a big bottle under my bed, which was supposed to collect infected blood. Lastly, a pencil thick steel rod was hammered and pierced three inches below my knee in the centre, projecting evenly on either side, from where two nylon ropes led to a pulley affixed to the bed's foot end frame top, with a traction weight dangling on the outside. This was to prevent any deformity, like the shortening of a leg.

But due to the loss of blood during the operation, and pain in the operated area, I could not afford even the slightest body thrust. Even clearing my throat felt as if the operated area would burst. I could not cough, sneeze or even laugh. When I laughed, it was like "Hah…Hah…Hah" with about a second and a half gap between every "Hah." I had to sleep on my back, unable to turn to the side or sit. Only my left leg was normal. I had come down from 62 kgs to around 45 kgs. I was so weak and sensitive that even a vehicle horn outside agitated my mind. The Doctor said that my sciatic nerve was cut near the hip joint during the accident, but it had a regenerating capacity. So there was no need to worry.

On the other bed, a carefree, middle-aged, villager named Manjanna with back problems had just been admitted. He had to continuously sleep on his back, with a small traction on both legs, but with no body invasion. The traction was strapped on from his ankle down and he would wriggle one of his legs out, and sleep on his side the moment the doctor left the room.

He was used to relieving himself in the open in his village and hence, would go downstairs to ease himself, lying to all that he was going down for food. Once, doubting him, the Matron asked him where he was relieving himself when there was a toilet in his room. To that he said, "Downstairs!" wherein the matron panicked, since there was a small lawn in an isolated corner on the ground floor. He reassured her that since our toilet was a Western type one, he used to go to the Indian one on the ground floor. The Matron heaved a sigh of relief, but complained to the Doctor who came over.

"I told you to relieve yourself on the bed itself," he thundered. He then lowered his voice, "Look, Mr. Manjanna, if you want to stay here all your life, you can do whatever you want and we can make good money. But if you want a cure, you should be on traction on both legs for a week, and never get out of bed even for the toilet or a bath."

From then onwards, Manjanna became serious and sincere as he wanted to get out of the hospital at the earliest. But regarding the toilet, he was concerned about the smell, ensuring that his wife lit an 'agarbatti' each time he wanted to relieve himself. There was a small portable partition screen between us, and all others had to leave the room with only the attendant remaining, when either of us wanted to move our bowels. His wife was trained by the nurses on how to handle the bedpan and clean it. His parents were no more, and he was attended to by his wife full-time, with his mother-in-law commuting for food, clothes etc.

Once, his mother-in-law got a welcome idea, and asked her daughter to use a scented spray instead of agarbatti, as the ventilation for smoke was poor. Manjanna liked the idea and told her to use it from the next opportunity itself. So when next due and while he was on the 'job', his wife sprayed the scent in the air with a 'tuss, tuss' sound. After she washed him up, she again sprayed 'tuss, tuss' in the air, while Manjanna smiled, looked at the ceiling, enjoying the aroma and feeling proud about this 'scented' idea put forth by his ma-in-law.

Suddenly his innocent wife had a brainwave and thought, "Why not spray it on the main source of the smell itself?" She sprayed twice on his open source and took the bed pan to the toilet. The unsuspecting Manjanna thought she had put some more water and initially felt cold, but within seconds, the scent's alcohol base acted on the sensitive area, which also had a piles wound, and it started burning like hell. He suddenly yelled, "Aiyyo, Appa, Amma," and kept slap-patting his mouth, fast and hard, screaming, "Ava va va va va…," to which both, his wife and I, panicked as we had no inkling of what had happened. He kept yelling and his tearful wife rushed out to call the hospital staff who were already near the door, having heard the yelling. On asking, he would only point to his bum, look angrily at his wife and yell some more, saying, "My wife and her mother are trying to kill me and usurp my property; somebody do something. I am dying! Help me, Help me!"

The nurses asked me what had happened, to which I replied, "I have no idea, but the last I heard was the sound, 'tuss, tuss', after which he started shouting." They asked his wife what this 'tuss, tuss' was, when she showed them the scent bottle and what she had done. On realizing what had happened, and since there was no ward boy present, a nurse went and brought a ball of cotton and some cold water, and applied it in and around the affected area, and then she noticed the piles wound. Someone brought ice cubes and asked the wife to put it in a cloth and keep it pressed there. After some time, the burning subsided and Manjanna, exhausted and breathing hard, cried out with folded hands, "Amma, Nursamma, you are a Goddess, amma – a thousand thanks!" To this, the nurse said, "Since you think I am a Goddess, just listen! Nobody has ever died due to a burning sensation in the bum. Ok? And don't be angry with your wife. She only tried to do what she thought was best for you and because of her, your piles problem is now known, and we will treat you for that also. Ok?" Manjanna meekly nodded his head.

I don't know how I controlled my laughter as any attempt to laugh, cough or sneeze would exert pressure on my right hip, making it feel as if it would burst.

-:-:-:-

Meanwhile, the Chief Medical Superintendent of Demblur Railway Hospital was transferred due to some issues, including his inept handling of the Railway accident victims. To add to the misery, the ruling State Government, which had announced an ex-gratia to the accident victims, was ousted in a political coup and President's rule imposed. So, all the doors of remuneration seemed closed just when we were undergoing a financial turmoil. I also received some inland letters addressed to me from the hospital where I had been treated after the accident. They were from advocates who wanted to fight my case to seek compensation for a 'small percentage' of up to 30%. Now it dawned on me why people had asked for my name and address at Lalitpur/ Jhansi. But thankfully, the Railway Accident Tribunal awarded us Rs.21,600, i.e., Rs.1,600 for loss of luggage and Rs.20,000 towards physical deformity, based on the immaculate representation of my case, by my father, since many false claims also were made.

My father met another man there whose son, wife and parents had died in the accident. This man was shocked to learn that he, as per some Railway Act, was not entitled to get a single Rupee out of the Rupees one lakh compensation announced for each of the deceased, as he was employed and earning, and not dependent. This is how the dead are valued in a Railway accident!

-:-:-:-

The matron was irritated that I had kept lots of pillows brought from home, beside me, below my back and legs for proper positioning. She kept grumbling audibly about something or the other. One day, my father went to the staff room and told her sternly, "Madam, I don't know why you are grumbling. If you have any personal problem, please don't take it out in front of my son. See, my son was injured in a train accident and we are all physically, mentally, especially emotionally, psychologically and financially drained. Already there is so much of suffering that the last thing we need is unwanted complaints. If you want to grumble, which is not part of your profession, please do it out of my son's hearing." To this, the Matron said with folded hands, "Sir, I am very sorry. Recently my sister's son drove somebody's bike and had an accident in which the owner was riding pillion and badly injured. I thought that your son was also involved in some irresponsible driving accident. I had no idea about the train accident. Please forgive me, and I will treat him like my own child. "After that whenever she came to my room, she would caress my hair and talk to me. She asked my parents to take back all the pillows and arranged hospital pillows instead, changing them daily. She also warned the ward boys against taking any tips. At the time of my discharge, she gave me a red rose and told me, "All these days, I've been seeing you as 6'2" horizontal. The next time I see you, you should be 6'2" vertical and walking."

4

THE SECOND OPERATION – THE TURNAROUND!

I was discharged with traction to be used at my home. Many visitors came, and as days went by, the right leg lost normal sensation and developed hypersensitivity. It could not withstand even the slightest touch or vibration, and pained unbearably. It also changed colour from brown to bluish black, as if it was rotting, and felt like a log of wood, a liability. Also, as I was continuously on my back, I developed a bed sore, on learning of which, my dramatics mentor gave us a water bed that was lying idle at his home. This was a great relief and prevented further damage.

One of my father's free homeopathic hobby patients, Mr Manohar, when learning about my cut sciatic nerve, was shocked that nothing had been done. He enquired whether I had been able to move that leg before the operation. He satisfied himself that the functioning of the leg before the first operation, though limited, was unlike a sciatic nerve cut, as it would have paralyzed the leg, then and there. He exclaimed, "My God, something happened during the operation and you have been misguided. The sciatic nerve cannot regenerate. Only some smaller ones do. I think it is a pencil thick nerve which runs from the spine to the toe, and is responsible for the blood circulation, as well as for sending and receiving signals to/from the brain to order the function of the leg. You should sue the hospital!"

To this, my father replied that his main concern now was to resurrect me. Mr Manohar brought his mother's orthopaedic, Dr Murali, to my home for a second opinion, and he immediately called the hospital owner who was also a doctor, and told him to schedule an operation on the coming Sunday (so as to do it at leisure and with a free, undisturbed mind). I was apprehensive about surviving more blood loss in the operation, as I was all bones. Dr Murali told me that there was no other alternative, and no time to delay. Even a 100 broken bones could be rectified, but a delay in attending to a sciatic nerve lesion or cut could have lasting disabilities. He was like a godsend because he personally conducted some neurological tests and operated on me without the presence of a neurologist. He did it in a novel way with minimal blood loss, which improved visibility during the operation also, duly searching for the cut sciatic nerve ends and stitching them. The operation was called 'Sciatic Nerve Exploration'. During the course of the operation, in the same area of the previous operation, he adjusted the position of the ball and socket, removed the rod near it and the tube for infected blood, and even the pierced rod near the knee. He said no traction would be required now. He didn't make any adverse comments about the previous operation, obviously due to professional courtesy. The same day, the hypersensitivity reduced, and there was some sign of movement on that leg's toes. Dr Murali didn't charge his fee and we only had to pay the hospital charges. Mr Manohar came to see me at the hospital and kept telling my father that he should still sue, and that if it was the US, he would have been a millionaire.

But my father kept insisting that my full recovery was of paramount importance, for now.

I wondered what drama was in store here after the previous hospital's experience, since again I was in a similar twin-sharing room. This time, my co-patient was under observation for liver enlargement and pain. He had the unique blessing of falling asleep within five seconds of his head touching the pillow, and he would start snoring, his mouth wide open. His wife and nurses had a lot of complaints about that, especially from the point of view of timely medication and food consumption. His house was nearby, and so, his wife would leave her five-year old son in the hospital with the knowledge of the staff. Once when she returned with lunch, she saw her son playing in the hospital lawn, in the children's area, where she had told him to be, but her husband was missing. Pandemonium prevailed within minutes, and all the staff members, including doctors, were running helter-skelter searching for him, blaming each other, speculating whether he had fallen unconscious or asleep somewhere. The issue would become serious for the hospital if he was spotted in any serious medical condition, apart from being missing. The son didn't know what was going on as nobody had asked him. After some time, he went to his mother and asked what was for lunch. She admonished him for being casual about his daddy not being around. "Oh, Daddy? I saw him getting into a crowded bus, travelling by footboard about an hour back. I'd even waved to him."

The most wanted man walked in coolly, in his shirt and lungi, and, when confronted, explained that the doctor came on his rounds and prescribed a medicine to be had immediately after lunch, which was not available in the adjacent Pharmacy. The pharmacist directed him to buy it from Demblur Main bus stand's famous pharmacy, about six kms away. As there was hardly any walking required here, or at the destination, he caught the bus which was readily standing near the hospital compound, due to which he could not inform anyone, except his son to whom he waved. The staff stood glaring at him, not knowing what to say, as he was a delicate patient. The Matron muttered that she would put him on a leash or maybe chain him or better still, make a head band full of pillows and fit it so that he would always sleep, for not only his own safety and sanity, but that of all the others as well.

-¦-¦-¦-

After my discharge, Dr Murali brought with him Mrs Mangala Narayan, a physiotherapist running the physiotherapy centre at Param Nursing Home, about 10 kms. away from my home. He told her to attend to me daily. As luck would have it, though she lived with her family in the opposite direction of our home from her hospital, her mother's house was near our house. During the lunch hour, she would drive down in her car, exercise me and then go to her ma's place for lunch. She had lost vision in one eye due to herpes, and was in danger of losing it in the other when homeopathic medicine given by her friend near our area saved it. That friend had told her that the medicine was suggested to him by my father, who practiced Homeopathy as a free hobby. Small world, eh? After that, Mrs Mangala didn't charge a single paisa from us and even returned whatever she had taken.

There were slow, but marked improvements in my leg and she sent across her regular contact to take measurements for heel to thigh caliper, for the right leg. He took the measurement with a lot of difficulty, even climbing onto my bed, as I could be in no other position than horizontal. But my apprehensions were dispelled when the caliper arrived after a week, perfect in many a way. They were fitted in a lying down condition in an ambulance when I was going for a check-up. I could sit as there was an unlocking arrangement near the knee, to bend it to 90° only for sitting. While standing, I had to lock it and was thrilled beyond expression that I could limp-walk, initially, with some assistance and bouts of giddiness/blackouts of course, as I had been horizontal for over three months and vertical, suddenly. The only catch was that my right pant leg had to be worn inside the caliper, but that was okay. It felt very much like Robocop, as the caliper was just like its leg and the walk also resembled it. I was thrilled and tears appeared at my progress, since I had seen on TV around that time that a similar patient had taken 22 years to get out of bed, and now drag-walked with the help of a walker. But the ultimate joy was to get out of bed and be able to use the western commode toilet in our house for the first time and say bye-bye to the bed pan. Whoever said that there is no place like home was right, but, additionally, there is no better feeling than clearing your bowels in the toilet at home.

Mrs Mangala also told me to avoid using crutches or a walking stick for support, as it would delay the progress, apart from making me dependent on them. After some time, I had to go to her centre daily for physiotherapy for which I was charged only Rs.15 per day as hospital charges, duly excluding her charges. I would travel only by bus, as vibrations in autos and other vehicles were greater, and could affect the operated area.

5

THE APPOINTMENT – THE RAILWAYS BACKGROUND!

Meanwhile, a retired official in the Railways who was from our community, during a visit, came to know that I had to forego my Defence job as only a three month extension had been given to join. My father's request to transfer the post or sanction equivalent employment at Demblur, was turned down. I had also passed a Bank Clerk's exam, but the interview in Demblur was when I was leaving for my second operation. Again, the request to conduct the interview at my home, as a special case, was futile. So, after consulting my father, he wrote to his colleague, serving in the Railway Board, who immediately sent a letter to the Personnel Department of Demblur city (Railway's Station Code – DBRC), to send a welfare inspector to my house, and to employ me as a clerk when I could manage to go for duties, on compensatory grounds for having foregone my earlier Government appointment due to the accident. It was some consolation for everyone, and most importantly, I would be in my home-city.

-:-:-:-

I got my appointment letter, joined the Railways on 4.10.1989 as a junior clerk, and reported to the Demblur

Divisional Office, four kms from my home and adjacent to the Demblur Main City Railway Station. After the customary oath taking in the Personnel Department (Human Resources Dept.), I was posted in the Mechanical Department in the same building, headed by a Divisional Mechanical Engineer (DME). But since there were no vacancies in that office, I was told that I would be posted to Chiroti, about 20 kms away, along with two others. The DME was insensitive, in spite of my condition, and the fact that I had to go for physiotherapy daily. He said, "We'll see – you go now and I will get you back if there is any vacancy here." He sounded very phoney, without an iota of sympathy in his voice.

I was dejected but the other two transferees were quite happy and consoled me. Later, I found that one of them, Mr Raju, had opted for a change to that place and the other, Miss Kavita, had her house nearby and was engaged to marry a boy residing in that area. We were to catch next day's train at 7:00 a.m. Raju told me about which platform and coach from the engine to get into as he had earlier worked there. He told me to get up at 5:00 a.m everyday to comfortably catch the train.

-:--:--:-

The train left at 7:00 a.m and Raju was my guide. I was relieved to discover that, after the accident, there was no fear psychosis of travelling by train. It would take about 40 to 45 minutes to reach our destination which was the fifth stop. The return train would be at 4:00 p.m. My first area of concern was addressed by Raju who confirmed, to my great relief, that the toilet in Sr. DME's office contained a western commode, whereas, in the Shed, all toilets were of Indian type.

The train was quite empty, but got filled up a bit by a noisy crowd at the second stop. The noise simmered down once all were seated. As the fourth station arrived, I saw the name 'Chiroti' and got up to alight, at which Raju stopped me, saying our stop was next as it was a special one, meant only for the Railway staff. Two minutes later, he told me to go to the door, and alight facing the same direction as while climbing on to the train. I understood what he meant as the train slowed down to a halt near a ten foot wall, about a kilometer long, very close to the train. To my horror, I found that there was no platform and we had to alight and limp-walk on the jelly stones. I got down slowly on the three steps, taking my right leg to the first step, and bringing my left leg onto the same step, following the sequence till I reached the ground.

Some staff members saw my difficulty and stood on either side of me, in case of loss of balance. They held me as I touched the ground, and asked me to lean on the wall till the train passed, as I could not walk steadily on the jelly stones, and also as the space between the wall and the train was barely enough for one erect man. As I held on to the wall and waited for the train to pass, regular employees from behind yelled as to why the line was not moving. To this, the person next to me shouted something which was a shock to me, but served the purpose and soon, all was quiet. He roared, "My dick has fallen down somewhere, so wait." When the train passed, and I said "Sorry," the others came to know about me and were very apologetic. I found that though the staff spoke very bluntly, sometimes roughly, using expletives liberally, they were very warm and friendly. They looked out for somebody to tell a loud, corny one-liner, preferably with some expletive to start the day's proceedings with a chuckle, if not a chortle, and today they had come up with a new one. As I surveyed the area, wobbling on the jelly stones, about 150 staff members were making their way to the narrow opening in the wall, which was the back entrance. It was a double-line and for the return journey, I had to catch the train from the other track, in the opposite direction. I ruled out alighting on the other side in the mornings, since, though there was enough of a gap between the two lines, balancing on the jelly stones without anything to hold on to, would be a problem.

-:-:-:-

This was the Diesel Loco Shed, Chiroti (Station Code CTI) which maintained Diesel Locomotives of 2400 Horse Power each, used for hauling passenger and goods trains. It was like a huge auto garage but with more complex, mind-boggling logistics. It had 90 acres of land, of which 30 acres were earmarked as working area, and the remaining 60 acres contained just 48 Railway Quarters and huge open spaces of barren land, enough to build three cricket stadiums and one football stadium. The entire 90 acres was bordered by a ten foot concrete wall with barbed wire on top, except for a small narrow stretch where there was a single track for Locomotives to enter and exit. The 30 acres was also earmarked by a similar internal wall. The Shed worked 24 hours a day on all days of the week through shifts. The Locomotive maintenance was done by 25 sections, each focusing on a certain Locomotive component or sub-assembly, or even the general check-up of over-all minimum working parameters. The sections were both mechanical and electrical, since the Loco had electric components also (hybrid) and hence, were technically called Diesel Electric Locos with mechanical energy generated by a diesel engine, powering up the mechanical as well as electrical components.

Hence, these Sheds came under the Mechanical Dept. and purely electric Locomotives came under the Electrical Dept. in the Railways. The Mechanical Branch used to dominate but with the electrification of tracks, the Electrical Branch was catching up. Hence, both were at loggerheads, each justifying that their Locos were more beneficial and the other's should be scrapped or phased out in the long run – a duel to the death.

The Shed was run by a Loco Foreman and was home to about 60 Locos at that time, and 250 staff members (understaffed since the yardstick was 6 staff members per Loco) with about 8-9 Locos in the Shed at any point of time in a day, for maintenance. A 24-hour Control room continuously monitored the location and condition of all Locomotives while being the nodal point for receiving and sending all messages.

The maintenance schedule attentions varied according to the term used, like Light Schedules for Weekly, Fortnightly, Monthly, Quarterly and Half-yearly attentions. Heavy schedules were those attentions which were Yearly (M12), 2 yearly (M24) and so on. The intensity of maintenance varied according to the type of schedule. After six to eight years, depending upon the kilometerage earned, they would be completely overhauled at nominated workshops.

The Shed also housed some complementary Departments which catered to several requirements, like Stores Depot for stocking, recouping regular requirements (called Stocked Items) and processing the purchasing of irregular requirements on need basis (called Non-Stocked or NS items). The Railway Protection Force, headed by an Inspector (IPF), also existed along with one-man operators of our mini Telephone exchange, Elec. Generators and water valves.

The Shed was controlled by a Senior Divisional Mechanical Engineer (Sr.DME/Dsl), the overall in-charge (like a CEO), along with 2-3 sub-ordinate officers, (DME, AMEs), whose small office building was located near the front main gate of the Shed. This office used to monitor/arrange the Shed's requirements, which were to be processed outside the premises, requiring approvals etc. from the Divisional Office, 20 km away, or the Zonal office (Southern Railway), 360 km away, so that the staff of the Shed could focus entirely on Loco maintenance work. The Sr.DME office had only about 10 staff members, excluding officers. But sections needing more interactions with this office were housed in that building, like the material control cell (headed by two Material Inspecting Officers (MIOs) – one each for electrical and mechanical), the Information cell and Store Depot Officer headed by an Asst. Material Manager(AMM) or Sr. Material Manager(SMM).

The Sr. Divisional Mechanical Engineer/Diesel came under the Divisional Head, the Divisional Railway Manager (DRM), and all Departments heads' offices were housed in the DRM's Office building at Demblur. Within the Division, departments were called Branches and the heads, Branch officers. The Sr. DME was to have his office there, but since his interaction and presence requirement was greater, his office was located near the Shed. But there was a Sr. DME in Divisional since there were other Mechanical Branch activities, like maintaining coaches, wagons, mobilizing Train/Loco crew, etc.

All the branches' fiscal and staff aspects were consolidated/policed by the Accounts Branch and the Personnel Branch respectively, in the DRM's office building.

The Zonal office, also called the Headquarters (HQ), was headed by the General Manager and the technical heads (Chief Mechanical Engineer for our dept.) of all departments in its divisions/workshops to monitor its proper technical functioning and for processing/sanctioning important/high value proposals, with due policing by the Accounts/Personnel Depts. at HQ and processing higher requirements at the Railway Board level.

All requirements, whether value-based, leave, write-off etc., were governed by the Schedule of Powers (SOP) which delegated sanctioning powers to various authorities/officials in the Zone/Division/Workshop.

6

THE DIESEL SHED – I LIVED TO BE DOOMED & HELLBOUND?

As I entered the Shed with fear, wondering whether I would be able to justify my appointment, there was a canteen on the right, and then the Time office where staff matters were dealt with, starting with the dropping of tokens of the technical staff. We and the technical supervisors had to sign registers.

We three went to the chamber of the Loco foreman (LF), the overall in-charge of the Shed. He knew Raju and asked about Kavita and me (Sachin Khanauji). By sheer coincidence, he had lost his sister in the same accident. It seems she tried to save somebody and got trapped. One more clerk, Rajat Kumar, survived with injuries and was at his hometown, recuperating, with the Railways treating the case as 'Injured on Duty'.

The LF said that, like various Loco maintenance sections, we, being the administrative staff, had also various sub-offices catering to the daily requirement and functioning of the Shed, working 6 days a week. These sub-offices were spread all over the Shed, focusing on a particular requirement of the Shed, like the Time office for staff, the Fuel office where Locos fuelling logistics and statistics were maintained (Kavita was sent there), General Stores, which dealt in drawal of the daily requirement of Stocked items of the various sections from the Stores Depot and accounting and distributing Non-Stock Items (I was to be sent there), the Tool Room, where hundreds of returnable tools were kept and the Control Room – as mentioned earlier. The clerks were called timekeepers, storekeepers, tool keepers, fuel keepers and so on. Only, in the control room, were they called phone clerks who worked 24 hours in 3 shifts.

Normally, transferees were supposed to report to the Sr. DME whose office was near the front main gate, out of courtesy for the controlling officer, before going to the Loco Foreman's office. But I heard that the Sr. DME was on forced leave as he didn't match the wave lengths of his bosses. It seems he did what he felt was right and was not the 'please the Boss' type called 'Buckets'. He was strict, principled, never misused his privileges, always stood up for the sincere and hard-working staff and was well-liked in the Shed.

As I was limp-walking, crossing tracks, towards my General Stores, I passed three maintenance bays of Locos on the right, which had a ramped platform to approach the Loco, and a pit underneath to attend from below. The height between the pit platform and the ramp platform was just above five feet. One Locomotive slowly passed half a foot from me and it was a heart-stopping moment. The Loco was gigantic and more imposing than an elephant, and the engine sounded like a lion's roar, along with its deafening horn. It was painted as WDM2 with a five digit identification number.

To my horror, I found that my store was located at the far corner, under the last bay, and I had to limp-walk under the ramp, with my body bent for 15 meters before entering our room. Its floor was below ground level, making it look like a dungeon. To compound the misery, only a 52-year-old storekeeper was there, with no assistants. I saw scores of bins with several unwanted items. It made me think that, since I had survived the train accident and its torturous aftermath, I was destined to go with what was left of me, back to the Railways to get incarcerated in this hell and die slowly. The job also appeared nondescript as there would be no induction training, and we had to "turn the page and learn the work." In other words, we were herded into service like cattle.

In the evening, I caught the 4:00 p.m train at the back gate without any hassles and the train was quite empty. It reached Demblur Station, from where I caught a bus for my physiotherapy session (7 kms away from there) and returned home at 9:15 p.m. This would be my daily routine.

-:--:--:-

But as days passed, I found that the work was interesting and challenging and the variety, size, smell and feel of the new material was great. My 52 year old storekeeper in the store, who preferred to be called 'Boss', was energetic and particular about the daily accountal vouchers of items issued the previous day. He would not keep any work pending for the next day. I used to indent for the depot items required by sections in the morning itself and look into the other work later. I wanted to streamline some documentation/ traceability and also make the stores look presentable. Unfortunately, we didn't have a permanent assistant as the one nominated was with us for less than three half days every week. Since our Shed didn't have a spectrometer for the lube oil analysis of incoming Locos, the samples were sent to Erode Diesel Shed thrice a week, and every time, the next morning he returned with the reports, worked for hardly three hours, readied new samples, and was given the rest of the day off, as he again had to reach Erode the next morning.

-|-|-|-

But we, in the Chiroti Shed, had to handle the materials ourselves, and in the evening, apply wax seals at seven places, including the tool room, where a handicapped person was present, and I would be deputed in his place when he was not there.

We had a lot of work to do and I thought of various ways to reduce our time, effort and inventory of unused items. I made innovations in indenting process, bin card arrangement, unwanted inventory clearance, registers' entries, files organization, documentation, labeling, etc. – all for proper accountal and most importantly, early traceability. I used to streamline work whenever deputed to the tool room since there was less work and disturbance there.

All this within two months really impressed my boss and foreman to the extent that, when I realized that my 12 casual leaves would lapse by December 31st and went to the foreman personally to request sanction of leave, he grabbed it from my hand and, without seeing the contents, sanctioned my first ever leave letter, smilingly, trying to create a reciprocating good impression on me. After I returned for duty from leave, the amused foreman exclaimed, without getting angry, "You had applied for nine days leave, eh? I thought it was only for one or two days. Your boss struggled in your absence."

7

THE TRAIN JOURNEY – MEDLEY OF JOKES RESOUND!

The train journey was also lively, with staff members making their own groups, and having something or the other to talk about – silly, corny, work-related or whatever. They would also adjust somehow and offer seats to the public, with three of them sitting in an area meant for single seating, looking like conjoined triplets, joined at their backsides and sitting on a commode. In case some person tumbled while trying to catch a moving train, it would trigger a discussion, lasting till we got off. Everyone would contort their faces and narrate their gory experiences of accidents, involving people with legs/hands cut off, and the like. Finally, while alighting, the last man talking would be someone who we didn't know at all, involved in the discussion to relieve himself of his loneliness, or to air his knowledge or his "better than yours" experience.

Once, on salary day, the train didn't start for over an hour, and a stingy but well-off 39 year old bachelor, squirming in his seat, announced primly that he would apply for leave and go back home, as his conscience didn't permit the loss of over one hour's service to India and so he would collect his salary the next day. He asked if anyone would like to join him. To that, his married colleague replied, "Appa, I am not like you, saving money for your next 'Janma' (life), I need money in this life, right now, to be precise, to buy home essentials for today."

A colleague said that he had to frame 25 questions for the quiz contest on Diesel Loco maintenance. So he jokingly told his gang that he would reveal the answers to one of them, and plant him in a team, so that they could all have a party with the winner's prize money. To this, his friend suggested that they could have a bigger party if they planted three people in three different teams to corner all the three prizes.

A staff member used to clear his nose, and especially his throat, with a loud 'Khoak' sound, shamelessly. We told him to stop that to which he pointed out, "On TV, you see your adored football and cricket stars spit on the ground. Nobody has questioned or pointed that out, so why are you hounding me?" To this, we said that that a TV is two-dimensional, whereas here, it is like four-dimensional with surround sound. We are not telling you not to do it at all. Do it out of our hearing, in the toilet, with minimum noise. Spare a thought for our feelings, please!

During the lunch hour, when we used to play table tennis, novice Madan was irritating, always insisting on playing singles while others waited their turn. Outside the room, when a first-time supplier came searching for Madan, Pranav told the surprised supplier to go inside and ask for the score – the one who was losing had to be Madan!

One of the employees, who was thin and had a flat behind, was looking for a marriage alliance. So his friend insisted that he should work out if he wanted to find a companion, as girls preferred to see something at one's back address location. "As of now, if you cover your face, no one can make out whether you are standing with your rear or front, upfront." He sarcastically added, "If I slap your non-existent behind, the swelling will be bigger than that zero-sized dwelling!"

A friend was teasing a new, first-time father, "Just imagine - how does "SO SWEET" or "CHO CHWEET" sound if you don't have front teeth? Obviously, it sounds like "THO THWEETH", and is definitely the "THWEETHEST" among the "THLEE." Tho? Thall I knock outh youl theeth?"

A colleague once joked, "I ate groundnuts from Bangalore's Groundnut Fair and got a free extended course on the Fart of Living." To this, his brother added, holding his nose, "He must've eaten too much to bear – he wakes up daily with a 'Hangover' in his rear."

-:--:--:-

A gum chewing colleague asked his friend, "You liked this new T-shirt for your elder brother. Now you're returning it because he didn't like it. It is the same as your size, so why don't you keep it?" The friend retorted, "I don't like second-hand stuff." At this, the others teased him. "At your home also, you are second hand, so you don't like yourself also?" "No," he replied looking at the first friend, "I don't. Anyway, do you have some gum?"

"Yeah, I do, but you won't like it."

"Why not?"

"Because it is second hand, you bum," putting out his gum tipped tongue.

-:--:--:-

An aged and senior technician used to have breakfast in the train, but before that, with immense pride, he used to take out his medicine pouch and remove all the strips of tablets and capsules, making sure everyone saw him pop them, one by one, into his mouth. Once, his friend espied the unopened cover of a big bar of chocolate in the pouch, which the technician tried to cover. Trying to be smart and expose it and probably expecting a piece, the friend pointed to it, asking in an audibly excited voice, "What's that? What's that?"

"That's a special medicine during emergency," came the calm reply.

"What sort of emergency?"

"Hunger!"

-:-:-:-

As I was being driven in a colleague's car at twilight, four girls suddenly crossed the narrow road and having noticed us, scampered helter-skelter, while one stood still. My friend braked and barely managed to avoid crashing into her. He then called out to the apologetic girls, "You're all pretty girls. Do you know the first rule to continue staying pretty? Staying alive and in one piece!" He advised them not to wear dark dresses while walking on the road in the night. At least one portion had to be light coloured so as to be spotted early by drivers in dark or dim lit areas.

-:-:-:-

One colleague also suggested a cheap, but highly effective medicine to exterminate cockroaches, which was non hazardous. He told me to mix equal parts of wheat flour (maida), sugar, boric acid powder and pour cold, unboiled milk to make round balls and to keep in strategic areas. It worked overnight, and he told me to repeat it every two to three months.

Another colleague had a simpler solution to a particular rat's menace in his house. The rat used to gnaw and cut computer and telephone wires. Traps, poison etc. didn't get rid of it. So he bought peace. He began to keep a bowl of rice with milk every night, and swore that the rodent problem had been solved forever!

My gym had closed down and dumbbells were costly, and so I put two-litre, one litre and half litre filled water bottles in a cloth, tied the opposite corners into knots and used them like dumbbells. I could remove or add weights... er... bottles, to my convenience.

Another friend told us how to test the intelligence or try and gauge how prone a person was in making mistakes. A simple method was to check out your fiancée. He said, "In a dark room, make your fiancée stand in front of a mirror, give her a torch and ask her to tell you her neck's exact skin texture. See whether she first points the torchlight to the mirror or on herself, and whether she realizes her error and corrects herself later. You'll know what I am saying if you check it out on yourself first to learn about your own intelligence or realisation power."

-|-·-|-·-|-

One of my most memorable moments in the train was the shock to learn and prove that a calculator was dangerously faulty, as it showed two different results when the same sum was done, using two different methods.

Another was to switch on the train lights and fans in coaches, which could normally be done only by sliding a rotary switch handle onto a projected rod and rotating it. As the lighting was to be switched on at stations, the concerned staff members were never there. The daily passengers said they had never seen a lightman, not even in their nightmares. So I used to wrap a cloth around the rod where the rotary handle was to be seated, tighten it, grip it and rotate it successfully. I used to educate the interested and grateful passengers on the technique and the exact switches to be rotated for lights or fans, duly dispelling their fear of any shock.

-|-|-|-

A group of employees used to regularly go for drinks, and towards the end, one among them shamelessly, would stick up his little finger, slink away and never pay. They could not avoid him as he ran a chit fund and gift fund for their benefit. So they got an idea to get rid of him, which succeeded. How? One night when his wife opened his lunch box to wash it, she threw a fit as it was strewn with various coloured, gum bottle dipped condoms!

-|-|-|-

Once three young women and a young man, holding a small baby, got into our somewhat crowded train, and somebody offered a seat to the man. He then passed on the baby to one of the woman who went further and got a seat. The baby was passed around till all the women were seated. My standing friend taunted the lady with the child to give it to an old man so that he could also get a seat.

-|-|-|-

My first interaction with Sr. DME was when he was on his rounds, and I was in the tool room that day. He was due for retirement the following month. He was dignified and enquired about me and my condition. He had received feedback from the LF and was considerate, remarking that our cadre's reins were with his counterpart at the Divisional office. He humbled me by saying that he was not liked by his higher ups or he would have transferred me to my dream destination within the next half an hour. I replied we all liked him as he had always stood for us even in trying hours. "I can retire feeling happy if I saw your face among the few faces I want to see on my last day of service," he said.

I felt a lump in my throat on learning that he was again asked to go on leave, and unceremoniously retired, while on leave, without the customary send-off. To add insult to injury, the new Sr. DME was posted a fortnight before his retirement. It was a clear message given by the higher ups as to what could happen if one didn't toe their line, even while acting in the best interest of the Railways.

-¦-¦-¦-

I once mentioned that I was very grateful to the toolkeeper for my being able to know the nuances of the tools and the tool room. Not because he taught me anything, but because he was absent regularly, and hence, I was sent to this self taught 'classroom'.

-¦-¦-¦-

In the Railway quarters, four families with similar food habits pooled and shared proportionately, and planning in advance to rotate the cooking. One did it daily, thereby saving time, fuel and money, allowing the three others to be free to get up late and/or relax or do something else.

8

THE SHED AND ITS ATMOSPHERE – SPELLBOUND!

The new Sr. DME was young, dashing, dynamic and highly diplomatic. Though he kept his higher ups in good humour, he maintained his individuality. He had this habit of picking at his thin moustache with a frown while listening, and had a favourite punch-line to extract work. It was, "Do this, or else I will squeeeeeze your balls until it is done!" said with a concocted sadistic expression. The gazetted officers changed every one to four years.

Our interactions were rare, but the daily routine in our dungeon was our prime focus. The Shed atmosphere was very rugged. We had to be vigilant, tactful and talk tough, for if there was any sign of meekness, they would dominate us. For example, when they would want some material urgently without a voucher signed by the section supervisor, my boss would try to chase them away for which they would get wild and growl, "Are we taking it for our home use? We will give the voucher later." My boss would insist say that most of the times they don't and he would have to answer for any shortage. I tried some damage control by telling the staff, "Look, I trust you like I trust myself. But I don't trust either your memory or mine, so please understand our difficulty if you forget to give us the voucher or if we forget to remind you." Though it helped calm tempers, the situation didn't improve, and so I opened a 'Loan' register.

Though my documentation was neat, I kept a lot of pending papers on my desk, as I found out the hard way that, keeping my desk neat or the papers safe, resulted in misplacing crucial papers. I would find them if they were in the mess on my table. So I coined the terms "Safety first, neatness next," and "There is an order in my disorder."

My rapport with my boss, and everyone else, was good and there were many unexpectedly humorous, tragic, sublime and ridiculous situations that we came across, every now and then. We experienced all the 'nava rasas' or nine emotions there. One moment it was hell and the next, heaven.

Once the job-writer (JW) of a section (who did the job distribution, documentation and errands other than working on Locos) came and complained to the Mechanical MIO that he was not getting items like bolts for their section. The MIO said that his section supervisor should place the requirement in the demand book, kept in our stores for convenience, since the MIO's office was in Sr. DME office building. "Anyway, what type of bolt do you want?" Caught unawares, the JW blurted "Er ...3/4 inch bolts".

"Okay, 3/4 inch diameter bolts, but what length, and fully threaded or half?"

"Er...er..." the JW, taking imaginary measurements, stammered, "One feet long." To this, we all started laughing uncontrollably.

Embarrassed, the JW corrected himself, at which we almost split our sides. He said "Okay then, half feet should be enough." Such howlarious incidents provided succor to our otherwise gruelling routine.

But this particular incident had me thinking, since many didn't know the size of the bolt, or the correct description of the location of its fitment, though they could identify it by looking at it. So I took a thin plywood board and made various dia holes, row-wise, and kept a sample of all the variety of bolts with us in them, and suspended the board horizontally with a light slant.

-!-!-!-

Our Shed's Locomotives mostly catered to passenger trains. The most dreaded aspect in the Shed was the receipt of a message in the Control Room that a Locomotive, given for passenger train service after the scheduled attention (and not overdue for the next attention), had failed enroute, and delayed a train. Phone calls would be received by our Sr. DME from HQ and the 'firing' would be received and passed on to the lowest level. Most of the failures would be material oriented than due to poor workmanship. The fact that the Shed was severely understaffed but still sincerely attended schedules properly didn't cut any ice. In some cases, Charge Sheets would be issued to the staff just to mitigate the heated environment and then, after investigation and enquiry, cancelled. Since this Shed catered mainly to passenger trains, the smallest of failures or even presumed failures, would get highlighted. As for most other Sheds catering to goods trains, their major failures would get diluted as they could be 'overlooked' or 'suppressed' since passengers were not affected. However, based on a survey of Passenger Loco failures in the Indian Railways, done on pro-rata or proportionate basis, it was found that Chiroti Shed had the least failure rate among passenger trains!

-!-!-!-

When I could limp-walk for a longer duration, I went for a long overdue sight-seeing trip of our vastly spread Shed. Wherever I went, the staff members were very warm, welcoming and accommodative. I was enamoured by the huge loco parts like pistons, cylinder heads, bogie frames, traction motors, turbos, wheels etc. in the various sections. The air compressors, 250 KVA Generators, forklifts, overhead cranes, whiting jacks for lifting Locos and their functioning were a treat to watch. The Laboratory and its activities were interesting, as well as nauseating. The control room kept track of locomotives' movements, and critical morning meetings were held there to plan the day's activities, shout out their problems, or justify/review any Loco/Machinery failures.

I even saw the Locomotive cabin through its window from over the ramped platform, and was as excited as a schoolboy to be able to reach, press the horn buttons and listen to its blare on either side of the engine.

Next, I trudged to the fuel point where two gigantic 2.42 lakh litres capacity HSD oil storage tanks towered over the atmosphere. Inside the office, books and papers were strewn around with four ladies literally banging on calculators for some complex statistics. Then there was the underfloor wheel lathe where the wheels of Locos or even coaches, are re-profiled or turned to bring them to the required evenness and radius. Next was the Load Box where the ready Locomotive's various parameters are tested in all the eight notches (gears) with simulated load. It was deafening at the higher notches. Then came the spacious staff room where there were lockers and bathrooms. To avoid the smells, the toilets were in a separate building, slightly further.

Then came the 'lennnngthy' Stores Depot – the size of a plane's hangar which stocked items regularly used, worth crores of rupees. There were over 1500 Locomotive spares, stored in concrete bins or sections made in the wall while constructing the building with huge ceilings.

I went to the canteen where minimum items for breakfast and lunch with tea, were served because the rates were reasonable but not subsidized, which I felt, they should have been. Outside the canteen was a dilapidated Ambulance, used for several 'other' errands, to keep in daily running condition. I imagined if somebody was injured, he would be told, "Just hold on for another ten minutes, the Ambulance has gone to buy vegetables for the canteen."

I then went to the RPF office which contained three Jails in which they kept arms, clothes for drying, and other stores, as it was safer there, away from the menace of monkeys. Alongside was the First Aid Post which contained a regular pharmacist and a dresser with a Railway doctor visiting for two hours a week on Tuesdays. There would be four plastic containers with tablets with the pharmacist during the doctor's visit, which would be the medicine for almost all the problems of the staff members.

The Shed owned a lorry, two material vans and a 'multi-utility' van.

Lastly, I went to the Sr. DME's office near the main gate, which worked only five days a week, and checked the water availability and the working of the western commode, in case of an emergency. As that toilet was a different entity, there was 24/7/365 access, thankfully, since, our Shed's timings didn't match with that office. Only the office, officers' chambers and ladies' toilet were locked after duty hours. This toilet was kept open for the Security at the main gate during night and day duty. I was tempted to go to this office for this and the 5-day week facility, but not for now, as its timings would mean missing my daily physiotherapy.

-:-:-:-

I found that bonus payments were being made by cash through a supplementary bill, and the cashier would come in the afternoon. Pandemonium prevailed and the payments would go on till 8.00 p.m., the main reason being that the employees' names were not in alphabetical order, but in the sequence of their Provident Fund Number, and so locating their name was difficult over 50 pages. There were six names in each sheet and I noted down the last PF number in each page, opening a counter next to the cash counter to help identify the page number of the staff based on his PF number. But still 75% staff didn't know their PF numbers, and I fed them in when the computers came, making a small program to identify the page as per their name in alphabetical order. This helped to save over two hours apart from reducing staff restlessness.

-:-:-:-

A visiting kid, enamoured by the Locomotives, wanted to know how to get employed in a Diesel Loco Shed. I was wickedly tempted to say, "Maybe break a leg in a Railway accident," but I didn't.

9

SHED DEVELOPMENTS AND SOME INCIDENTS - EXPOUND!

In April 1990, came the biggest single block of 150 appointments to the starving Shed, of class IV staff called Khalasis, since, till then, the technicians had to do odd jobs like carry/transport things on their shoulders, clean up and even go for material collection from the Stores Depot or from other Sheds or even collect parcels from the Railway Stations or the Lorry offices, etc.

They came from different communities, in batches of 20-25 everyday. They came well dressed to impress. They were told to stand in a line, and, after an introductory speech by the Loco Foreman, Mr.Raghunath, they were all given mops, brooms, brushes and shed-fabricated scrapers, and told to clean the shed floor, locomotives, its components and scrape out the embedded oil muck etc. "What we expected is not this!" They groaned. One of them moaned that he was employed in a private electronic company in a higher post with a better salary, but his parents and would be in-laws forced him to take this job as it had a Government label. The Trade Unions provided their offices as temporary accommodation, until settled.

In the evening, I had to pass the Divisional office to catch my bus for physiotherapy, and I came across a similar looking batch, who were to report to our Shed the next day. I immediately counseled them not to wear their best clothes, and informed them about the train timings, their stop, canteen and accommodation, and also that I would be in that train. The next day, all of them crowded into my compartment. I made them sit elsewhere in the coach and yelled out when our stop came, telling them to alight from different doors, due to the paucity of stoppage time. On arrival, I told the Trade Union leaders to send their representative daily in the second half to the Divisional office to counsel all the subsequent batches of new appointments and make them feel at ease, especially from the point of view of accommodation and food. .

Till these people came, Tamil was the dominant language since experienced technical staff members from southern Diesel Sheds were required at the time of the inception of the Shed. Initially hesitant to come from the South, they now didn't want to go back as they enjoyed the climate, among other things.

-:-:-:-

Once a year they had Volleyball and Kabaddi as sports activities on the occasion of India's Republic Day on 26th January. The 90 batch, as they lovingly called themselves (since it also meant an extra large peg comprising of three pegs of 30 ml), indulged in a lot of activities which would lead to the formation of a Railway Institute at Chiroti with several sports and cultural activities.

-:-:-:-

One day, both, my boss and the toolkeeper, were on leave and on the previous day, I was told that the LF would be arranging someone else for the Tool Room. At 11:00 a.m, a Junior Engineer (JE) came and said he wanted some tool and to open the tool room which was closed. I politely refused saying I couldn't be at two places at the same time. He went and came back in a couple of minutes saying that the LF had told me to open it, which I refused again. The JE came back again and said this time that the LF has ordered me to open the tool room. I lost my cool and said, "Bloody Loco Foreman, what does he think of himself? I am dying here itself and I have to drag my corpse there for your work, and drag whatever is left back here? No, I won't come."

The JE, who was aged, took objection to my language, and threatened that he would report me to the LF. I iterated, "Bloody LF! He can't give one permanent assistant for our store and instead, he wants us to work everywhere! Am I a prostitute or what and he my pimp?" The JE left, flustered.

A technician came and told me that I had been summoned by the LF. I locked my room and went to his room and found it also locked. It seems he was on leave. I was wondering whether he had phoned, in which case he could have called me on my store phone itself, when the technician waved, saying that the acting LF had called.

As I entered this well built, imposing but calm man's chamber, he retorted, "So I am a bloody LF, eh?" to which I said, "I'm sorry sir, I meant this for the regular LF and didn't know he was on leave." He next asked whether the matter should be taken to the notice of the officers and I said, "By all means, Sir, let them come to know the circumstances under which I said this, and what is going on here. I lost my cool because the regular LF knew yesterday itself that I was alone in the Stores, and said he would arrange somebody for the tool room, but I was upset today thinking he has knowingly done this." To this, the acting LF said, "Is it? Your boss is on leave? I didn't know that or else I would not have troubled you. Go to your store and I'll arrange someone else for the tool room."

The JE came to my store and shook my hand, to my surprise. "I am glad you didn't deny that you had used the word 'bloody' otherwise, I would have been taken up saying I had something against you. However, I didn't mention about the pimp and prostitute!" I thanked him profusely as, otherwise, the matter would have turned ugly.

On returning to duty, the next day, after his morning rounds, the regular LF phoned me, "Heat of the moment outburst, eh?" to which I told him that I had meant it at that time, considering the prevailing situation.

The same afternoon, after finishing lunch, I saw 52 year old Nagendra Reddy, an Ex-Serviceman, who had sought employment in the Railways, come to me and salute, "Nagendra Reddy – posted as your permanent assistant from now, reporting for Duty, Sir."

My boss was ecstatic when he came back for duty after two days, "What I could not achieve in four years by requesting decently, you did by using the words 'Bloody', 'Prostitute' and 'Pimp'?" Till then I had earned his respect for my sincerity in my work and innovations. From that day onwards, the way he treated me, I had became his hero. So, bad words are not bad if they are used in some situations, but with lots of luck, of course!

-:-:-:-

One day, my parents told me that we have to attend a birthday party in the evening, quite far away from my house. I was told to skip physiotherapy and instead, from the same bus stand, catch any bus on my own, going to either of the three stops mentioned in a slip given to me (Gama Bank or Gaynagar 9th Block or New Extension 1st Stage), with directions to proceed after alighting. The buses would start from platforms 13, 14 & 15, they said.

Those were the notorious days when there was hardly any proper display of destination boards on buses. As I limp-walked to those platforms around 5:00 p.m, a TC (Ticket Checker), who approves the departure of the bus by signing on its trip sheet, was standing near the platforms. He saw my slip and concerned about my condition, immediately pointed to a somewhat empty bus, whose engine was running and had no destination board. He hastened me on to it though he didn't tell which of the three stops it would go to. I hurried towards the back entrance and parked myself on my favourite seat – at the window next to the entrance, as I felt most comfortable keeping my right leg slanted on the raised curved floor, over the rear wheel. The conductor had gone to take the TC's signature, when, I heard the thumping of running feet on the platform beside me, as a short, stout, bald man asked me as he panted, "Does this bus go to South End Circle?" I replied, "I don't know."

After a small pause, he asked, "What is this bus route number?" to which I again replied, "I don't know." He took a longer pause and I dreadingly anticipated his next question, he queried, "Where does this bus go to?" I replied, "I don't know," to which he had a stunned expression on his face when, thankfully, the bus left. I could still feel him staring with his mouth open.

But I realised the ordeal was not over since, at the next stop, passengers were bound to ask the same questions, and the Conductor was busy issuing tickets in the front of the bus. As I braced myself, an idea suddenly struck me. As the bus neared the bus stop, the passengers jostling to enter the bus would find a lonely figure near the rear entrance window, dozing off, pretending to be fast asleep. Ironically, later, I had to take the same passengers' help for myself on where and when to alight.

***

Another morning, I boarded from the back of my bus along with two other men and a lone lady from the front – all regulars. This stop being the end of one of the fare stages (each fare stages have two or three stops with the same fare which changes in the next stage). I always kept the exact ticket fare in my hand. The bus would halt till all the tickets were issued and entries made in the trip sheet. It was 6:30 in the morning, the bus started moving and the conductor issued us three tickets, took out his trip sheet and started entering when I signalled that one more lady was at the front door and who was holding her fare in her hands. The next stop neared and as luck would have it, a strategically positioned ticket checking squad of three boarded – two at the rear and one at the front - and started checking. The poor lady was trapped and the TC called out to his colleagues who dropped everything and rushed towards their prey. No amount of reasoning or pleading convinced them and they wanted to make most of their 'auspicious' start and were all over her. They said that it was her duty to go the conductor and buy the ticket. At this point, I intervened, politely saying that I too boarded the bus with two others at the same stop and the next stop neared while tickets were being issued to us, adding that being a lady, we should not expect her to come to the men's section which was somewhat crowded, and buy her ticket. I looked at the conductor for support but from the look on his face, I could make out that he was pleading with me not to reveal that he had been aware of her, earlier. They did not relent and started abusing. To rub chilli powder on our already salted wounds, one of the men who boarded with me, approached her saying, "What, madam, couldn't you buy a ticket and avoid all this?" I told him with folded hands to move away and mind his own business. The bus neared the destination and all of us alighted, arguing vociferously even as some of the passengers and public gathered around us. I noticed that all the three TCs were white-haired and over 50, one of them chewing paan. They showed no mercy towards either my leg condition, or her tears, and kept hounding us. At one point the paan eater went out of bounds, taunting and gesticulating, "Looks like this hero wants to pay the fine on her behalf. No problem as long as someone pays." I told him to mind his tongue for which he aggressively headed towards me, chest thrust out, arms opening and as I clenched my fists, he snarled, "Maybe I should teach you how to respect people of our age," to which I snapped back " Oh yeah? Maybe you should first teach yourself to respect your own age, and then expect respect." My Shed's rugged atmosphere and morning one-liners seemed to have rubbed off on me.

At that point, the other TCs pulled us apart as I continued at another TC, "Sir, when you approached her, she had her ticket fare in her hands, didn't she?" He nodded and I continued, "OK, then, that is proof that she was going to buy a ticket since, being the first person you asked on entering the bus, she wouldn't have had the time to open her purse and take out the change to pretend to buy the ticket." I then looked at her and said animatedly, "Madam, I have to catch a train and I can't run. Please don't pay any fine as I am a witness, and one of the TCs himself knew that you meant to buy the tickets. If they are still adamant, I know the Assistant Commissioner of Police for Traffic, Mr Prabhat Alekai, who is also my relative and very strict. He was felicitated with the Rajyotsava award by our State this year. I will see to it (I looked at the TCs with disgust) that these three musketeers are dismissed or given compulsory retirement on grounds of sexual harassment." I left, not knowing what happened.

The next morning, as I was approaching the bus stop, the lady came over and profusely thanked me. It appears that they knew about that ACP and asked her to pay only the ticket fare and let her go. "You really had them going about the ACP stuff," to which I told her that he was actually my relative. We looked around to see that the other 'devotee' of those TCs was standing at a distance, looking away, and didn't board the bus we caught.

-:--:--:-

One night, at 9:15 p.m, as I was returning home after physiotherapy, I heard a commotion in front of my neighbor, Prasanna's, house. He was out of station and his widower father and his aged friend, Mr Bhaskar, were talking animatedly. It seems Mr Bhaskar's moped was missing. It was parked in front of the footpath opposite our apartments of 24 houses. I found that there were two other scooters, along with another moped of same model and colour, parked nearby. He dismissed the idea that the other moped's owner could have mistakenly taken his vehicle stating that it had an American Steering Lock, almost impossible to open. Mr Bhaskar was thinking of going to the cops.

Based on a hunch, and since I had had some snacks on the way, I decided to visit all the other 22 apartments. I limped from door to door asking whether they had had any visitor with a moped.

I struck gold at Flat no.18 at Mr Sindh's, and as I was explaining, Mrs Sindh asked her son, "Beta, which moped did you bring inside?"

Apparently, they had had a visitor who could not locate his moped's ignition key while departing, and came back, searched again in vain and gave the steering lock's key to them, stating that it was late he would go home by bus, and come the next morning with the duplicate ignition key. He requested that his moped be parked inside.

After some time, their son went and tried in vain to open the first moped visible in the dark. Being burly in size, he lifted it in and parked it at the back.

As I could not run, I told Mr Sindh's son to rush to Flat no.1 as they were planning to call the police. By that time, Mr Bhaskar had not only called, but had scampered to the Police Station, about a km away. Just at that time another resident was entering our gate in her car, and was generous enough to reverse it and take us to the Police Station. Half-way through, we spotted Mr Bhaskar coming with two policemen and he was gesticulating while explaining.

We stopped by his side and announced that his moped had been found, at which the policemen seemed relieved and they turned back, not even bothering to ask for the details.

-:-:-:-

I heard Mr Rajat Kumar, the clerk, who was 'injured' in my accident, had reported back for duty after eight months of the accident. It was rumoured that he had only a hairline fracture, and had availed of special paid leave, citing 'seriously injured on duty with mental trauma'. He enjoyed a paid eight month honeymoon with his wife who was working in Delhi. I went to meet the 'Honourable' Sri Rajat and, to my surprise, recognized him as one who had been in my coach. He initially didn't recognize me, and then recalled that Varalakshmi had screamed about her almost stolen necklace, and his was the first head to pop into our compartment. He then remembered me and asked me about the accident. I refrained from giving him the gory details, fearing that he might pretend some 'mental trauma' for revisiting the scene' and again run away on special leave.

After a year of great progress, my caliper was cut upto just below my knee, and I could now wear my pant over it. Though I was thrilled, I kind of missed the missing portion. I still had to undergo physiotherapy for foot drop, and other improvements. Dr Murali told my father that he had just taken a chance on my second operation, and that everything went better than expected.

10

COMPUTERS, CRICKET, SCRAP & THE SICK (ENING) FOREGROUND!

Then came the Computers, and a small room was earmarked as the computer cell. It had a floppy drive with a floppy as big as the palm of my hand. We were told that it would bring about a revolutionary change in managing and manipulating data and record-keeping. We were very afraid of it and never went near it. But a computer training centre hired by the Railways conducted a test of reasoning for interested shed staff, and I topped it. Six toppers were sent for training of Awareness, DOS, Wordstar, Lotus and dBase+++, crammed within a space of ten days. But our trainer on all days, Mr Sudhir, taught the basics so well that the computer became our friend and we could build on our level of knowledge. At the end of the course, we were told to rate the course between 1 to 10, and I rated the trainer's rating as '12' by mentioning 11 and 12 beside 10.

-!-!-!-

But computerizing the data, and with liberty to make programs of my choice, I began to plan, design and program our Stores requirements. I started working late everyday to catch the six p.m train which also stopped for us. I neglected the Physiotherapy but luckily it did not hamper my progress, and in early 1991, I could remove the caliper fully, and found I could even run slowly with my foot drop being very negligible now. Only the toes on my right leg could not be lifted much. There was some kind of a strange sensation along the sciatic nerve path from the operated portion onwards till my ankle. From below the ankle joint till toes, the sensation was abnormal. It remains the same even today, but what the heck, I could play, and played like hell.

-:-:-:-

TENNIS BALL CRICKET

It was called poor man's cricket or a poor cousin of the conventional leather ball cricket, and frowned upon by the elite, with no media glare or publicity hype, as it is more difficult to score runs or keep your wickets here than its snooty cousin. So what? This game is more affordable in terms of time and money. The game can be played more safely, with minimum fuss and formalities, and even on smaller grounds. Several matches can be played in one ground, simultaneously and parallelly, within a few feet of each other. One can elicit and exchange smiles, make friends and even earn mutual respect by just one small gesture of returning another team's ball near you or if you appreciate and give high fives to some other match's player who has held a great catch, near you. One can comfortably play three matches in half a day with 10 – 12 overs a side. So, if you fail in one or lose, you get another chance within the next hour, whereas in leather ball cricket, you have to wait for another day. Many frustrated youths are able to drown their negative feelings during the course of the game, while bonding with friends and rivals, and have a more positive frame of mind in the end, a much better option than to hit the bottle or smoke or find other unwanted means of redressal. Many famous cricketers owe their humble beginnings to this game before climbing the ladder. I preferred it being played as a friendly game with healthy competition, as this game would not make it big. I loved the game as it is - virgin, undisturbed, unexploited, but played in the right spirit and serving the players' purpose, quietly. It may be less entertaining but is more humane. Leather ball cricket may be great in terms of viewing or professionalism or fame or to make money. But if you are a decent player and when it comes to playing for some serious fun, nothing can match tennis-ball cricket!

For me, tennis ball cricket was like a therapy, played for a few hours on Sunday mornings, which would unwind me from the stress wound up over the week. I would feel invigorated and raring to go work early, with not an iota of the Monday morning blues.

I found another worshipper in a technician by name, Gopala, in the Shed. We formed a team, practiced between four and six, and caught the 6:05 p.m train.

For Republic Day, we conducted the first ever tournament. Our first match was with the Railway Quarters Team, and the match resulted in an exciting tie. As this probability was not anticipated or planned, and we having a hectic, daily schedule of upto 25th January, the only option was to decide over toss of coin since Super Over was not conceived then. But seeing everyone's faces, it seemed unfair and after discussion, we replayed the match on the next morning at 10:00 a.m, duly taking permission from the concerned who were amused but sporting. The Quarters' boys bunked college/school. This time, me and Gopala had a bigger opening partnership and took the match away from them.

We won that tournament because all the other teams were weak. But this cricket led from one activity to another, including a fierce rivalry with the Railway quarters team whom we regularly beat, more with tact than our limited skill, and finally we formed our own Railway Institute, Chiroti. Till now, over the last 15 years, about 12 non-sports quota players have played/are still playing for the Demblur Division cricket team (conventional leather ball) and such is their contribution that we are not allowed to form a separate team at Chiroti.

-:-:-:-

One day I was told to witness the loading of auctioned scrap of wheel turnings and borings, in the form of steel strips and chips, since my Boss, though on duty, was just recovering from a stomach upset. It required me, along with RPF, Stock Verifier & Depot Store Keeper to witness the loading. I was told that the buyer would be hand in glove with all and that I had to be careful. I was nervous that, that being the case, I may be compelled to play along. But I wondered how they would con because this item was the costliest, weight-wise, and any other ferrous item, even if loaded stealthily, would fetch lesser value. The non-ferrous scrap like copper and aluminum were kept safely in locked custody and there was no chance of that being loaded.

First we had to weigh two empty lorries in a private, but reputed, weigh bridge (WB) quite near to the Chiroti Railway Station. The buyers came in their car, and we were sent by our Railway vehicle since their two 9-ton lorries were parked near the WB. The first lorry was placed exactly at the centre of the bridge, and I noticed, due to my height, that six labourers were sleeping on the lorry bed with their equipment. The four people in the buyer's car, including its driver, coolly climbed and stood on the weigh bridge. The idea was to get maximum tare weight of the empty lorry so that when the loaded lorry's gross weight difference was worked out, you would get lesser nett weight of the load.

I paused to see the expressions of the witnesses. Only the sub-Inspector (SIPF) was objecting with conviction, while everyone else was expressionless. I was delighted the person who mattered most to me was on my side. I shook his hand and joined him. We also saw, to our pleasant surprise, that the lady operator of the weigh bridge came out of her lookout cabin and shooed the labourers, refusing to record the weight. The buyer had to relent and then the lorries were taken to the Shed for loading.

The loading was brisk and by 5:30 p.m, we left our gate with the SIPF in the first lorry, and me and another RPF constable in the second. Everything seemed fine, when my lorry stopped suddenly about half a km from the weigh bridge and the driver ran away. I was stunned, but recovered soon, and told the constable to stay with the lorry, while I went to the weigh bridge. There was drama there also since that lorry driver placed the lorry with only the right front and right rear wheel on the weigh bridge, and the other two wheels outside, on the pavement. The SI ensured that it was placed properly while I narrated what had happened. As he could not leave the spot, I volunteered to go to the CTI Railway Station nearby and called his boss, the IPF who immediately came over on his 350 cc bike with MIO/ Mechanical. He parked in front of my lorry and called out for the Driver. The buyer said that he had gone to answer an urgent nature's call, and subtly requested for weighing the first lorry again, but with this lorry's Registration Number, as it was getting late. He would bear the loss since this lorry contained less volume, whereas the first lorry's volume was more, which was correct. The IPF sternly told him that if the driver was not there within three minutes, their next nature's call would be answered in his jail, minus a toilet or water but with plenty of fire extinguishers to clean up themselves and their mess. Within moments, the driver appeared out of thin air.

The first lorry's nett weight was 8.7 Tons and our lorry's nett weight was 13.8 Tons! This is because the item was cleverly loaded with long, coiled strips in the first Lorry and small, straightish chips in the other. The IPF told the buyer to hire a mini-lorry and unload and send back the excess to the Shed. The buyer obliged by paying a premium for the mini-lorry and his labourers as it was beyond 7:30 p.m and his labourers refused to work until their money was not doubled by the hour. After weighing the mini-lorry several times and 3 trips to the Shed, accompanied by the constable and 3 labourers, the drama ended at 11:15 p.m, with us having street food and peeing in the bridge's toilet. The buyer never lost his composure and shrugged understandingly (which indicated - ok, if not now, next time). I felt great as I had a wonderful winning story to tell in the train next morning. Inwardly, I thanked that honest people like the IPF and SIPF still existed and that I was lucky to experience them.

-+-+-+-

The procedure for reporting sick in the Railways was ridiculously meticulous and sickening, with only some liberty allowed. For us, one had to normally take a sick memo from the work spot, go to the nominated health unit 12 kms away, get a sick certificate from the Doctor, ensure that it reached the work spot and then give attendance, every alternate day, or once in a week, according to the doctor's orders. Then one had to get a Fit certificate, signed by the doctor before attending duties. If one's sickness was beyond the expertise/facilities of the Railway Hospital, they were sent to either the Private Railway Referral Hospitals or to the Railway Hospital at Perambur, allowed to travel by a Medical Pass with one attendant.

However, inspite of waiting in the crowd and the cumbersome procedure, my colleague found relief in his problem of a growth in his nose with simple treatment by the Railway's Doctor. He had earlier thought the free treatment and Railway Doctors were inferior and the wait, procedure and applying leave would prove costlier. He had become wiser after having spent a lot of money in vain on hi-fi treatment by a showy doctor, which had rather left him, his finances and his nose in a state of stupor.

On the flip side, several years' absentees could present 'medical certificates' from Private Doctors and Hospitals and get reinducted in service whereas, during General/ Assembly Elections, whether you were engaged in election duty or not, even genuine sick cases would not be entertained by the same or any other doctor, since it could attract police intervention.

-:-:-:-

Someone had earlier said, "God is the best doctor and Prayer is the best medicine." To this I'd said, "Very true, especially in Dembluru; that is until the Ambulance negotiates the traffic and reaches the faraway referral hospital."

11

A.I.O.S – INBOUND AND OUTBOUND!

On September 5th 1993, I was admitted to the Male Nephrology ward of Railway Hospital in Perambur with a blood pressure of 220/130, after a horde of symptoms spread over a month, like 12 days of fever up to 104^0 immediately followed by right ear hearing affected for 9 days. Then there was nausea, vomiting, swelling of the face and feet, breathlessness, bloating of the stomach, limited urine passage and an increase in body weight by 10 kgs. in about 15 days. Seeing my blood report, the doctor directed me to the Railway Hospital at Perambur (RH/PER), as it depicted urinary infection and/or renal problem.

At RH/PER, I was looked after by an MBBS doctor since the Head of the Nephrology department was in London, attending a Seminar. Within his limitations, he looked after me very well along with a good support staff. He first gave me a diuretic for passage of urine and tablets for High B.P, duly consulting the doctor at London who used to call everyday to check on his patients. Consequently, I urinated bucket loads in the next few days, my B.P also came down to 160/100, and my weight from 78 to 64 kgs. From London, he told the junior doctor to conduct a biopsy of my kidney and not wait until he came back. It required taking some tissues of my kidney and this was his first biopsy attempt. A needle-like cylindrical tube was inserted from my lower back to suck the tissues, and the path of the needle viewed in a sonogram kind of machine. The first time it penetrated more than required and injured the kidney. The needle was cleaned and inserted a second time, within a minute, and this time it sucked the tissues from the outer layer of kidneys successfully. It was sent for analysis which included something called a Lupus test. Daily I wrote about my symptoms and progress on a paper, silently suffering painless bleeding in my urine due to the injury during biopsy. The colour of blood differed with each day.

My parents had come down leaving our pet cat home (with Prasanna to ensure its feeding) and stayed at a relative's place since the apartments for outstation patients' relatives were always full. My North Indian co-patient had seven people staying?! I was on a strict diet – not more than one gm salt per day and 500 ml of fluids. This was not a problem as I didn't drink coffee or tea and controlled it to 150-200 ml per day, monitoring my intake in a small book. The canteen served simple but nice tasting 'pongal', 'idli', 'upma', and 'Idiyappam' as breakfast, and south Indian meals, custom-made for diet. The only issue was that their canteen closed at 5:30 p.m and a packed, cold dinner could be had at 7:p.m in our ward. There was a small colour TV in an isolated corner only in the Men's ward and the female patients also came to watch it there. Thankfully, the Nurses allowed to watch songs or comedy films only, and not depressing serials which could affect their psyche and B.P. The US Open Lawn Tennis tournament was on at that time, and after 9:00 p.m, the TV was all mine. I would sleep on the empty bed next to it, legs near the pillow area, watch on a very low volume till late in the night, sometimes joined by the doctor and the male-nurse on night duty who were pleased as they had no idea about the telecast details, and had never watched TV at night, ever. Of course, the male-nurse didn't know the game and learnt it with our help. But all was not hunky-dory as it seemed that, daily in the early morning, three names would be shouted out aloud from the door to get ready for undergoing dialysis on that day. That would send shivers down my spine.

My Doctor finally returned from London and I learnt he was from Demblur. During his rounds with the intern doctors, I impressed him with my recorded symptoms from one month before coming to the hospital, during the stay, and also the colour of blood in my urine each day, like potassium permanganate colour, whisky colour, beer colour, coconut oil colour. He asked whether he could borrow it and returned it shortly. My symptom sheet became so famous that doctors and nurses from other wards also came for it, wishing all other patients would also follow suit. My doctor sent for me later in the afternoon.

As I sat down in his chamber, the first thing he told me was to not to see my fellow-patients and get the wrong impression. He said that all the other cases were direct kidney failures, whereas mine was secondarily infected. From what I could make out, it was like the opposite of AIDS. Here, the antibodies in the body, which are meant to fight and ward off diseases in the body, multiply automatically within the body with no external influence and, so far, no identified cause. They get restless when they don't have anything to fight and, in turn, attack some organ in the body, causing some kind of inflammation around the organ. In my case it had attacked my kidneys. Luckily, my Lupus test was negative and hence, there was a chance to retrieve the kidneys. If the Lupus test had proved positive, I would have a permanent medical problem just like, say, a thyroid problem and have to live with it all my life. He said there is no medicine for my present condition and that but he would have to put me on Corticosteroid which would suppress all activities of the body, including immunity (and he really meant every activity of the body!) and hope that in the suppressed condition, the disease got cured. I had to start with high dose of 60 mg, tapering off over 11 months. There would be several side-effects, but mostly pleasant (peace of mind giving a false sense of well-being and some water retention in the body due to which I would have chubby, puffed up and shiny cheeks). My B.P would be on the higher side. But I should not get addicted to the corticosteroid as it would make my bones brittle in the long run and also thin my hair. He told me to have normal food with only one gm of salt per day and no limit on fluids now. Lastly he told me that this had no connection with my accident, and was a rare occurrence on humans. Once cured, there was only a 5% chance of recurrence in one's lifetime, and I didn't need to have any inhibitions on having a normal family life as it was neither contagious nor hereditary.

I felt the last few words were like the Sanjeevani, the life-saving herb, and the Doctor was Lord Hanuman who, in this case, administered it aurally.

I was so thrilled that I christened my disease as AIOS (Auto immune overefficiency syndrome) as against AIDS (Acquired immune deficiency syndrome).

-|-|-|-

Every hospital had some howlarious experiences, and why not this one? First let me tell you the not-so-funny one. One day the Matron came into the ward and announced, "One of you has not flushed after using the toilet. You people take the free services for granted and that it is your right. Is this the way you maintain cleanliness at home? I know who the guilty one is (though she actually didn't). But this is a message for all of you. The next culprit will be forcibly discharged so that he can go to a private hospital and pay lakhs of rupees to survive. Then he will understand the value of our hospital and his responsibilities as a patient. Shame on you!"

An old patient of about 58 years, whose bed was next to me, was playing with his grandchildren, running around the ward. I saw my mother laughing uncontrollably and noiselessly, her hand covering her mouth. I asked her if it was because the old man was playing. She told me to observe his pyjamas, which appeared to be short, as they were inches off the ground. When closely seen, it could be noticed that it neither had the drawstring to tighten and hold it up, nor were there buttons on its fly. So the clever old man had tied a big double knot in the front, using the unstrung ends and lifting the fly portion also, which solved both the problems!

As the doctors' rounds were announced, the children were whisked away and my mother too had to leave, as the old man lay down on the bed. My doctor entered along with the other junior doctors and interns. This time a Gastroenterologist accompanied them and went straight to the old man's bed. A junior doctor acted as the interpreter. He was asked to sit up. He slowly got up as if he was very weak, and with an expression as if he had just drunk castor oil. I was surprised because moments ago, he had been frolicking. Later I learnt that he preferred the hospital to home, and was admitted here because of lack of space in some other ward.

The Gastroenterologist asked how he was feeling. There was no answer.

"Does it pain anywhere?" – Still no answer.

"Does it pain here," touching the abdomen – after a long pause "Yeeesss!"

"Does it pain here," touching the sides – after a long pause "Yeeesss!"

"Where else does it pain?" – after a small pause "Evvvrywhere."

Fed up, the doctor said, "We will discharge him as he is not interested in the treatment here." To this, the old man suddenly found his voice. "Saar, please don't do that, Saar."

After discussing and seeing his report, the doctor told the interpreter to communicate to the old man to be physically and mentally prepared for colonoscopy and endoscopy the next morning. So the interpreter conveyed, among other things, that a long tube would be inserted through his anus upto the large intestine to check for some problem, and likewise through his mouth into the stomach, duly pointing the areas of insertions. The old man nodded his head, and murmured something into the interpreter's ear with folded hands, and then using both hands to point at his mouth and backside. The interpreter looked up at the doctor with a very weird expression – neither laughing nor crying and trying to control his expression.

"Why, is there any problem?" The Doctor asked.

"No, Sir," he managed a reply, "He has agreed, but has only one humble request that, in case the same tube is being used both the times, he wants it to be inserted in his mouth first!!!"

-:-:-:-

After 22 days in the hospital, we returned home to find our cat, Jimmy, had become very emotional. Prasanna said that he was not eating properly and he had to feed him by hand. Jimmy sat on my lap and never went out because we had left home for the hospital when he had gone out. He would now go out to relieve himself nearby and immediately rush back. To take him out, we used to walk him like a dog without a leash. But he passed away some months later, falling into an open well. My father, a heart patient, also departed, having inculcated strong values in me. He believed that the country would head towards uncontrollable corruption, population and unemployment. He added that hope was there if families consciously opted to have only one child, as a start, which could spark the turnaround! He was one of those who lit that spark! The Country lags in its progress, never in its population. Earlier, it was the more the merrier, but now it is the more the messier.

-:-:-:-

Fortunately, my problems got cured during the medication period and I was off all medicines. The indication of my cure was when the presence of albumin in my urine became negative in three continuous tests. But my regular BP now was 130/90 or 140/90 as against 120/80. In my office, a visiting Insurance agent insisted that I go in for life insurance, but I did not hide any of my ailments. The agent said that they may charge some extra premium called 'risk premium' against the 'normal premium' and sent my original X-Rays and medical reports to his Zonal office. In a few days, I got back the medical reports in a dilapidated condition, threw a fit in their regional office, and got a compensation of Rs.90/-! Further, I received a letter stating that my life insurance application was 'DECLINED' which meant that I was not likely to last the term of my insurance of 20 years!

12

BACK IN SHED – THE BATTLEGROUND!

There used to be one Type-V Quarters for the Sr. DMEs which was more like a bungalow. The Sr.DMEs and other officers got changed every one to four years, and each time the new one had some unique feature and there was no dearth of mimics in the Shed. If one was about 'squeezing balls', another was very casual, sleeping in the office in the afternoons. A third was selfish, full of theory and not practical at all. So during the morning meetings, if something was wrong, he only kept asking how and why without being considerate or involved. Each meeting, he would target one supervisor who would become famous for the day, known as the 'man of the meeting' or 'man of the match'."

I once went to this Sr. DME to inform him that I had registered for his five-day week office, and that someone who had not even applied was posted there. On entering his chamber, I greeted him and starting to talk, when he interrupted me and asked me who I was. "How will I know if there is no introduction? You could be the Prime Minister of India or the President of America," he said with sarcastic seriousness. I was shocked since I thought I was a popular figure in the Shed, having worked hard and involved in organizing sports activities. He had worked for more than a year at Chiroti, and interacted at least 10 times in the Shed, and above all, given many sports awards to me (and shame on my 6'2" frame, being the tallest in the Shed). Later I came to know that he didn't even know most people from his own office and how many people were working there. He would only call somebody if he wanted to fire them or swear at them even for silly mistakes. Even hard-working people wondered why they should work and get a firing – it was better not to work at all and he would call only the Ch.OS and fire him. Despite his snobbish attitude, we found he was ultimately a cheapskate when he utilized the Shed people on his transfer for transporting, unloading at Delhi and even setting up his furniture, without even offering them a cup of tea or thanks or even a smile. "Ok," he said sounding grouchy, after his requirement was over, "You can leave now." He didn't even bother to see if their return journey seats were confirmed though he had signed their Emergency Quota application. Their seats were not confirmed but they talked to a peon in our office whose relative was a Train Ticket Examiner, who arranged seats for everyone. So a peon was more useful or powerful than a Sr. DME, at times.

Once, at Demblur Division, the Mechanical Department Sr. DME's ticket was not confirmed. So, moments before the train was to leave, he declared an air conditioned coach as 'sick' and to be detached with no replacement available. Immediately, officers from the Commercial Department literally fell at his feet since reserved passengers could not be offloaded, and that would cause a catastrophe. So the Sr.DME got his ticket confirmed and the 'sick' tag was removed.

-:-:-:-

The next Sr. DME was the best we ever had. He was Mr. Anmol Ratan Kumar or ARK. He was very strict, but rational. ARK would make surprise visits to the staff toilets and call up the Engineering department, who were responsible for its maintenance, and fire them for not allowing his staff to relieve themselves in peace as there was water leakage, defective flush tanks, holes in urine pipes which would 'urinate' back on the user, etc. He was keen that a concrete platform was built on either side of the tracks at our rear entrance, and though the proposal was never entertained, he kept sending it again and again, citing that five lady employees also boarded and alighted there.

He didn't have any inhibitions about taking the files personally to Division or HQ and meet our technical heads, CMPE and CME, during his official visits to get them signed there. Instead of sitting in the officers' chambers, he would personally interact with the concerned sections and get any pending proposals or doubts clarified, keeping small diaries in which he would take notes, consolidate into a big diary and keep end-to-end track of important duties. He was keen to computerize whatever possible and very much into sports, and hence, kept a spare track suit and sports shorts in his drawer.

Once he was at the HQ in Chennai for the monthly Stores Review meeting, and after finishing the meeting and lunch, served there itself, he went to the Office of Dy. CMM of the Diesel Section. It was 2:50 p.m, and there was only one staff and he was playing SOLITAIRE on the computer. He consciously ignored the Sr. DME who sat down in a chair. At 3:00 p.m, the Sr. DME asked, "Dear friend, what time does the lunch time get over?" To this, without taking his eyes off the monitor, the staff member said, "2:00 p.m." The Sr. DME said, "I just wanted to ....," but he was rudely cut off by the man saying, "Look, you are disturbing the timing of my game and I may make a silly mistake, if distracted. Go have lunch and come." When the Sr. DME said he had finished his lunch, the man retorted, "Shit, I missed a card and I lost again," and looking with irritation at the Sr. DME and asked, "What's your hurry, man, can't you wait for sometime? I am alone here and there is so much of work." (He pointed to the mountain of files on each table). Then pointing to the empty chairs, he said, "My assistant has gone for lunch with her group and must be offloading her personal problems – better she does it there than here. And this lady has gone shopping and this man has gone to ready his Chaat-Cart to supplement his 'meager' income in Railways. Anyway if you are a supplier asking for a favour, we can negotiate now itself; otherwise you can come after 4:00 p.m when some staff members will come over. Anyway I think you are a supplier since you called me 'Friend' earlier and no Railwayman will do that."

"Shall I come alone or with the Dy. CMM?" asked the Sr. DME.

"Oh? Big party, eh? My Dy. CMM has finished lunch and gone home to have a siesta. He will be back at 4:30 p.m. He will not degrade himself by coming here even if anyone was dying. He will call me to his chamber. Meanwhile, if you feel uncomfortable, we can deal with this in his chamber. Anyway, which company do you belong to and what is your designation?"

"I belong to the Indian Railways and I am Sr. DME/ Dsl/Chiroti," to which the staff member got up with folded hands, "Sorry, Sir, Sorry, Sir," and removed his feet from his slippers as if he was standing in front of a sacred figure, "What do you want, Sir?"

"You are supposed to attend the meeting, aren't you? I didn't see you during the meeting, but I saw you had lunch there, stuffing three gulab jamuns in the end."

"Sir, I am sorry Sir, how can I help you Sir?"

"Wear your slippers and open your palms – it is not going to compensate your wrongdoings - and give me the technical scrutiny file of Lube oil coolers which requires my approval of the upgraded specification given as the counteroffer by the least quoter. My Locos are waiting for the same."

The man immediately jumped at his assistant's table and started going through the files saying "This lady is useless, sir. I gave the file three days back to send it to you, but she has not yet done it." He spotted his assistant ambling across, with a bored look on her face. "Amma, Gunalakshmi, if you have finished playing your harmonium, come immediately and give me that Lube Oil Cooler file," to which she said, "Sir, it is on your table. I gave it 20 days ago as the file was not initialed by you when put up to Dy. CMM."

He rushed to his table, rummaged, throwing all files helter skelter, some falling on the floor and finally found it, and gave it to him, standing respectfully, bent like a courtier addressing an Emperor. My Sr. DME opened the file, read the contents, took out his pen and remarked, "Alternate specification is approved as it is an upgraded version and more beneficial to Railways."

Next he said, "Now type the draft purchase order and keep it ready and don't wait for Dy. CMM's orders to type it. Show him my approval, get the draft signed and release the Purchase Order by 5:00 p.m and I will come personally and collect it."

"Yes, Sir," he said loudly, like a soldier answering his Sergeant, and then lowered his voice with cupped palms, "Excuse me, sir…," to which my Sr. DME interrupted him and assured him, "Don't worry, I will not tell your Dy. CMM, who is like your big brother. But if I find delays in our cases, I will get you all transferred to some office where you will not interact with suppliers." He turned towards the lady, "Madam, have you finished telling your personal problems to your friends so early? You should come early one morning to my office. I will need a full day to tell you only about my Shed's problems and then you will enjoy telling them to your friends! Along with the harmonium, you can also play the violin!"

-·-·-·-

Once, my Sr. DME was fed up with improper guidance by our Accounts and Law Branch about the interpretation of Service Tax Notification on Tax application/exemption for repair by a contractor. He phoned up a Director in the apex Service Tax office in Mumbai. On asking, the polite, gently speaking voice at the other end stated, "Your Railway Minister wanted an exemption in Tax, so we gave exemption for Train tickets and Train freight charges." When my Sr.DME said that the clarification was not about tax exemption for Railways' Services but Services provided to Railways, the Director kept saying the same thing. So, my Sr. DME told him that he would write a letter seeking clarification, he was told that we were welcome to write not one, but a hundred letters, but no reply would be received!

-·-·-·-

I will be sinning if I didn't mention about the gastronomic delights in the area. The Shed canteen's quality was always fluctuating. About 2 kms away, was a low cost Andhra meals hotel with limited, but all individually tasty items, served on a plantain leaf. Their vegetarian meal, by itself, was a delight and they also served Dal Roti, Chicken curry and Biryani. On request, marinated lake fish would be fried which was tastier than sea fish. But the taste, though homely, was so good that we could not eat the same item daily and had to leave a gap of 10 days for each, to relish and to savour. The highlight was the double-yolk egg omelette which tasted differently better than the regular. My folks didn't believe the double-yolked egg until I took it home and they looked at it as if it was the eighth wonder.

-:-:-:-

Our Road vehicle repair was a problem. The authorised service agent would not give credit, so I had told the concerned to purchase new vehicles only after taking an undertaking from those who would give a credit period of ten days. The existing ones would act hep and rigid about payment against delivery but if you could see through them, they would bill you for cleaning of the AC ducts and AC gas charging when the Air Conditioning itself was not there.

-:-:-:-

Many of the inefficient/insecure staff members boasted of their 'achievements' of doing this or that, or even telling off supervisors or officers by giving them a piece of their minds while actually they would have been roasted by them. They whiled away their time with like-minded cronies and, on noticing higher-ups, 'pretended' to 'work hard' by gesticulating, making audible sounds or talking loudly to their colleagues or wiping their hands or sweat. They also loved to point out to the boldness of new appointees or their impudence by referring them to as not even half their age, remarking "but look at their arrogance". They took immense pleasure in making the comment, "Look at the audacity of that new boy – his service is less than the number of days I was absent on duty – and see how he works – he wants a trolley to transport the lube oil pump, while we used to carry it on one shoulder." or, "He is young, well built and eats 14 idlis for breakfast, but is unable to torque a bolt even with two hands. We could do it with one hand."

13

THE NEW OFFICE & A TASTE OF ACCOUNTS – PROFOUND!

The first best compliment I received from Sr. DME Anmol Ratan Kumar was when I went to tell him about my application to his office, with the earlier bad experience fresh in my mind. As I peeped into his chamber, I saw him busy talking, surrounded by nine staff members standing around him. I was about to turn back when he noticed, called me in by name and insisted that I sit before I talk. When I told him my purpose, he assured me that he would surely take me into his office in about two months when one of his Office Superintendents retired. If he took continuous leave, I would be called earlier. I apologized to the others in the room, thanked him and turned to leave. As I neared the door, my eyes became moist as I heard the Sr. DME apologizing, "Sorry guys, but some people should be given priority and their time should never be wasted! Now, where were we…?"

But within a fortnight, I was told one morning to immediately report to his office after lunch. My LF wished me and told to report first and that the transfer order would follow. Then I came to know the sudden development was because, among seven Ministerial staff, as we were called, no one was available that day, due to one OS finishing his leave before retirement, the Ch.OS undergoing rehabilitation for alcoholics, one clerk on maternity leave, two absent, one sick and the last one phoning up for leave. The Sr.DME was left fuming. When most returned from leave, I 'thanked' them, and hosted a mini-party of Masala Dosas and coffee.

-¦-¦-¦-

I was given the Stores portfolio here too among other sections, all of which were housed in one room. Here, the nature of work was different. It was to obtain necessary approvals and sanctions for procurement/repair of Loco spares after verification by our Accounts Department, pass bills of accepted NS material, scrap correspondence etc. Since there was shortage of staff, procurement of Rolling stock, performance of Loco spares, Maintenance of Loco instructions, Pollution Board aspects, etc. were conveniently added to my portfolio which was akin to buying one shirt and getting four more free.

The basic work, among register entries, filing and other cumbersome protocol procedures, involved drafting of letters to our Accounts and then to the Sanctioning Heads at Division or HQ for further process. All the proposals processing levels was governed by the delegation in GM's Schedule of Powers (SOP) which was compiled by HQ Accounts with technical consultant being Engineering Dept. which mainly dealt construction of assets and track maintenance. They had no inkling of other Departments' requirements and which were not addressed properly in the SOP. We, Diesel Sheds, suffered the most because of this. Having worked in the Shed, I knew the problems faced and hence, had that respect for the Shed, with the attitude to reduce their problems to the extent possible by working hard, and smart.

-¦-¦-¦-

Noticing traceability and other problems like one letter pertaining to three files, and where to file or to make three copies and file in all the three files, I made another innovation here called 'Combined-Single Filing System', which was liked by my Sr. DME. I filed all the letters pertaining to 42 files in one single file. Then, using a computer database, I made records for all the papers with data entry of skeletal details of the filed letters.

Tracing a filed letter was done through a Computer search program by selecting the kind of search from the Menu displayed (e.g. Datewise or Subject/Matter wise or File wise or Source/Destination wise etc.) and keying in the Searching string (of key words or date or file code).

Once, an officer from HQ wanted the date of his own letter (to trace it) about grease nomenclature sent to various Diesel Sheds, two or three years ago. He was very stressed but greatly relieved and impressed when I told him to hold the phone and gave him the details within 35 seconds.

But the next Sr. DME told me to revert to the old system as most of the staff were not computer savvy and would end up physically searching all files to trace an old letter, in my absence or in case of change of my portfolio.

-:--:--:-

Our office Ch.OS used to keep chewing 'Paan Masala' or 'Guthka' and could not answer his phone. When it rang, he would make an 'Oooooooo' sound to draw our attention and point to his phone to attend it. Another problem was that he was continuously drunk or off-duty, and the only phone in our huge room was on his table. It mostly rang when only another lady and I were available and I had to get up and attend it, with most people asking for the availability of the Sr. DME in his room. I would have to go and check that at the end of the corridor. It was so frustrating that I told my Ch.OS to provide me with a motorized wheel chair, and also a sensor on the Sr. DME's chair so that a bulb would light up in our office when he sat there.

Now, of course, we have two phones on each table with the facility to pick someone else's call or even transfer it. Instead of a sensor on the Sr. DME's seat, we hung a cowbell on his door which chimed while entering or exit.

-|-|-|-

I learnt that my first proposal for winding of some Induction Motors was returned by Accounts. Feeling insulted, I called up the dealer, Safina Begum, saying that I had enclosed the necessary budgetary rate reference from a firm for the estimated cost, and described the motors and its quantity. To this, she asked for details like which SOP it was proposed, the motor's make, rating and other specifications, where it was used, whether work would be affected or whether there was an alternative/spare, cost of motors, when procured and cost now, whether warranty is over, normal life expected of new motor and life expected after repairs and whether the repair is feasible or to procure new. She added that the budgetary quote did not mention a guarantee for workmanship or warranty for spares, and whether the removed copper wire and other items would be returned to Railways, the number of days for the rewinding, whether Railways would transport them to and fro, or if the firm would do it, how we would manage the work until the motors were repaired etc. She hit the nail on the head saying that "E" type of superior winding was normally recommended but the firm may have quoted for an inferior type. This really opened my eyes and feeling ashamed, I apologized and thanked her for her depth of involvement, and ensured that all my future proposals contained pucca, to the point information, and were self-explanatory. While making a proposal, I imagined I was Begum and also our HQ officers, in case there was any technical inaccuracy, or the Audit or Vigilance officer who could find faults and also as the end user and what he wanted and even as the motor itself and what it wanted. I would cover all angles.

Thus began a long relationship of mutual respect for each other as she, being good, was in that Section for many years and also as others didn't want that risky portfolio which required direct reporting to her Sr. DFM and not any sub-ordinate officers. I used to tell her which proposal was genuine or to return/reject unwanted proposals which my Sr. DME was forced to send, on telephonic pressure from HQ or a directive from the Railway Board or RDSO, based on some 'influence' of some Companies.

She once even concurred for the purchase of two turbo chargers which should never be done under Revenue account but, because its repair in Revenue by replacement of three of its damaged, critical, irreparable components, were costlier than a new turbo. The three components' replacement, plus its rotor balancing cost and transportation to and from the Company's workshop would cost Rs.22 lakhs for one turbo, whereas a new turbo just cost Rs.15 lakhs each! . By this, we could condemn those three components whose scrap metal fetched us a good price and other components could be kept as spares for future repair.

But one day we saw that Begum had returned one proposal with questions difficult to answer. I called her when she said that she had tried to contact me previously but I was on leave that day. I asked what had happened, to which she replied that the DRM had fired her boss for agreeing to some other proposal, and accused him of not going through proposals and accepting them blindly. So, to prove that they were going through them, her boss asked her to return all proposals at least once. I was thinking of what to do when she came with an idea, "Do one thing, Sachin; while sending proposals, leave out one or two points and I will ask for them in return." So before sending any proposal, I would give her four points, out of which she chose two. I wanted her to officially visit our Shed one day, but that never happened, and she got transferred from Demblur Division to the Construction Dept. where our office had no connections.

-!-!-!-

I heard some complaints about supplier's bills sent by me were not accepted and/or delayed. So I took a bunch of bills by the four o'clock train to see for myself. The dealer said she didn't take bills after four on weekdays and after one on Fridays. I protested that our office was the only office far away there, and that it was difficult to send our person before four, but it had no effect. I told her to at least treat our Shed's papers as a special case, but she refused. Then I lost my cool and we were talking in raised voices, when I noticed that arrangements for a retirement function were being done. So I toned down and left. But, eventually, we became best friends since I used to send the bills, enclosing proper details, avoiding minor irritants and even helped in the calculation of price variation formula etc.

-!-!-!-

Our heavy duty lathe was broken down and a nearby company did some critical loco components lathe work at reasonable rates. Once, a newly recruited Engineer fired the owner for no mistake of his. So the lathe owner told us that our business was peanuts to him, and to terminate the contract. The next alternative was very inconvenient and uneconomical. Our good relations managed to calm him down. We called the erring engineer and told him in layman's language that the lathe owner was like bridegroom's father while he was like the bride's father and should deal with him with humility and not hostility.

-:-:-:-

A new lady clerk, who had a good command over English and wanted to impress, was finishing her talk over the phone to an MNC which had delayed supplies. She raised her voice and said, "If I do not get a positive feedback shortly about the supply of the spares for the motor, we will stop buying motors from you and approach other companies." She slammed the phone down and looked at us, proud of herself and expecting to be appreciated. I said, "Madam, next time, before you speak, kindly tell us the name of the Company because the one you spoke to is the only manufacturer of these type of motors in this world!"

14

HOOKED, BOOKED & MY GOOSE IS COOKED? – LIFE'S NEWFOUND!

In August 1995, I gave my consent to my mother for marriage, and within three days, I was told that, Hema, a graduate from Bailur village, who was Prasanna's wife's paternal cousin, would be coming to see me on 6th Aug on a Sunday evening, along with her father, Mr.Rao. The match-making was done by her paternal Aunt. The meeting was arranged in Prasanna's house whose kitchen window faced ours. I had made a list of questions to be asked, and was keen on sharing my strengths, weaknesses, temper and medical issues as well.

I waved to Prasanna and his wife, Usha, in the kitchen as I made my way to their front entrance, alone. In the hall, I met Usha's parents, whom I knew, and Mr.Rao, who I found to be very humble, coming from an agricultural background. Prasanna joined us while Usha stayed inside, probably with Hema. Usha's parents started the conversation and told me about Hema's family, her elder brother and younger sister. Hema was a homely girl with not much exposure to the outside world, six years younger than me. I was told that she was soft natured and warned not to divulge the gory details of my accident/illnesses which were known to everyone in the room. I was to talk to her alone.

Usha brought Hema and sat her down while everyone, including Usha, left the room. She was tall and lean and had a very simple, friendly but attractive face. She had a narrow forehead and a long face which matched her frame. She kept staring down, hands clasped, sitting on the edge of the chair, nervous. Seeing that she was more nervous than me, my nervousness vanished. This was her first alliance too. I didn't know how to start the conversation as I had prepared questions and the list was in my back pocket. I said, "Why don't you sit comfortably? Are there any red ants on your seat?" At this, she became more nervous and fidgety. "Yikes," I cursed myself, "That was a brilliant start!"

I asked her whether she liked to watch movies to which she nodded her head, but did not specify the language. So I asked "Hindi?" She nodded again but did not open her mouth or look towards me. For "English" she shook her head and for "Kannada" she nodded. Further, she did not answer any question and only nodded or shook her head. "This is getting nowhere," I thought, "We're supposed to be here to make the biggest decision in our lives, not play Dumb Charades!"

So I went and called Usha and made her sit next to Hema. "Look, she is not answering or asking me anything, so you ask me the questions you asked when you met Prasanna and what your expectations were from him."

Usha asked some questions which I answered sincerely and even mentioned my weaknesses and strengths. My questions were again met with silence. So I asked whether she was ready for marriage when I first heard her soft voice. She said looking down, "Whatever Poppa says," meaning her father. I told Usha, "Look, I am not marrying her Poppa so it would help if she talked." She didn't, so I told her that

I would go home, discuss with my mother and come back. I told Usha to ask Hema's opinion about me, alone, without anybody's presence, especially her father's.

As I walked home, I saw Prasanna in the kitchen and gave him a Thumbs up sign. I went home and told my mother who had not come earlier because she said that some consider a widow's presence during these occasions as 'inauspicious'.

After some time, we made our way back to Prasanna's and while passing their kitchen, I saw Hema, Usha and Prasanna. Usha, on spotting us, smiled broadly and gave me an energetic double Thumbs up, joined by Prasanna.

As we all assembled and sat in the hall, I spoke. "From our side it is a 'Yes' with a capital 'Y', but her personal opinion is important too," to which Usha confirmed it as I continued, "But she should be ready for marriage and get adjusted to city life to the extent of running home errands, related to the bank, electricity bill, filling forms etc. since I don't have siblings to run around for me, and can't expect my aged mother to keep doing it. Also, I don't believe in dowry and prefer to have only a Reception at Bangalore after a temple wedding, or just a registered marriage."

They discussed between themselves and asked me if I had any objection if they conducted the marriage at their home in Bailur which had a big compound. This is also since she was the elder daughter and this was the first marriage in her family.

We relented, understanding that a traditional wedding celebration would have a good bearing, especially on Hema's younger sister's marriage alliance in future, since Mr.Rao was a highly respected person in Bailur. The engagement date was fixed as 5th September at Prasanna's place, after which she would stay for about a month in her Aunt's place about two kms away, to get 'acclimatized' to city life. The marriage and reception dates would be decided in due course. All of us were snacking when Prasanna came over and announced, "You are luckier than me, Sachin. When I went to see Usha the first time, it was like seeing a doll, which did not even blink. At least Hema spoke one sentence and did move her head." Later, I found why Hema was avoiding opening her mouth. Apart from being shy, she was conscious of an extra small projection of a tooth, a la handsome actor Shashi Kapoor of India, and her teeth were large in proportion to her face. But that smile actually complemented her face, and did not look bad at all, and I told her so. But she was still affected by it even after I remarked that one should believe any opinion given about one's physical appearance, especially if it came from the opposite gender. I had found something I could pull her leg with, all my life. When I asked her in general what she liked, I didn't know what expression to put on when she replied, "Sky blue colour, the smell of petrol and naphthalene balls!"

So they extended their stay by a couple of days and I called office the next morning for two days leave and told them about the developments. They were more than happy to give me leave and joked that even if I came, they would not allow me inside the office.

-:-:-:-

The next morning Usha, though free, excused herself from joining us even though we needed some moral support. I picked up Hema from her Aunt's place. The whole family came out to say goodbye as if we were going on a long tour. We saw the film 'Zamaana Deewana' and quite liked it, and then had Idli Sambar, Masala Dosa, Rasagulla and

Badam milk in my favourite Vishu Bhavana hotel which I used to frequent during college breaks. She loved every item but I got emotional when I learnt that it was going to be demolished to make way for a swanky shopping mall.

She insisted on paying the bill this time, which I didn't allow saying, "If you pay, it will be embarrassing for me. Anyway, after marriage, I will only have to do all the paying, so let us practise it now itself."

When we went back to her Aunt's place, there was the customary pulling of our leg about whether we actually saw the film, and requests to describe the story, etc. Then they planned to shop for her when she would stay for a longer time after the engagement. They were planning to buy a big suitcase for her, and I told them to buy a smaller one as I would be its carrier most of the time. Hema also wanted a pimple cream for which I said that the small pimples actually looked good on her simple, friendly face. When she insisted, I told her to retain a few of the pimples for my sake. I, however, suggested a big tooth brush, the size of a shoe brush, for effective brushing. The next day, I dropped them to the bus pick-up point and found that I had instilled lots of confidence in her. Her father was very pleased and, thankfully, my sense of humour stayed alive and came good at the right moments, which found favour with everyone. I was invited to their place.

A few days later, I told my mother and Prasanna that I had to go for my checkup at RH/PER by the night train. The next morning I woke up a sleepy Prasanna, "Hey, Prasanna, help me, I am phoning from a coin booth and I don't have more than three coins. I am in Murudeshwar – how do I go to Bailur from here?"

"What? What are you doing there? What about your checkup?" It all came to him in a flash and said "Okay, there is only one hotel near the bus stop. Ask for Anil, the travel agent's small shop cum home. He knows Hema's place and will arrange the auto rickshaw for you at a fixed rate of Rs.100. Lastly, ENJOY yourself, you mischievous fellow! I will tell your mother that you have reached safely," and then remembering something, added. "Take a litre of milk from the hotel as they have a problem of supply there."

Anil was happy to know about me, as being a travel agent, I was a potential regular customer and would bring him many more. After a five km drive on the National Highway 17, and a two km bumpy ride from Bailur cross to the left, off the highway, the auto reached the small gate of the Lakshmi Temple and the driver directed me to go to the compound adjacent to the front of the temple to a house named 'Gowrishankar', at which I asked, "Everybody knows everyone here, is it?" to which he replied "It's a small village of 6000 people, and Mr.Rao is a respectable man." As I paid the amount, I reflected, "Over 500 kms in a super-deluxe bus at Rs.120 and 7 kms by auto at Rs.100. Super!"

It was 7.15 a.m and a man was sweeping the temple premises, his back towards me. As I greeted "Namaskar," I found him to be Mr. Rao, my future father-in-law, who exclaimed, "Arre! Come, come! You should have informed us, we would have come to receive you!" to which I said, "All the fun would have gone if I had done that."

As we went into their compound, he called out, "Shali, Hemu, look who has come." Some lights lit up in the house and there was a flurry of activity. Obviously, Hema and her sister, Malini, were rudely woken up and told to brush and become presentable, while their mother, Shalini, and brother, Gautam, were already awake and came out. "Bhaiyya, give it to me," Gautam snatched my suitcase and as we went inside, I saw Hema and Malini come out, wiping their faces, sharing the same towel. On seeing me, Hema snatched the towel and covered her face, while Malini giggled and greeted, "Hello, Bhaiyya," and I greeted back, "Hi, Malini!" I turned towards Hema, "I am here for two days and if you wanted to keep your face covered, I would have brought a veil or a Goddess Durga's or Kali's mask for it." She slowly removed the towel and looked fresh and good, without make-up, smiling coyly when I asked why she didn't do this while in the city.

But what I felt refreshingly humbling was that it was as if like I was already their son-in-law, and being away from the concrete jungle and the hip, hectic, synthetic environment in my city to this green, fresh-aired, down-to-earth atmosphere, was a welcome metamorphosis from our city's over-hyped, still hyping and ever griping world.

To the enquiry about the bus journey, I said there was no problem but since I have travel sickness, I felt a bit groggy and would have a nap after breakfast. I prayed the broad gauge conversion would be over soon so that I could travel comfortably by train to and from Murudeshwar, where there was a stop.

They had another Aunt, Mr Rao's elder sister, visiting them and she came out and we exchanged pleasantries. She told me that Hema was a very shy girl – so shy of men that whenever she got down from the bus on the highway, while returning from college, she would put her head down and walk straight. Her impression of a male was, when she saw the edge of a pant or a 'lungi' from the corner of her eye, she would walk faster. Every time her father or brother went to pick her up at the Bailur cross, she would often walk past them without seeing their faces. So I said, if this happens after marriage, I will wear Bermudas or three-fourths pant or joker's oversized shoes, for an identification to make her look up.

Breakfast was 'dosas' with potato curry with gravy which was superb. They prepared only the basic bland food on a gas stove and all curries, rice porridge and spicy items on a clay stove using firewood which retains the original flavours of the ingredients, to give it a rustic, homely but delicious taste of which one never gets fed up.

The sea was just five minutes' walk away and could be heard from their house. Humidity was high, but one felt hungry because of the high rate of digestion due to the healthy, coastal climate. After my nap, we went to their huge garden overlooking the sea, and had tender coconuts, and then a look at their fields which mostly grew paddy, and later groundnuts, in the same patch. Rice porridge was served as filler just after noon and the 2:30 lunch comprised of fish curry and fry with boiled rice. Sea food was fresh and cheap and my mother-in-law was a fantastic cook, with her daughters helping with preparatory activities, stone grinding the 'masala', batter and 'chutney'. Hema didn't know to cook but said she was keen on learning to which I told her to cook only on Friday evenings at my home so that I would have two days to recover, in case of any culinary distortions. She once prepared an easy sweet dish called 'Sheera' or 'Kesari bath' to impress me. It was tasty but so sweet that my middle finger ended up doing 'overtime'. She'd created an impression alright – a little in my heart, a bit more in my mind, but a lasting one in my behind.

Mr Rao's generation consisted of 11 siblings, all staying separately outside Bailur, who altogether had 22 offsprings. I had memorized the 11 in order of emergence and their present locations, to impress all.

-|-|-|-

After two days, pending works started to haunt me and I was back to work with mouth-watering details of experiences that caused envy. I had put on some weight and my face was puffed and glowing, and on asking, I left it to their imagination, remarking that it must be the lipstick that Hema uses which must have contained a lot of vitamins and protein.

"So it's going to be the taming of the shrew, eh?" a colleague asked, to which I replied, "No, in fact, she's too tame, I have to untame her!"

-|-|-|-

The engagement preparations were on and, as it was at 4:30 p.m on a weekday, it was monopolized by ladies, teasing us incessantly. Except for Gautam, my brother-in-law in waiting, everyone else attended from Bailur as they could not keep the house locked. On this auspicious day, I had earlier taken Hema and Malini out for an early non-vegetarian lunch which they ate and relished, after a lot of initial protesting about having non-vegetarian that day. I told them that, having ordered the items by phone to save time, we would have to pack it, bring it home and hide the smells, which were easier hidden in their tummies. Prasanna had assured me he would just make it on time from work. When the discussion came to the matching of horoscopes, I said that my mother and I didn't believe in it, nor had we consulted any astrologer. "However," I said, "Rather than mine, Hema's horoscope must match with my mother's which is more important, as she would be spending more time in the day with her, than with me." As all became seriously attentive, I continued, "In fact, even if Hema gets an average husband in me, she is blessed in getting a gem of a mother-in-law, unlike those in today's TV serials, one who is very caring, supportive and accommodating, and will stand like a pillar by her side in case of the smallest fault by me. In fact, she is so understanding that recently when she came to know that we both like sky-blue colour, she went shopping and without informing us, and brought three underwears of sky blue colour. They were small for me and probably meant for Hema. Isn't my mother a sweet gem?" As they all screamed with laughter, a couple of them playfully hit me with their purse saying, "No non-vegetarian jokes on this auspicious occasion," to which I said, "Then why did you laugh? You devoured it, savoured it and will expend it later, and now you call 'foul' which is unfair."

As the rituals started from the Pooja Room where I stood near the door with Prasanna behind me, the 'Pujari' came out, 'vibhuti' applied on his forehead and arms in three horizontal lines. Reciting mantras, he held up the bowl of red 'kumkum' to me and I took a pinch of it with the tips of my ring finger and thumb and, noticing he didn't have kumkum on his forehead, applied it there, much to stifled giggles from the back. For a moment the Pujari stopped reciting, looked at me, patted his forehead, disappointed at my ignorance, and continued reciting. This time, he took the kumkum, smiled and applied it on my forehead and continued ahead. I slowly pushed Prasanna forward, as he was more aware of the formalities, and sneaked behind him, to imitate his actions and avoid future bloopers.

-:-:-:-

The wedding date was fixed on 7th December, 1995 at their residence at Bailur with a reception on 25th December, 1995 at Bangalore since most of the relations from both sides were there. Before that, she would stay for a month and a half at her Aunt's place. I started gymming to put something onto me, having seen my lean frame in the engagement photos.

The unique and blissful moments experienced during the intervening period of the engagement and the marriage in an arranged marriage, were the best ever, and can never be relived. The trust we gained, and the natural interaction, made it like an arranged love marriage. Suddenly, the grass was greener, the sky more blue, I was on cloud nine, all too good to be true.

Everything - the surroundings, the office atmosphere, the ribbing by friends and relatives – everything seemed to complement the feeling.

A friend noticed that I had put on some muscle, especially on my behind. So he joked poetically, "I guess it must have been, the effect of lipstick with vitamins and protein?" He stood and took a bow.

"No, yaar, we haven't gone that far, it's just plain gymming, over and above par."

They all said, "Wow, time for you also to take a bow!"

-·-·-·-

When Hema finished her stay, I went with her to Bailur. We had just reached the house when our match-maker Aunt called to give the good tidings that Malini's horoscope had matched a boy's – also from my city and he was staying just six kms away, working with the Customs. So Malini and her father accompanied me on my return journey. And, since it carried some weightage, I was also told to accompany the contingent to his house.

As we sat in the hall waiting for the boy, for a change, Malini's Aunt told me to not to crack any indecent jokes, and watch my mouth, as the boy's family were very devout. I nodded and assured her in sign language that I had my mouth zipped. She had also given strict instructions to the bold Malini to sit with her head bent, and her mouth shut.

As the boy, named Saikiran, made his way, clean shaven, looking dapper in a 'kurta pyjama', I leaned and whispered to Malini who, with her head down, had not yet seen him, "You were teasing Hema that she was marrying a 'Moochmunda' (moustache-less man), eh? Now let's see what you've got to say." Malini's face became red and as I was shushed by her Aunt, I told her that the blushing would help.

In no time, the alliance clicked and they had a Pujari ready with them as they were in a hurry to finish the wedding by the end of the year. We sat the couple on the swing on the first floor and got down to business. The engagement was to be in the following week, and taking cognizance of mine and Hema's rituals, the Pujari, after browsing his 'Ready Reckoner', fixed the marriage date on 10th December, as against my 7th, with the reception on 24th December, a day before mine, at the same venues.

For a moment all seemed fine, when it suddenly struck me that my elaborately planned Goa honeymoon and advance booked tickets/hotel had gone for a six along with my post-honeymoon travels to Pune and Mumbai.

While all started to gorge on the delicious food, I caught hold of the Pujari and Hema's Aunt and started bargaining. I said I didn't mind sharing the altar and having both the marriages on the 7th, which would save on expenses and other logistics. The Pujari said the date was not right for Saikiran. I asked the Aunt whether I could postpone my wedding to the 10th which was refused. "Instead," she said sympathetically, "Why don't you postpone all your programmes by exactly three days," to which I said my program was so hectic that if I postponed it even by two days, both I and Hema would not be available, either for Malini's reception or for our own! And to fill my cup to the brim, I would be relegated from the boy's side to being the girl's within a day of my marriage.

Finally, after a lot of bartering, I took my place on the victory podium for the Bronze medal whereas both the Pujari and Auntie shared the Gold. "Okay," I consoled myself, "At least Hema will be coming here to attend Malini's engagement next week," and the thought lit up my face. I went over to Saikiran and told him loudly so that all future prospects or their parents would get educated by my message, "You hardly have time between the engagement and the marriage, so make the most of it by ensuring regular interaction with Malini during the period, as these beautiful moments of getting to know each other and that chemistry can never be experienced after marriage."

-:--:--:-

For the marriage, I had hired two vans, one for my mother and relatives, and the other for my office friends, including some sight-seeing. I went by bus two days before December 7th along with a cousin of mine and, while alighting, three of her uncles came to Murudeshwar to receive me. I impressed them, addressing them by their names and asking about the welfare and the presence of their other siblings. I booked a corner room on the 1st floor of the temple's huge guesthouse cum hotel which was built on rocks, overlooking the sea, with a wonderful sunset view from the room's 'L' shaped balcony. If we sat or stood in the balcony, it felt as if we were sailing on a giant ship, like the 'Titanic', with the friendly sea waves nudging the rock structure below it. The rates were nominal and I booked it for a week till the 11th morning, as I knew Hema's place would be crammed, especially for the night stay. For my office gang, I booked a couple of rooms on the fourth floor for two days in another corner, to avoid any 'disturbance' to me from them, and also from me to them.

On 6th night, since many would've left by 7th evening, all youngsters and couples partied on the first floor at Hema's house, celebrating our marriage, as relatives and friends got together, duly not inviting us, the couple, as we were to keep ourselves 'pure' for the next day!

They had erected a big 'mantapa' made out of thermocol; the open areas were fully sheltered with ceilings made of knitted coconut tree leaves with two corner 'Pandals' - one for a temporary kitchen at a corner, and the other for placing 12 dining tables. On D-day, the rituals went smoothly and we were married. They were announcing lunch when I was told that there was one last traditional formality pending.

I had heard about hiding the groom's footwear, but this one took the cake – they would hide the bride in the big house and I had to search her out. They hid her and said that if I didn't find her in ten minutes, I would have to pay money to them, to get her. I was desperately hungry and necessity was the mother of ideas. So I went to my unsuspecting brother-in-law, who was serving lunch, and told him that the Priest had remembered some other ritual and needed me and Hema immediately. "Where is she?" to which he replied, “In the Puja Room.” So I hurried through all rooms and went into the dark Puja room, and brought Hema out to some wicked adjectives mouthed by the ladies’ brigade following me, like “Cheater cock”, “Spoilsport,” “cunning fox” etc. to which I promised to compensate for the disappointment, if any, during Saikiran’s search three days later. As decided much earlier, Saikiran and his family didn’t attend our wedding for obvious reasons and I too felt that some charm would’ve been lost if they had.

Later in the evening, around 7:30 after an early dinner, the Raos had arranged a gathering which would showcase their talents in the form of songs, skits and jokes related to marriages. It was nice till 8:30 when I wanted to poo but didn’t get up, out of courtesy. I didn’t even feel like reciting the romantic poem which I had laboriously written. At 9:00, they went out of context and started singing Bhajans and the ‘knocking’ in my backside had turned into a ‘pounding’ or in other words, the ‘courtesy’ was turning into ‘gallantry’. If it were to ‘explode’ I would’ve become a martyr who had died of embarrassment, and probably the first one in history for unpleasantly morbid reasons. Thankfully, my father-in-law came to my rescue and told us take leave as we had to go to Murudeshwar. So we went in one van, followed by my office friends in another. As we rushed to our room, one friend, who was unaware of my ordeal, remarked, “Look! They don’t want to waste any time! Anyway, see you tomorrow if possible!” They were to do some early morning sightseeing and reach Demblur by evening.

I was in the toilet for 20 minutes when Hema saw some creeping shadows on the windows adjacent to the room’s main door. The shadows were magnified due to some light in the opposite corridor. She recognized one of the shadows to be my cousin's and hence, didn't panic. She tapped softly on the toilet door and whispered about the proceedings. I came out and announced loudly, "Our show starts in three minutes and I am coming out to sell the tickets." I suddenly unbolted and opened the main door, as a couple of them, bent, with ears to the door, fell in and four others, on their knees, grinned sheepishly. They had brought a conch, a temple bell, hotel watchman's whistle and finger cymbals and had come in another van, to make a din at some 'opportune moment'. To make up for the anticlimax, Hema and I took them and the van drivers to an ice-cream parlour to cool down, and then had some 'paan'. I told them that if they wanted to curse their luck or themselves, it would have the best effect with paan in their mouth. When the 'paanwala' charged me for some cigarettes they had taken, I told him that as a policy, I don't sponsor such lifespan reducers, and asked him to take that money from the smokers. We then went back to our room, giving ice cream cones to the watchman and hotel reception on the way, cautioning them against entertaining any more revellers.

The next morning, we went with our van to receive Saikiran and party as their bus would terminate quite near to our hotel. On their arrival, we found they were 19 as a group, and didn't know that if there were 15 or more, the bus could be extended till Bailur. The bus transport operator obliged and so we all and a couple of other thankful passengers, alighted at Bailur where we took the bus crew to have breakfast with us. The bus then returned to Murudeshwar, giving a free ride to some more villagers.

Saikiran and Malini's marriage went well and the time came for hiding Malini! I told Saikiran that I would help him. Her friends hid her among a heap of mattresses while

I noticed that her cousin's wife was of similar height and face cut. She was wearing a shiny saree and I put a couple of garlands on her and hid her in the dark Puja room, exactly at the same spot where Hema had hidden, three days earlier. I told her to keep her face down at any cost, and not to look up at anyone entering. I then hid myself in a very sensitive place. Saikiran started his search, walking slowly, followed by the ladies' brigade. Thankfully he missed spotting her among the mattresses and moved on to the toilets and lavatories. As he opened the second lavatory door, I suddenly stood up from inside and came out, screaming "Aaaaaaarghhhhhh," and 'covered' my sensitive areas, acting as if my 'modesty' was 'outraged'. I joined Saikiran in the hunt and as we neared the Puja room, I indicated with my eyes that Malini was inside. He entered slowly and in the darkness, 'spotted' her to his right and triumphantly headed towards 'her'. As he went out of view, his hands were raised.

In about two seconds, we heard a scream and the woman came running out, face down, blushing red, but smiling. Saikiran came out behind her, his face even redder. I mockingly asked, "What did you do to her, I say?" to which he squeaked, "I...I...I just went to hold and twist her ear...nothing else," to which I said "Are you sure? We saw you going towards her with both hands raised as if to catch her, whereas only one hand was enough for her ear, which definitely is not big as an elephant's." This episode became more famous than mine.

-:-:-:-

My mother and relatives left in their van immediately after lunch. Saikiran and family left early next morning for a pilgrimage and soon after, Hema and I left for Goa for our truncated honeymoon of five to two days, and then to Pune and onward to Mumbai. In Mumbai, in my relative's place where we were staying, they wished us good night and I reciprocated, waving good night to everyone and mockingly to Hema also, who said, "Hey, what do you mean? I am sleeping with you," to which I said, "Is it? Thank you, and so very kind of you!"

We returned back to Bangalore on 24th morning to attend Saikiran's reception and, of course, for ours on 25th. As our house was very near the venue, we told Saikiran's family to come over to my place in the morning, and then go to the venue from there. By chance, our conversation veered towards the evening menu and we were pleasantly surprised to find that, though the caterers were different, Saikiran's menu and mine were exactly the same, except for the sweet item. Everyone was enjoying the humour in it when I suddenly gasped, "Gak! That means that common relatives attending my reception tomorrow will think they are having today's leftovers!"

Both the receptions went well and many of my Shed's staff members also attended. They were quite surprised when I attended office the very next day. I joked that I was taking a break from a hectic wedding and honeymoon and had come to office for some fresh air.

15

HONEYMOONED - OUT OF BOUND!

I told my colleagues that I needed more leave for a proper honeymoon. I went later to Kodaikanal in 1996 with another newly married Shed technician and his wife, sharing all the costs. This was more fun than just the two of us going. Two newly married couples going outstation together, I feel, is a better and safer option as our agenda was quite common - enjoy without being miserly, but book two different, but preferably adjacent rooms. As there would be same gender support also, we could feel so free to the extent of painting the town red. We didn't take the package tour and went on our own, dodging brokers, who would fleece us as well as the service provider. For sightseeing, the car arranged by the broker would cost us Rs.600. In a travel agency, their van would charge us Rs.150 per head, which worked out the same. To attract us, the travel agent's boy said, "In addition, at no extra costs, we will show you some suicide points!" I told him that the first suicide point was their travel agency itself. We went to the petrol bunk corner as advised by our hotel help, where three cars were standing, totally uninfluenced by brokers. The cost was Rs.350 and the tour was proper, with no curtailment whatsoever. The driver also refused lunch or money as his house was nearby, and had it there and came back.

-:-:-:-

As we checked out of the hotel, we generously tipped the help who requested us to take his photo in front of the hotel, and post him two copies so that he could send one to his family back home. As we waited at the bus stop to go down to Madurai, we were joined by another couple who were also proceeding there. A car stopped some distance away and its occupants got out after paying the driver. I guessed it had come on a one-way trip and could return empty. It had a Madurai Registration number. As I confirmed with the driver that he was returning to Madurai, three brokers came from nowhere, elbowed me away and spoke animatedly with the driver. They looked at me and asked me if I was going to Madurai and how many people. I said only two to which they said Rs.300, which I paid to the broker, after the driver nodded. The brokers shared Rs.225, gave Rs.75 to the driver, and vanished. I sat in the car and told him to take it to the bus stop. I called out to the third couple to join us which they did happily. I told them only five of us could sit comfortably and one's wife would have to sit on the husband's lap. They were all more than willing and, in fact, there was competition for that. Then we decided that all the couples would do it by turns on the way, only that in their eagerness and enthusiasm, they should ensure they sat on the correct lap. As we started, I asked the driver whether he was free in the afternoon and would take us sightseeing in Madurai, which I had not mentioned in case the brokers took advantage of that also. The driver was more than happy to do that for Rs.400 and thanked me for not telling this to the brokers as well as indicating only one couple, earlier. I also told the driver to take us to a clean and tasty vegetarian hotel which need not be fancy, for lunch. He took us to his favourite hotel which was quite okay with old wooden tables and chairs and food served on plantain leaves. The full meal was typical Tamil Nadu tasty food with no baking soda to feel 'full', costing a 'princely' Rs.18 per meal! We overate, and the driver even dropped us to the Railway station, refusing any tip.

-|-|-|-

In the computer room, three months later, Mr.Jaipal Singh, a Junior Engineer, was browsing through the Railway time table. On asking, he lamented that all his marriage leave was over in travelling and in rituals. He had had no time for a honeymoon and he planned to go to Ooty, applying a week's leave, wanting to make optimum utilization of time and expenditure. I told him that there was a once in a lifetime scheme for that now in the Railways, which I missed three months earlier, adding that I could join him with my wife, as I preached that two couples would always be best. In that scheme, the Railways would give us a first class pass instead of IInd class which we were otherwise only eligible for, along with one week's leave on their account. They would even book the well-maintained Ooty Railway holiday home for a week.

His eyes lit up and, without any hesitation, he agreed and asked me to plan at the earliest. "How do we go about it? What do I have to do?"

I said, "Nothing, the Railways will do everything. We only have to fill a form each with the time when we reach Ooty, and a nomination with contact details."

"What nomination and what for? In case something happens to us?"

"No, no, we have to nominate either our name or our wife's."

"For what?" he asked, getting impatient.

"For undergoing Family Planning Operation!"

He chased me down the corridor and we had a good laugh when I told him that this scheme was on just for now only. Normally, after the operation, apart from a week's leave, one is only given a sweet lime or 'mosambi' and a transparent pack containing four glucose biscuits as nutrition to aid 'early recovery'.

I narrated this and two other incidents during Jaipal's promotional transfer send-off, which had the gathering in splits.

-:-:-:-

One day, in the Control Room, after the computer room was closed, Jaipal and I were checking on some data in the Computer and then went to cross-check it in the Loco History book kept on a shelf. After some time there was a panic attack sounded by the telephone clerks that the computer was not working. We were worried as we had worked on it last and being the only computer, it required to be working continuously. We had a look at the monitor and nothing seemed to be wrong. A clerk said that they wanted to enter an incoming Loco's details like the number, date, time etc. but nothing was working though the program was opening. I noticed that the Number Lock key 'Num Lock' was off as I had pressed it earlier. Now I pressed it 'on' and hey presto, the computer worked to their liking! I asked them how long they had been using the computer and was stunned by their reply, "Over five years!"

-:-:-:-

Another day, I was typing on the computer when Jaipal came over, wished me and bent down just next to me to check the networking cable junction on the floor. I asked him if he had had breakfast to which he confirmed, "Yes." I then asked him what he had for breakfast to which he said, still bent, "I am in an awkward position, Sachin, shall I answer your questions later?"

I replied, "I am in a more awkward position, Jaipal, and even if you mind, I need to know for sure what you had for breakfast now, because, if you let go from behind, I am sitting at point blank range, as you will find." He stood up and we had a hearty laugh.

-:-:-:-

We had a promotee officer, Mr Balachandra, who was very arrogant, always threatening even senior supervisors that he would write adverse remarks on their Confidential Report and see to it that they were retired early with no pension etc. Even confronting him, saying that he had also been like them until recently, or complaining to the Sr. DME, did not change him. He was harsh on my office colleagues even if they were eight minutes late. Even Trade Union representatives were treated shabbily. Everyone was looking for an opportunity to teach him a lesson.

One day, in the absence of the Sr. DME, he ordered our office driver to take his wife, residing in the Railway Quarters, for shopping. The driver, who had also felt the brunt of his loftiness, communicated it to the Trade Union.

As the vehicle with his wife, Anshu, and his nine year old kid, was nearing the Shed's exit gate, a Trade Union Leader came in front of the vehicle and signalled it to stop, as the security at the gate looked on. He 'admonished' the driver for using the vehicle for somebody's private use.

"What, madam, going on your honeymoon without your own husband and your own vehicle?" asked the leader in the local language, knowing she didn't understand it, and ordered all to get down or be arrested. Quickly they obeyed. Anshu was a grotesque figure – very fat, wearing a blood red T-Shirt, blue jeans, a straw hat, and thick sunglasses which made her look like a gaudy old bat. He told her to get a palanquin from home or walk back home and as they did, called out, "Feel the road for a change and watch out for bulls and snakes on the way!" Not having walked at all, nor observing the route whenever she had travelled, she lost her way and somehow found it later with the help of her son, as she didn't have the courage and humility to ask anyone the way to her own house. To the curious, she said she was taking a walk.

Mr Balachandra, who had no inkling of what had happened, received a phone call from Delhi which could be overheard in three other parallel connections. It was from his father-in-law, who yelled, "I gave you one crore as dowry and you didn't use your own car and its driver meant for the purpose. I even got you the officer's promotion through my contacts, and this is how you repay me, you cheapskate. I am sending your mother-in-law to console our daughter who is still in shock, and wheezing. At least send your own car with its driver to the airport this time, you idiot!" The next day, on the wall of the office urinals, one could see the graffiti like 'Red Bull' and 'one crore idiot' and 'Bala- the elephant mahout'.

16

ACCOUNTS & OFFICE PROBLEMS RISE & POUND!

One day a bill was returned by the Accounts department seeking a warranty certificate and a calibration certificate pertaining to the item in the bill. I phoned Accounts saying that it was the end user's prerogative to check that and, if in order, he would certify it, after which the bill was passed. For this, she said to meet her officer who was adamant about it. So I went to the Divisional office, setting aside all my pending work. The officer told me to calm down and to first sit down. Then he told me why he was insisting on them. It seems when he was an office superintendent some years back, he had passed a bill of Construction department for a lorry which was never purchased, though the minimum required papers for passing the bill were in order. One year later, he passed a repair bill for the same lorry, when the Vigilance department got to know of it. His condition was pathetic as he had go to the Vigilance HQ at Chennai several times and justify for both - the prosecution and defence - as to why the bill could be passed and why it shouldn't have been passed. He was issued a charge sheet as he had not delved deeper into the papers. Due to this, his promotion was delayed and was still under probation and he didn't want to take any chances. "So, until I am here, kindly send whatever I ask." And I used to always say that whenever Accounts or Audit wanted some details, give the reply or documents to the extent what they ask and nothing extra, because they would find something wrong or 'interesting' in the extra details sent.

-|--|--|-

Our Sr.DME (Mr ARK) called all the office staff to his chamber for his monthly review of our work that he had noted. He asked one by one about the status of the work for which he mostly received replies like, "I'm on the job, Sir," or "Tomorrow I will start, Sir." When my turn came, it was like, "That indent is already verified by Accounts and approved by DRM. It is in your HQ pending papers with a covering letter to HQ, as you said you said you will take it personally" or "That repair proposal was sent to Accounts who returned it as the new dealer had some doubts which you wanted to personally clarify along with the resubmission letter already made and signed by you, Sir." After getting similar answers for four of his questions, he looked at me and asked me a question which was the best compliment I received for my proactive, hard work. He asked, "Am I chasing you or are you chasing me?"

-|--|--|-

He then blasted my colleague, Nagraj, for not having done a single task of whatever he had noted. As we came out, I asked Nagraj why he didn't do them as he had been on duty for the whole month. He casually replied, "Arre, I will do it when I feel like doing it. By doing it early, it is not going to give me any promotion or extra money or praise." I remarked that it was not about promotion or money, but about doing something for the country, or at least for the salary one took. He said it was about promotions or salary because he compared his progress with that of a Stores Dept. office clerk on the 1st floor named Murthy.

Nagraj was a science graduate while Murthy had only passed his tenth standard. Both were from the General Quota and had written and passed the same Railway Clerk exam in 1990. Both were from Demblur and had opted for Demblur as their first choice among the others given. But since Nagraj had scored more marks over Murthy, he was posted to Demblur in the Mechanical dept. and Murthy to Mysore in the Stores dept. But Murthy was absent continuously, citing medical reasons which he worked out cunningly and got a transfer to Chiroti, whereas Nagraj was posted to Chiroti right from day one. After 7 years, Nagraj was still a junior clerk whereas Murthy had got two promotions. Murthy's gross pay was almost double to Nagraj's as of now. It was an issue about promotion and salary also for him. Additionally, one Junior Engineer from Shed who had a paralytic stroke was medically de-categorized and posted in Chiroti as a Head Clerk, with seniority above Nagraj. He was unable to do any work due to the paralysis. And, to rub salt on the wound, a Station Master from the Commercial Branch was medically de-categorized and placed in the Mechanical Branch, posted in Chiroti, again with seniority above him. At least they should have posted him in the Commercial Branch, was Nagraj's valid point. The Station Master also had given a letter reporting that he couldn't read, write, type or use computer which, when forwarded to DRM for transferring him, was returned with a handwritten remark - "You manage somehow!" Nagraj said, "There are several RPF staff also waiting to exploit the medical rules and come as clerks. Class IV employees are promoted and posted as clerks and don't know to draft or use computers. This is the way vacancies are filled up with no skilled staff, and there is no creation of posts for clerks being made saying the computer will do the work. Instead, they are surrendering clerical and other posts to create officers' posts. In our office, there are four working clerks and four officers, whereas the same office in the Division has 21 clerks and four officers, with many clerks working for more than 15 years in the same office. Check this deploring fact - in our office, we go for a rare outing, and that too on a holiday for one day, whereas they make groups and go to Kashmir and other faraway places for 7 to 10 days at a stretch.

Suppose there is a problem identified in a stocked item, the Stores Dept. places it for our remarks or redressal as they follow a very organized but narrow path of work. Anything slightly out of the way will be dropped on our lap and all the dirty work like removing the diaper, cleaning up and putting a new one, is to be done by us. Do you know that satellite Stores depots in diesel sheds have got a very definite and detailed yardstick for each and every post whereas the main Shed's yardstick of Ministerial staff is incoherent and open to any kind of interpretation? Also, the Stores dept. has faster and many more promotions and, ironically, their salaries are paid from our budget. At least you got your first promotion in three years but nothing for me. Where is the motivation to work? It is a thankless job with no prospects. You will get some nice words from your officers when it suits their plan, that's all. The more you work, the more responsibilities will be given to you. Here, in this office, the substitute for hard work is more hard work – no improvement or streamlining in the system, nor time for us to do so. Those who enjoy themselves continue doing so with no or less work but full pay, and their work is given to us. Those who don't work or pretend not to know computers, are transferred to an office which turns out more convenient to them, whereas people like you, Sachin, are exploited and never transferred, being the golden goose. Let him transfer me if he doesn't like my working. Do you remember the junior most lady clerk who was posted to Chiroti on a one-way transfer from Mysore and then, within two months, transferred to some other department in Demblur Division, with a five-day week office, by the then DRM, for her convenience. What is the meaning of having a lien in one branch while being transferred to another? While we wait for years, this lady gets a plum one-way transfer and inspite of being the junior most, also gets a choice posting while we, several years senior to her in Service as well as in the Division, are not transferred even on having applied years back. For years, we hope that the DRM will throw a crumb whereas this lady not only gets the cake and eats it too, and that too topped with icing and a cherry by the top administrator in the Division. Most officers are bothered only about their interests, comfort and problem-free working during their tenure, faking numerous 'achievements' for the sake of showing achievements and improvements in their annual self-appraisal exercise. When they get transferred, they want to go with their head high and bum intact. Our work or achievements mostly cannot be quantified nor exhibited, and are stomped and swept aside. Our cadre is becoming extinct in Railways with no or very feeble representation at any levels for resurrection. In the staff creation proposals made in our office, in which, at every stage, even after justifying and convincing, the clerical or Ministerial staff are struck down at the next level, and only the technical staff are processed and that too shoddily reducing their numbers. An officer or a Shed technical staff member can point to someone and get emergency or excess things done whereas, in our sphere of work, we have to point to ourselves or our own ass to get work done. If we go on leave, almost all our work we only have to do after we return. We are an endangered species, but officers safe-guard their cadre at any cost, since all policy decisions are made by them, and they can toy with the lower level. Once, to give promotion to an officer, a Sr. DME post was redesignated as Dy. CME, and another post created as Sr. DME. The office name was changed with great difficulty and then reverted to Sr. DME after a few months, withdrawing the Dy. CME post. This played havoc in our correspondence and other aspects and we suffered in unimaginable proportions, much more than the officials. Our own Ch.OS also didn't support us. He was busy drinking and at the mercy of the Sr. DME and would not represent or solve any of our problems, also because he had attained the highest possible promotion with no need for any botheration. But he had the courage to make inflated bills during some occasions and shamelessly pocket leftovers of cashew nuts, biscuits or leftovers, uneaten by visitors. During dignitaries' visits, I think he wore two pants so that he could pocket more. When going for tea, his inviting all and sundry and never paying is legendary. He is not a Chief OS, but Cheap OS."

I could empathize with most of his frustrations but I told him that this Sr. DME was different, to which he said, "Okay, so he is different, but can he make a difference? His higher ups will snub him if he goes off their comfort-zone. For example, just now when we were inside, CMPE called from HQ, gave instructions and disconnected before our Sr. DME could even speak one word of his requirements from HQ. The Sr. DME has got too many bosses who'll torch his backside for one small mistake, or if he seeks any official good or gets into their bad books. You may also remember we gave a representation of our problems when the DRM was here, but he threw it out of the window, as per his driver, saying, "Why are they approaching me now, why not the earlier DRMs?" This was the same DRM who travelled in the luxurious tourism train, Golden Chariot, with his family, free of cost, costing the exchequer lakhs of rupees.

You may recall your friend, Naidu, who had a genuine Railway quarters problem about to be solved by the previous DRM, who suddenly got transferred. When Naidu humbly approached the new DRM with his problem, this DRM suddenly got up from his chair, gestured Naidu to sit there and told him to do his work while he would go and run around to solve the Quarters problem. Naidu ran out of the chamber, embarrassed. Is this the dignified way of solving a genuine problem? Even when we approached Accounts and Personnel Depts, who are meant to cater to us, they wanted us to come personally and would pour out their woes and problems rather than solve ours. Sometimes the dealers would not be in their seats nor pick up the phone or would have gone out and disappeared from there itself. The Salary bill clerk for the Shed never came here and worked at his discretion. A staff member's excess recovery of rent was continuing inspite of going personally and requesting. But it was solved when the staff member found the bill clerk in a bar, chased him and beat him up in front of the public. They also held annual Diesel Maintenance Group Meetings on weekends at tourist spots, staying in swanky hotels, for high level officers and their families. Who was footing the bill for that? After all this, you expect me to be sincere? I am being like most of them. And it is better not to have a good reputation in the Railways or else you will end up being exploited."

I had nothing to say to this Nagraj whose hatred was deep rooted. It was the same Nagraj who, while in the tool room, put tools found short in some staff members' account, and they were shocked to see buckets and spades in their account. The same Nagraj, who, during Control room night shifts, used to defacate just beside it out of fear of encountering snakes or rats, while going to the toilet. He was caught once and for all, with his pants down, by another night duty staff member. He was the same Nagraj who was transferred to our office before me, without having applied for it, while I had done so, and also the same Nagraj who, when the morning newspaper anticipated an earthquake around noon in Demblur area, went and stood alone near the main gate for 45 minutes from 11:40 a.m, watching and waiting for our office building to collapse. There was no point in counselling him. He could, instead, brainwash us to become inefficient.

-|--|--|-

Our Sr. DME also cited an example of shameless exploitation of loopholes by a lady staff member in some other Government entity. There was this 45 day paid leave facility for miscarriages. As the rule was not framed properly, this lady used to bring a medical certificate of miscarriage every year and avail it, for years. Finally, a lady boss got a clarification and put a stop to that. Now it is upto 45 days in service.

-|--|--|-

A perennial late comer and a bad worker, a lady clerk used her 'weapon' of shedding crocodile tears to exploit the protective environment for ladies. So the disgusted Sr. DME conspired with the equally fed up new Ch.OS and solved the problem to a great extent, giving her a dose of her own medicine - of that of emotional blackmail. The Sr. DME would call both to his chamber and not say a word to the lady, but shout at the Ch.OS for her not having done the work, saying he was a useless administrator. He would fire him left, right and centre, using even unparliamentary words and advising him to quit the Railways. Lastly, he would tell him in a booming voice to "Get Out!" of the room. Once out of the room, she apologized and promised to work, but suggested that he should complain to the Trade union about the language used by the Sr. DME. The Ch.OS refused and 'rubbed salt into his own wounds' by saying that in his 35 years of service, he had never got fired for somebody else's mistake. He would then emote further in an 'about to cry' tone, "See, ma, I have a daughter and you're also like my daughter. No father would like to see his daughter humiliated for her mistakes, by some other person. Instead, he disgraced me, your father, and I don't mind if my dignity and honour got molested, all for you, my lovely daughter." And this 'daughter', when compared to his age, was only 12 years younger!

-:-:-:-

My favourite Sr. DME got transferred and his parting message to the Shed, said, "Remember! Officers will come and officers will go. You are the ones who stick around and run the show. You all own this Shed while we're on loan here to keep the interest."

-:-:-:-

The next Sr. DME was the one who told me to withdraw my computerized, single filing system. He knew how to please his higher ups, and was very shrewd in extracting work from the staff by delegating all staff interaction to his sub-ordinate officers. He would hardly be in his chamber, to avoid calls from HQ or Division. He would roam around and be behind the staff when they went to the toilet and came out; he would ask - why twenty minutes? He also would sit on low tree branches and observe the staff. Once, based on a tip off, he went to the staff room, during the lunch hour, as he learnt that some staff members were playing cards. My colleague from the stores depot, who could see the staff room from afar, narrated that he saw the Sr. DME entering from one side and after a small pause, the staff came out in several numbers, simultaneously from three other exits, running helter-skelter resembling a fountain. They had run for their lives dropping their cards and money. Afterwards, except for one, all other exits were sealed. The joke that went on was that this Sr. DME was found to be everywhere in the Shed except in two places – his chamber and the ladies toilet!

Once the Trade Union leaders came to meet him, on knowing that he had indirectly given instructions to open the staff token dropping board only at 4:00 p.m, instead of 3:55 by which some staff members missed the train. He argued that the Shed's actual rostered closure was at 4:15, to which the leaders said that they were completing the work and then only leaving. This was not accepted, at which the leaders told him to anyway keep the Shed open till 4:15, but change the train timings so as to reach the back gate at 4:30 since it was anyway delayed after Chiroti and reached its destination late. To this, the Sr. DME said, "You buggers are too much, I say," to which a leader said, "Sir, we are not beggars, so please apologize, or we will call for a strike saying that you abused us." The Sr. DME contested, "I said buggers, not beggars. You buggers means you fellows." "No, Sir, you called us beggars and we heard it." At that moment, a shadow could be seen outside the translucent glass door. "Okay, okay, I apologize – somebody's coming, so no more discussion about this." The token board opening was reverted to 03:55.

-|-|-|-

Once an officer, touted to be a genius, shocked me and our draughtsman when we went to wish him on the verge of his transfer. He told us to escape and get out of the Shed somehow. He had worked for over three years to understand us this way and finally come up with such a nasty remark? A cowardly, cheap, genius?

I had heard of officers 'transferring' themselves to their convenience and outside the Railways, to remain and stay put in a particular city for their own sake. But this one takes the cake - efficient Railway officers like our favourite Sr. DME were deputed outside the Railways to other cities and unrelated entities like Food Corporation of India, Container Corporation of India, Coffee Board etc. Was it the price for overefficiency? Dump the few good ones outside the Railways and restore parity?

-|-|-|-

Sports quota appointees were posted to Chiroti Shed, and were frequently out on sports duty, or permitted half day off, everyday. Since the Shed was far away from the main city, neither could they contribute towards work, nor focus properly on their sport. Sports quota personnel should not be posted to Sheds just to make up the numbers; they should be in the main city where they can have more time and balance work with practice much better. However, after getting the job and found relaxing or exploiting, they should be given the fear of transfer with no permission for their sport.

-¦-¦-¦-

Once, during our Republic Day function at our Shed which our DRM had attended, while taking refreshments arranged in a room, he saw me and asked in the presence of all, "I have seen you somewhere," to which I replied, "Yes, Sir, about two years back when you beat me very badly." As eyebrows were raised and breaths stopped, I continued, "Even the back of my pant got torn at that time and it was very unfair, Sir. The occasion was the Divisional Sports meet and the game was table tennis. You beat me so badly, I had no chance at all and my pant tore while reaching for a ball. Luckily, there was no space for spectators behind me so my modesty was intact. At your age you play so well, which is unfair."

17

DIVIDE AND CONFOUND!

In 2003, since Railways was raking in huge profits (called surplus), instead of creating new income-generating avenues, infrastructure, facilities and amenities for the Public and Employees, huge amounts of money was spent in forming new Railway Zones by bifurcating existing Zones, citing better efficiency and management. Demblur came in the new South West Coast Railway which comprised of three Divisions - Demblur, Mangalore and Palghat. Initially, the Zonal Headquarters was in Demblur and then, by political compulsions, it was shifted to Mangalore. In this HQ, only scores of officers' posts were created and, for non-gazetted staff vacancies, the existing only were deployed and Engineers worked like clerks. Instead of posting the best officers at top levels, to lay a proper foundation during the teething stage, they posted the most inefficient ones. The HQ Accounts was a mess. They told us to follow the SOP of Southern Railway and came up with their own SOP only in 2008. There also they took the SOPs of Southern Railway and South Central Railway of 2003 and selected the worst of the individual item's powers among the two and made it at 2003 monetary values itself, without adding any inflatory costs over the years.

The HQ was more like a post office, and when any technical queries were made by HQ Accounts, our HQ, being the Technical Head with CME, CMPE, Dy.CME, AME – all provided with individual chambers and computers - would send it with a covering letter asking us to reply, as there were only two ministerial staff there – a office superintendent and a Senior Clerk – both fighting to play Solitaire on the only computer available in office. High level individuals at HQ took stupid, paralytic decisions of writing to firms about a high cost warranty failed engine repair to be shared 50% each by the firm and Railways, which was not possible. Our Accounts cited there was no policy to approve, nor would they approve one paise for a warranty claim to be paid by the Railways. The firm happily latched on to that 50% letter and is still waiting for Railways to commit half the expenditure, while the asset lies unutilized.

The new Zone was supposed to be a paperless organization but instead, Demblur and Chiroti, proportionately, had more documentation than earlier.

The gauge conversion from Demblur to Mangalore, which was languishing since 1994, suddenly was over in no time, because Demblur was a modern city and many officers would come on Duty from Mangalore with their families, on Fridays, stay on Saturdays, and leave on Sunday night to HQ. The poor Demblur officers had to follow the 'Protocol' of receiving their higher-ups early in the mornings, entertaining them and ensuring to cater their hour-to-hour needs, and some of their eccentricities, became the order of the day. A CME loved to watch movies in Multiplexes and that too alone, and in Gold Class, without lightening his wallet! A wife had a sudden craving to eat watermelon at midnight! Another wanted wine and onion pakodas!

While forming the new Zones, options were given to the staff to opt for their zone and all optees were put in the Headquarters, and enjoyed fast promotions. We heard that a Bungalow peon was to become a supervisor in the Mangalore HQ with five promotions within ten years, while I waited for 15 years for my 2nd promotion, and that too was given as ad-hoc. Nagraj's prospects were even worse. In Southern Railway, promotions to Engineers were kept in abeyance to filter out the prospective Engineers to other zones and then given, with retrospective effect of 1.11.2002, before Zone bifurcation of 1.4.2003. The actual affected Engineers in the new Zones united, put a case and won, getting the promotions while the undue benefactors were stripped of the promotion, and the guilty officials identified, suspended and punished. If the illegal promotions were effected from 1.4.2003, they would have been saved. But greed, overconfidence and underestimation cost them dear.

-!-!-!-

A few years back, an old Office Superintendent was at no. 4 and a much younger one at no. 45 in the Zonal Seniority List. Since the younger person went to other divisions and after 'the 'modification' or 'interpretation' of rules, he now stands at no. 3 with the old one still at no. 4. When no. 4 approached the Personnel Branch for settling the matter, inspite of knowing the injustice done, they took the easy way out by asking the old man to seek legal succour.

-!-!-!-

A lorry repair proposal in HQ Accounts took three months for them to agree after queries, not bothered about the vehicle downtime or the owning Department's hardship. The old Zonal HQ had got into a groove and proposals were cleared fast. Now, everything moved at a snail's pace.

The monthly Stores Meeting was a farce with Stores Dept. dictating the proceedings and end users suffering for want of material. The HQ Accounts would snub the Divisional Accounts by misinterpreting the policies or playing too safe, thereby making Divisional Accounts also wary of giving the initial approval for processing further at HQ Accounts.

Soon, the profits went to losses. The new Zones, the bureaucracy and inefficiency had made the Railways appear like a pregnant white elephant.

-!-!-!-

One fine day, the platform at the back entrance was sanctioned and the work was completed in about three months. It was about the length of three coaches, and on either side of the tracks. I remembered the Sr. DME ARK's adage, "In the Railways, keep throwing endless stones at a mango, and one of them will find the mark, which we will not know then, but only when the mango falls much much later." Next, our Accounts did not sanction a shelter for it and the Shed fabricated its own and erected it. This reminded one of another of ARK's sayings, "With great difficulty, we manage to get a gun but the same Accounts, later, does not agree for buying bullets, not even one."

-!-!-!-

One Monday morning, the Sr. DME changed our office working from a 5-day week to a 6-day week, citing new zone rules. This was done unceremoniously, without involving the Personnel Branch, who had the right to issue such orders. Of course, any change could be done mutually but this was a one-man show, as if to say "I am Rambo." We protested for which he said that he wanted people on Saturdays also, to which we offered to be available on rotation basis. He did not budge though our suggestion made sense. We were wondering what happened to him so suddenly, when a subordinate clarified in confidentiality that the CME had come on a personal visit on Saturday for some 'Darshan' nearby and since it was over early, had dropped in to see the Sr. DME who was neither in the Shed, nor in his Quarters – he had gone to play golf. When the CME contacted the Sr. DME, he was told that Saturday was a holiday for office. The CME thundered that a Sr. DME should have a morning round in the Shed on Saturdays to which, as a knee-jerk reaction to salvage some brownie points, he said he would convert the office routine to a 6-day week.

This decision de-motivated the staff and I could see that due to the forced implementation, the overall work output suffered, with the affected staff doing only surface work, not taking any initiatives or being proactive. Further, I proved to the Sr. DME that working time itself got reduced, i.e., the daily routine of two extra tea-breaks and readying formalities at the start and the end of the day additionally took away 45 minutes on the 6th day every week. So 45 minutes x about 15 persons of our office and SMM's (excluding officers) was a loss to the administration. Also, extra travelling and fuel wastage on the 6th day was a loss to the Nation. And, for some personal work which could have been done on Saturdays, we had to apply for leave now to get them done. The Sr. DME agreed that it was his mistake, but did not roll back his decision, as it was a prestige issue for him. But he said that if we approach the courts, we would certainly win the case to which we said that we didn't have the time nor the inclination to go to courts. The Trade Unions also made a feeble, vain attempt and did not pursue it to make it a strong case as they were Shed oriented and we were a minority, comparatively.

Seeing how an individual officer's ego and whims could affect the shed staff or the shed's working, I feel that the concept of Trade Unions is very much needed, but then all cadres and administrative concerns should be represented equilaterally to create an amicable and just atmosphere. It should not be about claiming credit or achievement for any benefit given to the staff by the Administration, but to share it and celebrate it with the staff and all the other Unions together. It should be like how different communities work together in the Shed to achieve a common goal; the same principle should apply to trade unions. However, like some officers, the leader's selfishness could also affect the reputation of the Trade Unions.

Once a Trade Union hurriedly put up a condolence message of a bereaved staff member on its notice board to be the first to do so (competition in such situations also? Alas!) which read, "HEARTLY CONDOLENCES – we sorry to tell the sudden death of Shri Kiranappa, Tech.I, heat exchanger section's father. May his SOLE rest in piece!" My friend was tempted to ask which one, the right sole or the left, and whether the technician or his father had died.

A Union leader found his neighbour's five year old daughter playing in the sand mound in the Railway Quarters. His request or order not to play was totally ignored by her. He solved it by lying that dirty stray dogs peed and pooed there which would cause itchy rashes on her body, and pimples on her beautiful face which could stay for life.

There were employees who also pronounced 'Chocolate' as 'Saklet', 'Public' as 'Bublic' and 'Pump' as 'Paamp'. Once a depot storekeeper confronted a fuelkeeper to return his 'paamp', wildly gesticulating. The storekeeper jumped and looked around, scared out of his wits since he heard it as 'Paamb' which, in Tamil, means snake.

-:-:-:-

I came across another newspaper cutting on the notice board which was superscribed by our union as 'Flash Good News for Railway Staff'. The article said that Central Govt. employees were to get PF interest of 9.5%. In early 2000, the Central Govt. had announced a drastic reduction of interest on Provident Fund deposits from 12% of several years to 8%. Our Railways has a separate body called the State Railway Provident Fund which also reduced it to 8%. As the PF of the Central Govt. employees was different, their trade unions fought and made it 9.5% for that year, and I found that many of our Trade Union leaders were not aware that the Railway PF had a separate governing body. This body never raised it to the level of the Central Government who always got 9.5% for about three years and then 9%. Ours remained static at 8%. This gross disparity was a shame since the Railways was a revenue generating entity, whereas most other Central Govt. offices were not. Hence, the Railways deserved the interest rates to be on par with Central Govt. offices, if not more. This glaring anomaly was not represented or addressed at all. If the Railways were incurring losses, it was because of its populist exploitation, mismanagement due to too many cooks (even crooks) and neglected inefficiency at all levels. In addition, the cross-subsidy plan was ludicrous. And it looked as if that subsidy burden was passed on to the employees. Instead of going to the root of the problem, a spate of 'austerity measures' were announced which saved droplets of money from a bucketful of expenditure. For example, a botched attempt was made when some company introduced a lubricant, which when sprayed on rail wheels on run at sporadic intervals, was claimed to reduce wear and tear. A research by the Railways did away with this exercise as it was found that the cost of lubricant and procurement, fitment and maintenance of the spraying mechanism was much more than the savings achieved. But years later, it was learnt that this was reintroduced, but whether due to improved parameters or lobbying is not known.

Whereas, we were told to reduce our Locomotive stores' requirements, stationery, sending staff on duty, our already insufficient budget grant, etc. which were not a consistent viable option for Diesel Sheds. But there was no reduction on our outage target of Locomotives. If we went for material assistance to other Sheds, we would send our people with a list and then they, in turn would send theirs. Instead, if both Sheds had communicated by e-mail/Fax of required or spareable items, one Shed's team could take and bring the items, knowing the exact items and people required. A lot of unwarranted activities could have been restricted.

My Sr. DME asked the Engineering Dept. officers why plumbing works were not attended to for years, and whether they were part of the 'Austerity measures'. The supervisors, called Inspectors of Works, cited shortage of hands and materials, but there was always manpower to attend to the works of the IOWs, to hold their briefcases and follow them or even take their children to school and back, and wash their family clothes or do shopping, in-between. The lower type quarters, occupied by the Engineering department officers, were well maintained and furnished, whereas the same of the others' quarters were treated like 'beggars' quarters' and its residents repaired or painted or furnished them at their own cost, fed up of waiting. The IOWs never lifted their phones or inspected their jurisdiction properly. When taken up, they talked about the shortage of staff and pressure by high level officers, causing them to drop everything and attend to their 'needs'. Some IOWs also complained of BP and sugar problems which were genuine, and squarely blamed on the official mobiles given to them, which were never to be switched off.

-:-:-:-

Our Draughtsman had maximum interaction with the Engineering department and hence, volunteered to be the nodal man in the shed for all communication with them. But whenever they delayed or created problems, our staff blamed the poor Draughtsman. Once, for a long delayed bathroom leakage plastering, a mason tried to use inferior materials, and the Draughtsman stopped him and told not to use that material. When a complaint of non-compliance was received, the Contractor squarely blamed the Draughtsman, stating he had stopped the work which was being done, without giving the correct reason. Good is bad in Railways?!

18

A BEAUTIFUL COINCIDENCE, UNBOUND!

A league type tennis ball cricket tournament was conducted by the Engineering Department of Demblur Division at the Railway Grounds at Demblur. As they had only seven entries, including our team, we were allowed to field another team and called it 'B' team and ours as 'A'. They formed two groups of four teams each and both our teams were in the same group. All the four teams were to play each other in the group, and the top two teams would qualify for the semi-final.

Our final group match was our Team A vs. Team B. We, Team A, had already qualified, having won both our earlier matches handsomely and Team B would qualify for the semi-final, if they beat us. So, all the other teams were echoing that we would 'fix' the match and lose to Team B, whereas for us the situation was different, because some of the Team B members thought they deserved to be in Team A. So we won the toss and asked B to bat first. We got them all out for a humiliating 11 runs with the chief destroyer being my namesake and friend, Sachin Rao. So as a reward, we sent him to bat first along with me.

As we were walking, the scorer asked for the batsman's name to which I replied 'Sachin'. "We know your name, I meant the other batsman," to which I said, "His name is also Sachin."

One of the umpires commented jovially, "Oh, Sachin squared, eh?" to which I said "Sir, if I tell you another coincidence, you will be even more pleasantly shocked." "What is that?" the umpire asked. I replied, "It is not about the fact that there are five Sachins in our Shed, but the rare and beautiful coincidence about us both Sachins in front of you now, both our wives' names are also the same – Hema." The umpire raised his eyebrows, smiled while bemused, and shook my hand. I still savour the moment because of the way it came up in a totally unexpected situation. Years later, I was to read a crime report of North India in which the criminal couple were named Sachin and Hema, and I felt that whoever said the world is small had made an understatement.

19

CONTRACTS & PROBLEMS THAT HOUND!

In Divisions, the concept of Work Contracts was restricted mainly to the Engineering Department for construction of assets, and to a lesser extent, to the Commercial Department. Now, the Railways wanted to outsource many non-core activities by awarding work contracts through transparent open tendering, as it was found to be more feasible and economical than doing it departmentally. Like many other branches, we also found some relief as staff shortages were never filled up and now we could use some on core Loco maintenance. So we outsourced unskilled activities like Shed Cleaning, Loco cleaning and Component cleaning as a start. Subsequently, the RPF Fire wing was closed down and the maintenance of Fire Extinguishers in the Shed and on Locos were also outsourced.

Since the Shed water was not potable, we had about 11 water purifiers whose maintenance (AMC) after warranty was also given to the OEM (original equipment manufacturer) through its franchisee. They didn't give a single rupee as discount even though we had 11 machines, and could save on visits by simultaneous servicing. The purifiers were good, but it seemed that the OEM did not have confidence in their own product. Also, every now and then, the franchisee changed even during the course of the contract, but which was honoured by the new one. One day, one of our technicians saw some wire-like arrangement sticking out of the back of the water purifier. On examination, he made a stunning discovery which could still be prevalent in water purifiers in India – especially where there are several purifiers at one location.

When switched on, the purifier conducts a self-check of proper functioning of all the stages of water purifying, indicating a yellow light, and then displays a green light when it is ready to discharge the processed water. At one stage, near the Ultra Violet light purifying stage, near the UVL chamber, it was seen that the wire was shorted using a diode, which would 'okay' the UV test, even if the light was not working and we could still have the 'purified' water! This 'arrangement' was found to be in seven of the machines! The manufacturer's zonal and Indian HQ could not be contacted at all. Finally the franchisee, blaming the previous one, agreed and did away with the diodes and rectified the problem. But, we found that, when the next franchisee took over, this diode had resurfaced in one of the machines. I fear to think of the outcome if the UV light had not worked? Cholera? Diarrhea? Slow poison? What if the manufacturer came to know and instead of preventing the problem, found it profitable to incorporate it in the machine? This flurry of thoughts made me develop goose bumps. .

-!-!-!-

Then, the newly manufactured Diesel Locomotives came modified to the digital type, very helpful in making a better assessment of the performance and problems of the Locomotive. In the old or analog type, some of the problems used to be identified through tell-tale signs like sound, smoke and other crude methods. The new digital Locos had a display which was a single window to check the working parameters and many other aspects, which added value to the maintenance, efficiency and reliability of the Locomotive.

The Railway Board found it so advantageous that it sanctioned for the conversion of existing analog type Locos to the digital type in Sheds who had to tender it and get it done. Though Contracts was not my portfolio, the incumbent Sr. DME wanted me to do it for certain technical reasons. I initially refused since the total cost was over Rs.3.5 crores for conversion of 15 Locos. But my Sr. DME got personally involved and we successfully completed this, and another 28 Locos' conversion, later.

The Audit department was not convinced about this digitalization, or its benefits, and considered it unnecessary expenditure. It was after it, hammer and tongs, seeking remarks from innumerable angles to trap us somehow into submission, in one way or another. But we were able to hold the fort, each and every time. As a last straw, we received a letter from the CAG addressed to all the Sheds who had undertaken this conversion, saying that against the expenditure of Rs.25 lakhs per conversion by Timothy Shed, all other Sheds had spent over 30 lakhs per conversion, having, in totality, caused crores of Rupees loss to the Indian exchequer. Initially I was disappointed, thinking how this could happen, since the order went to one particular Company which was charging standard rates. However, by chance, we had used Timothy Shed's rates as the rate reference while finalizing the offer and took out those rates. What had happened was that 25 lakhs was the basic rate and Audit had conveniently left out all the other aspects like Excise Duty, Sales Tax, Installation charges and freight, which, when added, worked out to Rs. 2000 more than our per conversion cost. We sent a letter to the CAG through proper channels, as well as an advance copy, and the case was dropped like a hot potato, much to the chagrin of the local Audit Dept. which had worked 'very hard' to compile and to show this digitalization as a national calamity.

This unwarranted situation calls for posts of technical auditors to be created or depute Engineers from the 'rival dept.' during Audit inspections since, as per the normal mental make-up of most humans, finding fault in others while hiding yours is the favourite occupation as well as pastime, and Audit does this all the time. For example, Electrical Dept. Engineers can be sent to the Mechanical Dept. and vice versa, as both will go in-depth to find genuine shortcomings in the other, and not be speculative or presumptive. But then somebody told me that this is not possible as the Auditors have to justify their existence and retain their prestige by making such observations and even stand by them.

The Accounts department received a directive that all bills' payments were to be made vide Electronic Fund Transfer, which was implemented suddenly, with no advance intimation or grace period. In fact, 47 of our bills were returned for entering the bank details of the supplier with all our pleas to pass them now, and ensuring future compliance, in vain. At least the Vigilance Dept. could have visualized this and given some grace time. The Accounts department dominates over all the departments but fears only two – the Audit and the Vigilance bureau.

Also, the printing of Revenue Stamps of one Rupee denomination was stopped only in Karnataka State, but Accounts would insist on the stamp on each bill, citing it was Government Revenue. They told us to return such bills to the suppliers as per the rules in force, which was that any bill to be returned should be done so with a proper covering letter, and should be mandatorily sent vide Registered post only, which cost Rs.25 each, apart from cumbersome procedures. So for the Revenue of one Rupee, one would spend over Rs.25! This encouraged black-marketing (Rs.1 stamps were sold for Rs.10 by nearby shops and by our staff too) and I would have none of it, so I used to get stamps whenever our staff went on duty to other States, to paste them on the bills. Some companies also would give 30 to 50 stamps free of cost with the request to help their brethren in the smooth passage of bills at least at this stage.

-:-:-:-

One day, I received a call from the bills passing Accounts SO (Section Officer) of Demblur Division asking if M/s. Istri Enterprises, Kolkata was one of our suppliers and how reliable they were, what our rapport with them was, etc. The questions were pretty weird and no details were given. I then came to know that a payment of Rs.7,235 of M/s Istri Enterprises, Bangalore had been erroneously sent to them by Accounts, and both firms had no connection. As there was no response from them, this SO had gone twice to Kolkata, to retrieve the payment but had failed to do so. Their ego prevented Accounts from admitting the mistake to us. But since bills were kept pending in the absence of the SO, I called the firm at Kolkata and requested the proprietor, Mr.Dass, to return the amount as he had high regards for my prompt compliance of his bills. Mr.Dass politely replied that he had a golden life-time opportunity and would not return it immediately. "I have suffered a lot for small payments with the same SO. If I ask him over the phone, he tells me to come there and find out, or doesn't attend to the phone itself, or pretends to be a peon and tells me that the SO is not in the seat or that his assistant is on leave. I am a retired Railwayman myself and know the shape of the hooks of these crooks. If I quote for Advance payment, your Accounts does not agree to it and then you plead and negotiate for payment after delivery. Even if you send our bill early to your Accounts informing about my compromise on advance payment, they will be least bothered. Even if I quote for a half percent discount if payment is made within 12 working days of the supply, your Accounts will claim that discount even if the bill is paid six months later. They know I will never go to court because of the high expenditure and multiple formalities involved. And when payments are finally received, there is no advice or remittance note for the same. My Bank pass book shows the entry as 'EFT' or 'EFTSWCR' and I cannot connect to it as it is received months later, among hundreds of my other payments. At least an e-mail advice would be appreciated. My accountant says that these unknown payments could be interpreted as Terrorist Funding also! Your Accounts holds back payments during October so that they can pay bonus to the Railway employees, whereas I am sometimes not in the position to pay normal salaries, and Durga Pooja in October is very critical for all of us. I don't want to disturb your DRM or GM for such small amounts. If I don't quote and the next least offer is very high, you will retender the case, begging me to quote. Also, in this case, the SO was very rude and arrogant, blaming us for his mistake, even asking how we accepted the payment and had not yet returned it, threatening to go to Court. I told him do so and gave him a dose of his own medicine when I didn't attend to his phone calls. Then, suddenly, he turned into a very humble person during his second visit. Let him experience the meaning of the word 'delay' for a change."

I told Mr Dass that two times was too much for him and that the SO would have learnt his lesson. Since his absence was also holding up payments of his fellow suppliers, as well as to his namesake firm in Bangalore until he returned the amount, I requested him to return the payment which he agreed to. I called up Accounts pretending to be from Istri, Kolkata, and they said the SO was not in his seat. When I said it was not about receiving payment but returning a wrongly made payment, the SO came on the phone before I could finish exhaling my breath. I told him what the moral of the story was, "What goes around, comes around."

-:-:-:-

We were given a meager sum of Rs.1,000 as per occasion for Independence Day Celebrations. This was not enough for ourselves or to cater to our satellite office near Demblur, or even the trouble shooting point at Demblur Station. So I suggested that we treat each location's flag hoisting as separate occasions and demand Rs.3,000 instead, which worked to our satisfaction. Initially Accounts were apprehensive, but obliged when we emphasized that we were not taking one flag and hoisting the same at three locations.

-:-:-:-

One Monday morning, I encountered four smartly dressed youngsters – three boys and one girl - in the corridor.

The shortest among them spoke arrogantly, pointing to the name board of my Sr. DME, "Tell your boss that the trainee officers have come; he's expecting us."

"I am sorry, Sir, he's in the Control Room's morning meeting and will come in half an hour. In fact, Sir, since you've come to study the shed, you can join him at the meeting as it will give you a gist of the Shed's daily review and planning."

Feeling somewhat insulted, the shorty roared, "Don't tell us what to do. Tell him now that we have come and are waiting for him in his chamber!"

"Sorry, sir, I cannot disturb him in the meeting wherein critical decisions will be taken for the day, and also being Monday, Sunday's activities will also be reviewed. I will leave a message with the phone clerk, who will communicate to the Sr. DME."

Like a person who doesn't take "No" for an answer, he thundered, "Just do what I told you to, and watch your mouth, I may come here tomorrow as your boss," he looked at his group, expecting applause.

"Then, Sir," I said, without flinching, "You will be proud that I didn't disturb you and maintained the sanctity of the meeting," thanking myself for getting the right words at the right time.

Seething, he noticed a peon and repeated his instructions to him. I told the peon not to comply as the Sr. DME was his boss and disturbing him could bring him a scolding. I also told him in the local language that these people were there only for a short time whereas his Sr. DME was his master, and not this bunch of jokers, and that he should choose who he wanted to please. As the peon stayed put, Shorty lost his cool, "I'll get you crucified you….. you…..," he stopped short of uttering expletives, noticing that I was not blinking, and that I too had my boxing gloves on and ready to punch him, word for word!

Later, my Sr. DME called me and instead of firing me, told me not to take it to heart as the Shorty was a General Manager's son, totally pampered in his life with the Railways' facilities and expense. While studying for his intermediate, he stayed in a posh Railway guesthouse with a car at his disposal and after his course, he got a seat in the five year Special Class Railway Apprentices course for which you don't pay a single paisa as course fee, and instead, were paid a stipend with good hostel accommodation and food, totally in contrast to all other degree courses where you have to pay by bleeding through your nose at every level. Then, job and time bound promotions or pay upgradations are assured. "They are like the son-in-laws of the Railways. These four are here for a week's study of the Shed."

"But, Sir," I said, "They should have some decency in their approach. What do they think of themselves? Anyway, thank you, Sir! If you had scolded me instead, I would have been totally demoralized."

"Don't worry, Sachin, this shorty complained to me and I told him not to order my staff around and that what you did was correct in terms of not disturbing me. However, when they finish the course and get a posting, they would have mellowed down." These considerations by a Sr. DME kept us motivated.

I later learnt that all four went to their respective native places the same day and returned on Saturday to take a 'Certificate' of their 'hard' training in the Shed. So much for the histrionics of our future leaders of the nation!!!

-:-:-:-

My portfolio got changed to Contracts. There also, I streamlined the passing of bills and other details to be user-friendly, traceable and for timely contract renewal. As there was no one who had the time to cross-check my calculations, I made some worksheets with customized calculation formulas in the Computer, to work out the billing details as well as to cross-check the figures. But I found the General Conditions of Contract (GCC) governing the contracts in tandem with the SOPs were more biased towards Engineering Department Contracts, and did not address many issues pertaining to other departments. For example, if we were to tender for a repair contract of a major component, we could make out only some surface damaged parts' repairs which could be viewed. But the condition of the other parts' could be made only after dismantling the machine. So we had no flexibility for any extra work to be done. We could only incorporate some Special Conditions of Contract, like penalty etc., customized to the contract requirements, but not those unspecified material/labour which would be required later and would increase the financial implication. The only other alternative, at present, was to float a quotation contract enquiry first, to dismantle, assess the damage and then float a repair contract tender later, which was ridiculous.

There was no cost variation addressed in the GCC for labour intensive contracts, and the Accounts would negotiate with the cheapest offering Tenderer and ruthlessly bring it down to contract rates, almost two years old. Future inflation for two more years or minimum wages revision every six months to labourers due to DA (Dearness Allowance) raise were not factored in. The Contractor manages for the first year, and then starts to suffer losses later and cuts corners, which affects the quality of execution and which, in turn, attracts penalties and adds to the woes of the contractor. My attempt to bring in suitable Price Variation Clauses and Statutory Variation Clauses, which would even help enter into contracts for five to ten years, thereby avoiding the cumbersome tendering and finalizing procedures every year or two years, failed to stir my Accounts or the Law Department of Railways, or even HQ which advised to continue within the existing framework. Suggestions for entering into Rate Contracts at Division level similar to DGS&D contracts were also shot down.

The Railway Board brought a genuine system improvement by asking production units to enter into Rate contracts (RC) with OEMs for overhauling or AMC of common standard components in Locomotives for all Locomotives in India and behalf of all its homing Diesel Loco Sheds. Since it was a bulk order, the rates were more reasonable than if individual Sheds went for tendering. This RC would be entered into with firms after the due tendering and finalizing process, as per the GCC, and the Sheds only had to issue work orders for their quantities and enter into the Agreement.

But our Accounts Department was adamant that we float tenders in these cases also, because the tendering and finalizing procedures were not done in the Division. So we made a fool of ourselves and the company who quoted higher than the rate contract, and which the Accounts did not agree to, and held negotiations, finally bringing down the rate to the same as the rate contract. The whole exercise was idiotic and unwarranted and wasted valuable manpower by not just duplicating, but multiplying our work as well as the Accounts' and even the Company's. This cowardly act was insisted on normally by direct recruits having come from among the prestigious Indian Civil Services, even after the Railway Board clarified that "RCs were meant to do away with the tendering process," citing that exact wordings of 'not to tender' were not clear. The promotee officers were more practical, having basic common and civic sense and understanding, and said that some direct recruits looked down upon them and nicely delegated their work to them, playing it very safe. They got involved only when their signature on the documents was inescapable.

For example, in the GCC, on receiving a work order, a contractor has to submit a performance guarantee amount within 60 days of issue of work order, or the contract stands terminated. The Accounts Officer interpreted that it is 60 days from the date work order, as that is what is considered as a date of issue like Govt. Gazetted notifications. We clarified that Govt. notifications are for complying the instructions from the same day, whereas our Contractor would not sit near our doorstep waiting for his work order, because the successful Contractor's identity would be known only after the work order was made and it had to reach the contractor by post. Even if he came to collect it, he had to see if there are any deviations and then accept the work order for execution of the work. That acceptance date was termed as the date of issue by our office. But the Accounts Officer was adamant on its stance. That is why, while making a policy, it should not be uni-dimensional. The policymaker should put himself in the shoes of all concerned and look at all angles before finalizing anything. Mistakes could happen by oversight, but early redressal was required, not dragging of feet.

Once an MNC, while making the digital component named DIGICOM of the Locos, argued that they need not replace a sensor system since it was not listed among the major parts of digicom in the contract made by the HQ, on behalf of the two sheds. We argued that the AMC is for digicom as a whole and HQ is not aware of all the components' parts and that the MNC had guided them and wreaked mischief by not indicating all in the list since some are costly. "Ok," said my Sr. DME to the MNC, "You give a signed undertaking that it is not a part of the digicom and also that there are other sensors in the market which are compatible in the slot, and then we will not ask you to replace it." The MNC quietly replaced it, without further ado.

The digicom and its AMC cost were very expensive as it was the only product available in the market, imported and supplied by the MNC. But its monopoly ended when an Indian company came out with a better version at a much cheaper cost and the rates could never be matched by the high overheads' structured MNC. The Indian company was very adjusting to Railway rules and soon helped avoid substantial imports by developing more high-end products. Very soon, we could indigenise our high horsepower Locomotives.

-¦--¦--¦-

Really, our Accounts! To agree to buy nine computers on the replacement account, they wanted one out of it for themselves. They made us promise that not on paper, but on the phone. We said we had no choice since our ass was always in their hands, which, anytime they could fry and leave us high and dry.

-¦--¦--¦-

The transfers' season was like a fish market, even at top levels. I heard that a branch officer was transferred but did not budge from her seat when her reliever, another lady, came over. The reliever took a chair and sat beside her, both causing embarrassment more to their subordinates visiting the chamber than themselves. So the incumbent absented herself from the next day and then suddenly turned up with a modified transfer order to her liking. The reliever took over charge without being handed over. Comparatively, in the Shed, the Storekeeper, especially the Toolkeeper had to spend days for handing over or taking over charge.

A tardy lady employee once asked her in-charge to give her a light job. The fed up in-charge said, "Come early in the morning, switch on the lights and switch them off in the evening – at least that way you'll be on time."

20

WORKSHOPS CROWNED, SHEDS FROWNED!

Railway Workshops doled out monthly incentives to its employees on increased productivity (based on the formula of the positive difference of time allowed and time taken for an activity), while there was no such thing for the more deserving Diesel Shed employees, who were more hardworking and worked in a tension filled atmosphere with health hazards of sound/smoke/oil etc. Talking about incentives, we were astonished to learn some facts in a goods wagon maintenance workshop which used to overhaul wagons. A new, no-nonsense CWM, due to take over charge next day, was telling his wife at dinner about the present and outgoing CWM's 'dirty tactics' as he had learnt from his sources.

"The workshop is headed by a CWM (Chief Workshop Manager) and the present one wanted the output of wagons to be raised from the monthly target of 150 to 210." To this, he was told that the maximum possible, after giving complete attention to all maintenance activities would be 180 with the present staff strength available. They were already giving about 175 per month and getting some incentive. As he was adamant, this was conveyed to the workshop staff, but the supervisors said that they would have to sign the job cards which indicated the detailed attention/replacement of parts and lubricants, duly recording the time allowed/ time taken, and that they would have to initial/sign after every activity. They couldn't risk the signing activity not done, and if found out due to any failure or derailment, they would be taken up and punished severely. In other words, it was impossible to give output of 210 wagons if they had to do all the jobs mentioned in the job card. To this, the CWM said that the public did not know how many wagons get derailed, which were more frequent than trains/coaches derailing. The wagons derailing details were suppressed or ignored as there were hardly any human casualties (though the derailment sound could wet the pants of the guard, alone in his last wagon, and maybe of the Loco's crew).

So the CWM stated that the staff would also get maximum incentives in a month and hence, to do away with job cards and instead calculate incentives on the simple formula of wagons output in excess of target. "Let somebody object and then we will see." So for over three years, the work was done without job cards, skipping attention, but without any reported derailments. The staff members were happy as they were getting maximum incentives. The new incoming CWM pointed his index finger at his wife saying, "But I will clean up the mess he did."

As the new CWM took over and during the send-off party of the old one, the incoming CWM praised the outgoing one for his 'achievements' and then personally walked him till the car, waiting to take him to the airport. He then came back to the party hall and ordered to lock the doors, indicating that only officers and Senior Supervisors should remain in the hall for his message.

"You bloody fellows," he began, glaring at the supervisors, "I know all about improper attention to the wagons and bypassing job cards! Are you all out of your minds? Don't you have a conscience? How dare you flout the procedures, compromising on the safety and efficiency of wagons? If I come to know during my tenure about even one instance of a job card missing or a job not done, I will dismiss the supervisor on the spot. I want every single activity to be done properly as per the specified instructions. Am I clear?"

"Yes, Sir," the supervisors echoed meekly.

"Louder, I can't hear you!"

"YES, SIR!!!"

"Okay, then," the CWM lowered his voice and continued, "Tomorrow morning itself, I want all the job cards to be back and existing wagons to be re-examined thoroughly and attended. I don't care how you do it as I want all procedures, all attention and everything to be done meticulously, but I want the same output of 210 wagons a month if not more! Not a wagon less!"

-|--|--|-

The stores depot in our Shed used to float quotation enquiries against our indents which were opened twice a week and which had to be witnessed by an accounts representative. As their office's personnel management was at Mysore, 200 kms away, the witness was deputed from there. Then, as a part of the austerity measures, since Demblur Divisional office was only 20 kms away, it was decided that the witness would be deputed from the Accounts office there. I was thrilled because the first witness was the new SO, Smt. Kalamani, who dealt and mostly disagreed with our proposals, and would come in my train in the morning. I wanted to impress upon her about the problems of our

Shed, during the train journey. On the previous day, she had enquired about the train timings, platform no. and the coach to enter. She barely managed to catch the 20 minutes delayed train and was in some other coach. So I met her only at our back entrance and it was 10:10 a.m.

We entered our office room at 10:15 where she paused, looked around and not seeing anyone else, suddenly took a dramatic posture of bent knees and raised arms and eyebrows, shouted icily, "You people are enjoying like anything!" It came like a bolt from the blue when I realised that she was comparing to her five-day week office which started at 9:30 a.m.

"Madam," I defended, "For your kind information, our office starts at 10:30 and works six-days a week. We are 15 minutes early. Please take back your words about us enjoying, Madam." She refused and still persisted in her accusation. I was seething with anger when I took her to the adjoining room and sat her down. As she had made a nasty remark, I told her that she owed me an audience as her witnessing work would start only at 11:30 and I would convince her, in the meantime, about who was really enjoying.

"Madam," I started, "Tell me how many times we have to send somebody to your Divisional office for a simple, straightforward, unreturned and accepted proposal till the bill passing of repairing a motor costing Rs.5,100?"

She didn't respond thinking it was not important, when I iterated, "Please take a guess, madam, because what I am about to prove is the unwanted misconception of us enjoying, by you and all our related Divisional staff, whereas for each of our proposals, it actually is a matter of life and death in terms of Loco maintenance."

She looked up, thinking and taking her time, trying to be more accurate than guessing and replied, "Umm ....three to four times?"

I lifted both my hands near to her face to make a dramatic impact and showed her my fingers, "Minimum nine times, Madam, which even our officers do not know and which I too realised recently," and at her genuinely astonished look, I listed out the sequence of events, counting on one finger at a time;

"1. When sending the proposal to you for calling quotations for work.
2. Collecting it back after your concurrence.
3. Sending a Note to ADRM for approval.
4. Collecting the file back.
5. Sending file to you again after receipt of quotations, for awarding work.
6. Collecting the file back.
7. Sending Note for ADRM's Sanction for awarding the work.
8. Collecting file back.
9. Sending bill for passing after work is done.

To this, add the two more times since you are following the rule of returning at least once, making it 11 times. For almost everything, we have to take your permission except for going to the toilet. Moreover, if you need any clarification on policies or commercial aspects like taxes or Excise Duty on our proposals, you ask us to get a copy of the notification though it is your job to obtain it or ascertain it from reliable sources. Do you know, madam, that if an Indian company supplies an imported material which is imported in fully finished condition, the actual Counter Vailing Duty paid at the time of import should be claimed as the excise duty, and not the one on supplier's cost price? Your office and many Accounts all over India have reimbursed it on the supplier's cost price along with subsequent bloated sales tax."

I continued, "Now that I have your fullest attention, kindly don't interrupt me till I finish, since most of your doubts will be cleared during the course of my enlightenment. Do you know what is probably the most difficult industrial activity in the whole world, as of now?"

As she shook her head, I said, "Mobilizing material in all Indian Diesel Loco Sheds!" I continued, "While I tell why, let me tell which are the two biggest factors making it so difficult – the first villain is the DISTANCE – that is, the distance of the Shed, which is away from the processing/ approving levels at Division or Zonal HQ at Mangalore, who think we are enjoying ourselves here, in this green, airy atmosphere while they sit in cramped offices. And the second main villain is YOU – the Accounts Department at Division as well as in HQ."

"We have seven varieties of Locomotives, each having thousands of spare parts, many different but with a limited supply of sources for each spare part. The good suppliers keep away seeing our rules and delay in payments and you don't entertain advance payment or payment while collecting materials. After supply, they become beggars for their payments and are treated very rudely when they follow-up with you. When we tell them to complain to the higher-ups, they say they don't want to do anything with the Railways. So second rung suppliers take over who charge more and/or supply inferior quality.

Our Stores Depot stocks over 1500 items which have regular consumption, and the yearly requirement is capped by Accounts' formula. That is, for each item, the next year's quantity estimate should not exceed 10% of the average yearly consumption of the last three years. Our consumption is haphazard and based on requirement at a particular time only, and its quality due to different makes or delay in supply. Your formula is ok for the likes of your office which uses only registers, files and other stationery, not for maintenance spares. Moreover, the items' cost is debited at the book average rate decided at the beginning of the financial year, while the procured rate differs and is mostly on the higher side. In January, the Shed, fearing less quantity sanction in the coming years due to less consumption, in a special drive, will draw all the items to make up for the current year's sanctioned quantity. So, in the month of February, this special drive amount, as well as the difference amount of the book average rate and actual procured rate, gets debited, and your Accounts Budgeting Section Head will start jumping at the enormous 'expenditure' without trying to find out the real picture. Once, in the Division, he started shouting at me in front of everybody when I told him to calm down, asking him to imagine that if he had seven departments or seven children with one child born as a freak, whether he would ignore that child or pay more attention to it? When he indicated the latter, I told him that our Shed is that freak child who is ignored, and that we both should have periodical reviews of the budgeting and expenditure, as the rigid policies and our nature of work make us a big freak, while we can be a much lesser one. Additionally, debits to be raised under Capital expenditure by the Production Units to Railway Board, are sent to the Division who even accepts it as Revenue expenditure. There is no indication of the nature of supply either in the sale issue note or delivery challan. A Rs.98 lakh debit is sent just like that, without any traceability references. In fact, these production units want our indents to be placed two years in advance, and the item comes after 4 years or sometimes one year in advance or not at all. We will not know for which year's indent it has come or whether it is a Railway Board directive item, since some items not indented/not wanted are also received. You might say that Electric Loco Sheds should also have the difficulties as Diesel Locos have. But the fact is that for Electric Locos, electricity is already available on the overhead lines and is just harnessed, whereas in Diesel Locos, the mechanical energy is produced in the Loco itself and those components and its wear and tear is the extra factor, which is not so in the case of Electric Locos.

In coaches and wagons maintenance, the mechanism or technology is peanuts compared to Diesel Locos. If a coach is unfit, the train can still go without it, but if a Loco is unfit, the train itself can't go." I paused for a while.

Kalamani, overawed, asked, "What about Railway Workshops where your Locos are overhauled, Sachin? Their budget compared to yours is many fold. How is that their budgeting is more accurate?"

"That is because, madam, they overhaul Locos, wagons or coaches of many sheds and when sent, 90% of their Store Depot items are must change items with 10% on need basis, during overhauling, whereas in our Diesel Shed's Stores Depot, 90% items are changed on need basis. Also, Workshops don't indent for as many NS items and their deadline is two months, and nobody asks if it is delayed, whereas our deadlines are daily, or sometimes hourly. Workshops will send back Locos without fitment or with an improper fitment of spares, asking us to do it, but who can we tell if we don't have spares? We have to somehow beg, borrow or even steal from other Locos stopped for long duration maintenance. And what's more, workshops and production units get incentives while we, who work harder and smarter, customized to the requirement, are shown only the middle finger in terms of monetary benefits. Our Shed's work gets little or no appreciation, but if one Loco fails enroute, we are crucified, and the news spreads around in 70mm and with stereophonic sound.

You also give priority to the Engineering dept. proposals because their officers sit above you, literally one floor above and come down and breathe down your neck and your boss's. Also, their construction work completion and inauguration help officers to 'achieve' something for their personal record too, apart from being splashed in the media. The Engineering Department strives to meet a deadline whereas a working Locomotive is the Railways' Lifeline! You should give top priority to our Loco related proposals, second only to the staff medical related proposals since staff good health can only add to the Railways' well-being and wealth.

Also, your office has entered into a contract with a Courier Service for sending documents at very low rates. You also send documents to our office. But if you had extended it for us, we could have also utilised their services. Also, when any of our office-related cheques are ready at your end, instead of sending them by a courier which charges only Rs.10, including tracking and giving back acknowledgement, you insist on sending someone from our office to collect it. Apart from losing his services for half a day, he is paid a minimum travelling allowance of Rs. 90. In your HQ Finance's annual system improvement letter, a level of cumbersome procedure was done away with and then reintroduced, a few years later. Whenever you have an ego fight with your HQ finance over our proposal, we feel the pain as we are the ultimate sufferers. Our mistake is our mistake, but an Accounts mistake is like our blunder. Also, I have seen how coolly other departments wash their hands off their problems at the first instance. In fact, they do it without soap or water.

Now let's come to the 'enjoying' part, madam. Of course, some people do enjoy themselves, and will continue doing so, and people like me and the draughtsman end up with their share of work. We do it for the country thinking there will be some respite or streamlining, or some good news or even a miracle, but day by day, the change is for the worse only.

Do you remember, Madam, when they announced leave encashment by applying for ten days leave and surrendering ten more days, and we had applied around the same day? You got your money before you proceeded on leave whereas I got it after eight months! Now tell me who's enjoying, Madam?!! Our Shed staffs who have applied for Scooter advance or Computer advance get it after two years, whereas the Accounts staff and Personnel Branch staff who have applied just two days before the announcement, get it! Accounts and Personnel Branch should root for and cheer us, not boot or jeer us!

When we got the new 4000/4500 Horsepower Locos, you never agreed for spares procurement as the unit cost was expensive. But this Loco is supposed to run for longer periods than the conventional ones before it can come for maintenance. Also, one Loco will suffice wherever two old Locos were used. You just can't reject an item saying it is costly. In the long run, this Loco is supposed to be more economical. I can easily fool you by writing some technical jargon in my proposals but I don't want to get things done by hook or crook. In the process of implementing austerity measures, you should only cut corners' not our jugulars.

In fact, we have never been trained on the new Locos and the other Shed, which has been trained abroad, uses the policy of use and throw, whereas our Shed tries to repair/ resurrect defective items, without the requisite training or staff or budget support. We have learnt all by ourselves and we had lot of teething problems, especially from the panicky Loco Drivers who were all at sea, and would phone our shed personnel at any time, during the day or night to seek guidance and redressal. It will take over five years to plan and standardize requirements and it is an 'on the job' experience.

Madam, you are sent on three-day surveys to see how much a Railways parking Contractor makes in a day or how much Sales does a Railway HOPCOMs outlet make, so as to increase the reserve price for the next rental contract which will be a few thousands more if not a lakh. Instead, you should come for a three-day survey to see the working/ expenditure of lakhs and crores in the Shed and spend one and a half days in the Shed, half a day in the Control Room, half a day in our office and last half in the Sr. DME's chamber. You will know how the Sr. DME has to be involved not only in the Shed's activities, but also receive nasty phone calls from higher-ups, payments pending, or also if there is no water in our Quarters or Contractor's problem, or a long absentee's counselling or meeting family for a staff member's marital discord, employee's legal or alcoholic problems or family insensitiveness. Once even the quarters' ladies had come with clothes and towel saying there is no water anywhere except in the Sr. DME's toilet and threatened to take a bath there. Another time, due to staff unrest, a Sr. DME was also locked in with a padlock from outside by the Trade Union members with their own lock and when taken up, they said that it was to 'safeguard' him from harm.

His Stenographer's wife also called him demanding why her husband was granted only three days instead of five days leave and whether she should travel alone one-way and whether the Sr. DME would provide and guarantee safety.

Madam, I don't blame you earlier since if I was in your place, I too would've made similar comments. I also know that you are overloaded without an assistant. But now, after enlightening, if you still think we're enjoying, then you're not a human being."

"Okay, Okay, I got your point, Sachin; I take back my words and will try to give priority to your proposals."

"As a start, madam, I request you to agree for us to send a repair proposal after calling of the quotations which will cut four trips to the Division." This was accepted as it reduced her work also and contributed to the 'austerity measures'.

At that moment, my Sr. DME asked for me and as I went in, he pointed out that I had forgotten to sign in my attendance. "All for the good of the Shed, Sir," and I told him about the SO and her turning over a new leaf." He asked to see her and gave her tea and arranged transport to the Division after her work to complete the 'new leaf' cycle and improve the odds in favour of the Shed.

-:-:-:-

After experiencing the six-day week for some time, some of the male staff said that they were ok with it, as, or else on Saturdays, their spouses would force them to take them out or shop or do some work. "We are able to save money," they said mockingly, much to the chagrin of the ladies.

21

RAILWAY'S PROBLEMS, UNWOUND!

The material control cell was always busy with varied tensions. They had to send their help outside, even outstation, regularly, to other Railway entities or Suppliers to collect materials. On two separate occasions, the mothers of the employees passed away and, by the time one of them came back, she had been cremated. The other one was a bit more fortunate as he was near Delhi, and the MP of his constituency bought him a plane ticket and gave him money (all returned later). He reached in time for the funeral. Sometimes they were sent alone and after collection and waiting for the train on the platform, they couldn't even risk going to the toilet with heavy, costly material which was useless outside the Railways. Sometimes, if the train came to another platform than displayed or announced, he had to somehow rush with the material since no one would buy his story if he missed the train or material was lost. One employee just brought some material from outstation in the morning and was told to go out of station the same evening. The employee was tired and fast asleep and missed alighting at the station at 3.00 a.m and alighted at another station at dawn. He somehow caught a bus and came back but the collection was delayed by one day, and one should have seen everyone jumping and having a go at the poor employee. Sometimes, due to a particular crisis situation in the Shed, even a genuine mistake was not tolerated. The tagline was 'Get the work done SOMEHOW'.

Once the Material Control Cell in-charge found time to talk to his help, Nagesh, and asked him where he stayed, and whether his father and mother lived with him and whether he was married.

"Yes, Sir, I'm married," said Nagesh.

"Any children?"

"How, Sir," said Nagesh to his stunned boss, in a stifled but frustrated voice. "How is it possible if you keep sending me outstation like this?"

Apparently, there was some fertility problem which was compounded by 'concerned', bawling relatives. So his boss put him only on local material collection duty and, shortly after, he became a grateful and happy father of two daughters, born in the same year – one in February, the other in December, another rare wonder.

-¦-¦-¦-

Some sections also, to play safe, place five-year or ten-year requirements in one go, which has to be curtailed. Some even don't bother to see the availability and still place indents when the Material Control Cell has to play detective to trace it out through records or even section visits.

-¦-¦-¦-

There was this newly appointed officer, an apprentice ADME in Chiroti, who was very snobbish and never interacted with the office staff, as if it was below his dignity to do so. He was not interested in learning his area of work but instead wanted to know about all the facilities and goodies he was entitled to.

The Railway Recruitment Board conducts exams on some Sundays and for which Railway officials are deputed to the exam centers, which are schools/colleges given on rent. This ADME was deputed as the officer-in-charge of one of the centers along with our OS (Office Superintendent) as the assistant supervisor. They both were to collect exam conducting material (mostly stationery) on Saturday from RRB office, and inspect the Exam center's numbering of the candidates on the benches where they were to sit and write the next day. The ADME took an office vehicle, a peon and went on his own on Saturday and didn't even bother to inform or take the OS with him.

Come Sunday, the OS reached the exam venue at 9:00 a.m and the ADME was already there and sat aloof. At 9:20, the sealed question papers were supplied by the Town officer to the center, and the ADME asked OS about the exam conducting material.

"What exam conducting material, Sir?" the OS asked innocently, "You went on Saturday without informing me so I thought you had collected the material."

"What? You expect an officer to carry the material?" he thundered.

"No, Sir, but I would have carried it if you had taken me with you yesterday."

"What? You have not collected it? I will have you suspended for the atrocity."

"Okay, Sir, but right now we have to conduct the exam first and how can we do it without the exam material?" the OS said calmly.

"You think of it, I say. It is your problem."

"I am sorry, Sir, using the material only is my problem. It's not being available is not my problem," said the OS, taking out the office order, pointing and saying, "See, Sir, it clearly says here that the Officer-in-charge has to collect the exam material with the Assistant Supervisor assisting him. This means you have to sign and collect it and I only can carry it." And he showed his watch indicating that only 15 minutes were left for the exam to start.

The ADME jumped up as if lightning had stuck him, started quivering and sweating and whimpered, "What shall we do now, ya? Do something. Help me."

"Sit down, Sir and calm down! You look like you are getting convulsions; do you need a metal or key to hold on to, Sir?"

"No, No, I'm ok, but do something ya, the candidates are already seated in their rooms."

The OS went into another room, purposely took about five minutes and came back with the exam material, much to the relief of the pathetically beleaguered ADME. "I knew that this could happen, Sir, so I told my friend going there to collect and keep it with him. I went to his house yesterday evening. You should know that we have been in the Shed for over ten years and working for its betterment, and not for ourselves. All should co-operate and have a good rapport. One officer showing high-handedness can spoil the whole atmosphere which is already sensitive. During the management training, you are taught to show who the boss is. In this atmosphere, it is better to be like a friend or a mentor, or else there will be no winners, all will be losers. Kindly keep this in mind when you feel like splurging your ego. If you talk about rules, and if we follow the rules exactly, and not work extra or late, all will suffer. But at the same time if you talk to us reasonably and empathetically, we may go the extra mile for the benefit of all."

-!--!--!-

Honnegowda was feeling very happy. Newly appointed as an RPF constable, he was posted to Gudipuru Station which was near his hometown. His widowed mother applied a tilak on his forehead and wished him luck. As he made his way towards the station, he recalled when he was twelve years old, at Bangalore Railway Station, while walking in the subway, he saw a tramp shamelessly defacating there. His father's shouting didn't help so they went through the other lane in the subway, holding their noses, not bothering whether actually there was a smell or not. They went up the stairs to the common pavement for platform no. 5 and 6, when Honnegowda noticed two RPF constables standing and looking ahead. He approached one of the constables without the knowledge of his family, who were still holding their noses, and heading towards a bench.

"Sir, somebody is shitting in the subway," said Honnegowda to the constable, who had both his hands in his pocket.

The constable only looked at the boy and looked away, without taking his hands out of his pocket and nonchalantly said, "Poor fellow, it must've been urgent."

Gowda was shocked at their attitude and after a pause, he added, flustered, "Yeah, poor fellow, there is no water there – maybe you could provide him with some," and before the constable could react, his father, who had spotted him, came and dragged him away, apologizing.

Remembering this incident, and vowing not to be like them, he climbed the platform to the small, deserted station of Gudipuru for his night shift. The time was 6:00 p.m and he wanted to impress the Station Master by being an hour early. From a distance he could see on a bald patch of land, just behind the Station building, that a white-dressed man was sitting down with his back towards the station building and relieving himself, covering his face from the side but looking towards the bushes in front of him.

"What a start! Yuck," Gowda thought as he rushed towards the man, hitting his baton on the metal poles, making a 'thak' 'thak' sound to drill fear into the man. As he neared him, Gowda shouted, "Shameless fellow! Don't you have any shame?"

To this, the man turned, looked at him and said with folded hands, "Aiyya Sami, you must be Honnegowda, the new constable. I am Sriram, the Station Master, who is expecting you." A shocked Gowda came to attention, stomped his right leg and gave a military salute, "Sorry, Sir, yes Sir, Honnegowda reporting for duty, Sir."

"At ease, my dear man, and before you get ideas, let me tell you that there are no toilets or water either for me or the public here. And I am here because my reliever in the afternoon didn't come, and I have to continue my duties now and the next shift also – totally 24 hours. There is no pointsman or flagbearer so I am doing their work also. Thank God you've come or I was to do your work also. I didn't go in the bushes, as there are snakes and rats around."

"Sir, can I help? Can I get something, some paper or water?" asked Gowda, concerned.

"Don't bother, I have that covered," said Sriram, raising two Goli Soda bottles from his other side, which had a marble sealing the bottle mouth and had to be pressed to open it for the aerated water to gush out. "Only, I have to remember to shake well before use, and point it correctly for best effect. You should try it too, the tingling sensation is some experience," and he continued, "In fact, you may have to, since I got a message that your reliever in the morning is not coming, as he is booked for train escort duty, and the only shop nearby closes shortly. He doesn't sell mineral water and this is the best option. Once I'm finished, you can return these bottles and take four more, asking the shopkeeper to retain the bottles' deposit which I've already paid. But don't tell him the purpose, even by mistake!"

Honnegowda was standing, wide-eyed, as Sriram continued, "Now go in and answer any phone call till I come back. The way you made your entry, my urge to purge halted out of its hurry!"

-|-|-|-

Once, an RPF office stenographer was travelling with us in the train where she spotted a groundnut vendor and signalled 'four', and in no time, four full paper cones were handed over to us. I was surprised to see that the vendor left without asking for payment. I went after him to pay, but he refused saying that if madam saw or came to know he took money, his livelihood would be affected and he would not be allowed to come near a train, and even be arrested if he did so. I put the money in his pocket and told him that he didn't take the money, as it was I who had given it to him. In fact, he would salute me whenever he spotted me and I was glad to learn that his two daughters were studying Commerce and doing very well for themselves.

-|-|-|-

Every evening, for about a week, our return train was reaching 15-20 minutes late. One evening, our train was very late, as it was halting at every station longer than required. The only good thing was that all four of our gang got seats. Two other young employees were sitting on the side single seats near the window. Only one 50+ aged lecturer, a regular, was sitting in our compartment. The delays were irritating, and to break the ice, one of my colleagues said that he knew how to read a palm and everybody made a beeline for him. I said that my question is single, humble and not time-consuming, and so I showed my palm first to him and asked, "Can you see my palm and tell me what time the train and I will reach the destination?" Everyone had a good laugh. I actually wanted to make the atmosphere jovial, but who thought that the next half hour would turn into an animated verbal altercation.

The old man at the window asked casually, "You are all from the Local Shed? Aren't you?" I said,"Yes, Sir, but it is called Loco Shed or Diesel Loco Shed," and got busy with the palmistry. After some time, a Shed boy sitting in the side single seat remarked audibly to his friend sitting opposite, "Have you seen the Local Shed? We should go there one day." Even as I signalled with my head and right hand to keep quiet and not to continue, the other one replied, "We are local boys and not yet been to the Local Shed, shame on us."

This really did it and the old man blurted out, "Okay, Okay! You boys are the only educated, knowledgeable and perfect ones here and I am an idiotic, old professor in a college, taunted for a slip of the tongue." Immediately, I apologized on behalf of the boys and told the boys also to say sorry, which they did unwillingly.

But the old man was not ready to calm down as he seemed to be waiting for a trigger, "Your Railways does not have respect for its own specified timings, and now the employees show no respect for its passengers. Daily the train is late and now I have to experience this, in addition to the ordeal."

The boys who were waiting for a chance to get back said, "Sir, we said we are sorry but we can't tolerate your remarks about the train going late. Do you know that the Controller in Division has to monitor and permit the trains? What problems lie ahead of us, who knows? Do you know the Controller can't even go to urinate sometimes? You cannot just say something without knowing."

To this the old man said, "Ok, you may be right but you have public address systems in Stations which blurt out recorded messages. Can't they announce why it is late or how much more time it will stop here? So local trains are like sheep van and we are all the bloody sheep, is it? The sheep don't know where they are going or what time they reach. When they have the facility to announce, why can't they use it? Your high level officers travel in swanky cars and when they inspect our train, it is ensured that it is punctual. Do you see that electronic display supposed to be showing the next train and coach number? It has been defunct for the last two years. The train stops only for five minutes in the station and what should the hapless passengers do to find their coach? Your Demblur City Railway station is renovated and renovated and renovated in the same areas? Why? And after all that, your main platform no. 1, which is rebuilt and rebuilt and rebuilt, is so slippery that if there is one trickle of water on it, which is hardly noticeable, the person walking on it has had it. If he is carrying heavy luggage, he will have such a fall that he will become the luggage. When it was metre gauge, we aged people could climb into the coach without much difficulty as the low platform was in level with the door. Now, with broad gauge, the coach entrance door is higher, and there is a clearance gap between the coach and the platform, into which many a person has slipped, got stuck or fallen into. In the morning also, we wait on the Demblur platform for information on the incoming 9.45 a.m train, which goes back at 10.00 a.m, but it arrives at 10.20 with an announcement only at 10.17 that it is coming in. But announcements are made about the arrival time of 11.00 a.m due Train, at 10.00 a.m. Who will be there for such an early announcement? We hundred people are waiting to know about our late train to go for work, and unwanted announcements are made apart from loud, irritating advertisements. The display board also keeps changing the late arrival time of a train by 10 minutes each time, instead of giving an approximate time of the actual arrival. I know you have unavoidable circumstances, but there are avoidable ones like timely and proper announcements which, if rectified, will help us feel that there is some care for us. I agree that our tickets are over-subsidized and I have to pay only Rs. five for a one way trip and Rs. ten totally per day. But I have to pay Rs.30 per day for the parking of my vehicle and there is no monthly pass also. Today, since the train is late and the parking will just exceed 12 hours, I have to pay Rs. 40.

Also, our train stoppage, actually meant for the Railway staff, was removed, making us alight at the next stop and again catch a bus back to our college. This stop was beneficial even to several IT Sector employees. We heard that it was for safety reasons, whereas there has not been a single incident or injuries or casualties in that stop over the years. When we teachers and some from IT sector people went to request to reintroduce the stoppage, your DRM asked us what rights we have for alighting or boarding the train which was meant only for the staff, and threatened that he would have us arrested. Why? Are we different from the staff? We also service the country by teaching youngsters and making them ready for the future. This liberty should be given to all, not only to the staff. We also take our ticket/pass till the next station. But what hurts is that the train was stopping there for 23 years, and then suddenly, it is taken off. Either don't introduce a stop in the beginning itself or if you have been stopping a train at a point since a long time, do not remove the stoppage suddenly, without feedback from the public or your own staff, for that matter. You suddenly change the train timings overnight without any hint or advance notice to the public or in the newspaper. Don't make passengers feel frustrated or like beggars. We also are sympathetic towards you. Your Railways make very populist announcements like 78 days bonus, but what you are paid is a measly Rs.8,000 or so, using some old base. Why give a bonus if you are making avoidable losses, and that too by holding back payments of suppliers and contractors? But if a bonus is to be paid, they should indicate the amount and not just the feel good factor of 78 days. Are they ashamed to announce it and leave the shame for the staff and his family to bear?

Many Railway staff members, school teachers, garment factory and small scale industry workers, IT sector employees, labourers etc. travel by these trains which are their lifeline. Some research for punctuality loss can be done. No doubt the Railways have come out with a fantastically designed, user friendly time-table and a beautiful computerized reservation system. But you cannot rest on these laurels and some perennial problems have to be looked into. The distance between Bangalore Cantonment to Bangalore City can be covered in ten minutes, but the time-table for some Superfast trains says 40 minutes! Once a teacher was complaining about the lack of time to do household work and was peeling vegetables in the train, but throwing the skin and unwanted pieces on the floor of the train, to which I strongly objected, telling her to practise what she preaches to her students. Once, at 07:30 p.m, in a delayed train for which you had switched on the lights, a familiar teacher was going towards the toilet. She took offence when I told her to trust me and to take her umbrella with her. But knowing me, she relented, thinking maybe there was some leakage from top. When she came back to her seat, she was red in her face and thanked me profusely. The reason – the glass of the toilet window was fully broken and one would notice it only when the train arrived at a station platform and see people. The open umbrella kept her modesty from being outraged, and there was no switch also for her to 'off' the light, at that moment.

Some of your fans and lights are only dumb displays which don't work. Better utilization, sustainment and maintenance of the existing facilities will help bridge the gap of many an unwanted problem and friction between the public and the Railways, like the perennial problems of toilet discharges while over a bridge, falling down on the road or on the vehicles/people below. You hold meetings with representatives of the public whom we don't even know. You should publicize and hold these meetings, involving us also. Once there was an overhead electric line failure just next to your Shed and their Electric Loco hauled train halted. But because it was an Electrical Branch related failure, their ego did not let them to request the mechanical branch to send your Loco and push/haul the Train till the next station. They instead waited for the line to be rectified, by which time, trains had piled up behind for hours, without a single announcement in the stations, causing a cascading effect of delays. Though the rules for the employees, facilities for the public and the general outlook look somewhat hunky-dory on the outside, things are actually rotting inside."

-:--:--:-

In the Industrial Exhibitions where products are displayed, Diesel Loco Sheds used to be given a free big stall to exhibit Loco parts to develop local or Indian suppliers. This time they were asked to pay Rs. 34 lakhs for the stall with Rs. 500 per extra chair with no free water or food. For 15 people, there were three chairs with the staff sitting on rotation or like musical chairs. At this cost, it was better to have a web platform where ideas could develop and/or exchange.

-:--:--:-

There was this Modified Assured Career Progression (MACP) scheme where long serving, non-promoted employees were given the next post's grade pay with three ensured such upgradations during 30 years of service. One was given an upgradation if he or she had served in a grade for 10 years. But this upgradation was given with effect from September 2008 only. The retrospective effect was from that date only. The ambiguity was that earlier such instances did not get justified. So the newer entrants benefitted more than the long-serving ones. For example, Mr. A was appointed in June 1990 as Junior Clerk and got his first promotion as Senior Clerk in July 2008. Whereas Mr.B, appointed as Junior Clerk in July 1998, got a Sr. Clerk pay upgradation in September 2008. Instead, the rule should have been that Mr. A should have got an upgradation after 10 years in June 2000 with monetary arrears only with effect from September 2008. Mr. A was complaining that the service and experience of the seniors were left in the lurch by the scheme.

Our Accounts Department Section Officer was complaining that she had passed the Section Officer's exam with great difficulty whereas, thanks to MACP, her one year senior colleague's pay, who failed the exams and working under her, was upgraded to her grade and drawing more pay than her. Her colleague had a different story to tell – "I work effectively and harder and better than her. For this exam, only my English is poor. But this lady, who whiles away her time, knows better English and passes these exams where rote knowledge is the criteria, not the actual working or ability. She studied for the exams during office hours and passed them while I didn't. He felt that the MACP was a godsend.

Last heard, people who had come from other Zones/ departments on one-way transfer willingly losing their seniority and grade, posted as juniormost in their cadre, but with pay protection, were fighting for MACP from their appointment date, whereas the Administration was adamant that it should be from their one-way transfer date, otherwise, this way, their pay is upgraded though designation is same, causing disparity in their colleagues who have served more than him in this cadre or Zone, but pay could be less.

There was also Restructuring wherein posts are created in the higher positions and reducing in the lower, duly surrendering some posts. While it had taken Junior Engineers to get promoted as Senior Engineers after 12-15 years, due to restructuring, recent Junior Engineer appointees got promotions as Senior Engineers in just four years.

-:-:-

Whenever Mrs.Kalamani used to call from Accounts asking how we are, I used to tauntingly say that we were still enjoying ourselves. She would then laugh and tell me that three of our proposals were cleared. Cleared meant it was cleared from her table, but it could mean the proposal was 'agreed' or 'returned', which was never clear.

-|--|--|-

Our ADRM, being an ex-serviceman, a retired Major to be precise, arranged for Sports for all interested employees of the Division. The chief guest of the day was to be his old junior, now a Major in the Indian Army. It was 45 minutes late and the Major had not yet turned up and the opening ceremony was yet to be done. So the ADRM called up the Major, who was still dressing up and told him not to come as he would set a bad example since, if he was late for a scheduled programme, then, as per his discipline, what would be the fate if there were to be a sudden war or attack?

22

SCAMS, PROBLEMS THAT ASTOUND!

Within ten minutes of a train being eligible for reservation, all its seats in all classes were booked. A gentleman who had purchased a ticket for that train on the same day, was shocked to find it was waitlisted within 12 minutes of the start of booking at 08:00 a.m and straight away handed it over to the Police Station. On investigation, the Demblur Passenger Reservation System was embroiled in a ticket scam by agents in connivance with employees. So they made some changes and made Agent booking to start only at 10 a.m daily. Last heard, inspite of all precautions, the agents had found a way to circumvent it and still, a similar scam is going on.

-:-:-:-

Moving further, the Railways brought in an E-Ticketing system which brought convenience, transparency, and much touted security in booking. But the fraudsters conquered even that hi-technology. It seems that a Control Room of a major junction received a message from a neighbouring station that a train, which was showing as cancelled in the passenger reservation system, had arrived at their Station. On examining what seemed like a small technical snag, led to a shocking discovery of a cyber crime which had caused the loss of crores of Rupees to the Railways. The modus operandi was that the agents would book long distance trains' E-tickets and, with the connivance of the Railway staff, get the train cancelled from its Originating Station for about 30 minutes, and then again get it restored in the E-system. So, when a train is cancelled, all E-payments are refunded to the Accounts of the agents. On restoration of the train within 30 minutes, the old Reservations stand good but the money doesn't come back to the Railways. The fraud came to light, thanks to a careless, conniving Railway staff member, who totally forgot to restore the 'cancelled train' and the alertness of the doubting Thomas of a Station Master, who received the 'Ghost train'- the status of which was still displayed in his station's system as 'Cancelled'.

-:--:--:-

Two gentlemen came to our office and I knew one of them was the Service head of a company which had done the work of the fitment of panels on our Locomotives, and whose bill had been pending with Accounts for months.

Before the Service Head could talk, the other man in a suit came over, extended his hand and introduced himself, "Hi, Mr. Sachin, I am the General Manager of the Company and pleased to meet you. I am very indebted to you for having passed my final bill of Rs. 35 lakhs to your Accounts without any delay. But I understand that some Audit para of your Divisional office Sr. DME pertaining to a warranty attention was pending. My man has personally gone and checked that the warranty attention was over long back, and a reply to the audit para was given to your Accounts branch, who, in turn, forwarded it to the Audit Branch. But the para is not closed. My man has also taken relevant copies from all your departments and given them to the concerned departments, and has been running around three floors. However, my bill is still pending for the last seven months. I have written to your DRM who has marked the letter to the Accounts Officer, who simply re-marked it as 'Audit para pending' and kept it aside. So I have come to you for one help. Please tell me the list of people with the order of approach so that I can personally go and fall at their feet, one by one, as that is the last option I have. We are not taking the legal course for obvious reasons of delay, and your Accounts jolly well knows that. They don't care even in cases of inordinate delay. They behave as if they are doing us some great favour by even talking to us. Please help me."

After pacifying them and expressing my limitations, they left for the Divisional office and I briefed my Sr. DME saying that we should have a Chiroti half-day in the Division wherein Accounts and other departments would dedicate half a day solely for our cases since he was the only branch officer far away from the Divisional office. My Sr. DME said that it was a good idea but it was still to materialize due to the indifferent attitude in the Division. Only with my individual rapport, could I get 50% work done, which was not much of a consolation.

-:-:-:-

The Vigilance Department HQ at Mangalore got wind of some irregularities in the scrap disposals of our Shed. The intelligence information received indicated that all the Railway officials deputed for the witnessing from all the relevant departments were in connivance with the buyer. They came with two palm size handycams to record the proof and their own RPF team in plain clothes, and waited in a hotel near the main road.

Chiroti Shed used to depute a Senior Engineer for the witnessing of lorry weight, loading etc., after my old, mind boggling experience where, luckily, the IPF and his SIPF were very clean. For some reason, that Engineer was on leave and an OS (Office Superintendent), by name Bholanath, was deputed. After the loading, two lorries went out of the gate, followed by the Contractor's MUV (multi-utility vehicle) in which all others, including the IPF with two of his constables, Bhola, the Stock Verifier and the Depot store keeper went. Once out of the main gate and on turning at the main road, the vigilance officials followed in two vehicles.

The MUV suddenly stopped near a Bar and restaurant while the lorries continued. Luckily, having brought two cameras, with one as back-up, the vigilance team also broke up into two, and one vehicle followed the lorries while the other team went into the bar which was hardly crowded at 5:30 p.m.

At 7.15 p.m the lorries came near the bar where all were still sitting, inebriated. Both the vigilance teams met, discussed and immediately gheraoed the Railway staff and took them to the Shed. Two plain-clothed RPF sat in the lorries and also took them to the Shed. All were taken to the Control Room, except the lorry drivers who were taken into the Sr. DME's Office which was opened. The lorry drivers, who were not aware of the proceedings, were under the impression that they were going to be served dinner there before proceeding further. "What, Sir, we could've had dinner and drinks at the bar itself along with you all. Anyway, we're hungry, and what's the menu?" asked one of them.

"Mutton Biryani and Chilly chicken," said the RPF, "Just wait, my boss is bringing it any moment."

"I hope something accompanies it, we're thirsty" said the driver, thrusting his right thumb from his fist, towards his mouth, indicating 'drinks'.

"All in good time, my friend, all in good time."

As the Vigilance Inspector walked in, the drivers were disappointed seeing his empty hands.

The inspector asked, "Tell us where you went between 5:30 and 7:15 at which the drivers looked at each other, winked and chuckled, "You know where we went."

The inspector slapped the sniggering driver so hard that he lost his balance and fell on the other. "We have video evidence, so don't try to fool us." Within two minutes they squealed that they took both the lorries to another waiting lorry and unloaded about eight tons of the scrap into it and then went to the weigh bridge and weighed the lorry themselves and came to the bar to hand over the weighment slips. The net weight indicated 5.678 and 5.836 tons in the slips against each lorry capacity of 9 tons and which meant they were overloaded to unload about four tons each.

The enquiry went on for two months at the HQ in Mangalore and all other Railway witnesses except Bhola, said that they were hungry and had stopped for food, vehemently denying having taken any money since there was no evidence of it. The 'professionals; that they were, they feigned ignorance about the lorries having gone for unloading.

Poor Bhola, under pressure, admitted to have taken Rs. 500 in the Shed from the contractor's aide. Ironically, just then he had got a monthly raise of Rs. 500 in his salary due to a revision in DA (Dearness Allowance).

At the end of the enquiry, except for Bhola, all the others were issued with a minor charge sheet and 'punished' with a 'warning' or 'censure' or with 'one Railway travel pass withheld' from the yearly account of three passes, having been charged under "failure to maintain devotion to duty."

But Bhola was issued a major charge sheet for "failure to maintain devotion to duty" in conjunction with "pecuniary loss caused to the Government" and was punished with demotion to the lowest grade of Junior Clerk for a period of five years with recurring effect. Bhola and his family suffered huge financial losses, apart from the stigma of being demoted as a Junior Clerk. The vigilance deals only with the wrongdoings by Railwaymen and not of the outsider, the buyer, so the instigators are not touched at all.

This incident really destroyed the reputation of the already neglected, beleaguered Ministerial cadre of clerks. Actually it was supposed to be an Engineer who was the main target, but a meek Bhola got trapped in a weak moment, this being his only case of deputation for scrap witnessing. After a couple of years, the trade union got his punishment reduced, but the damage was already done.

While others got away with as much as a pass cut, for poor Bhola, it was as good as if his ass itself was cut!

-:--:--:-

Once, the least among the tenderers, in a Loco cleaning contract, lost his cool and was educating the merciless Accounts member during a negotiation in the rates of his offer. "What madam, you want me to bring down my offer to the same rates as two years earlier, or, if not, you are only willing to increase it upto 10%, sounding like you are doing me a favour? Are you bargaining for buying bulk quantities of fruits and vegetables? Anyway let me educate you about your own raise in salary income. In the last two years, you have had four raises in Dearness Allowance and Travelling Allowances at 8, 10, 10 & 7% respectively, apart from two increments each of 3% which raises other allowances also. Effective raise is over 40% in the past two years and for another two years, it will increase at least by another 25 to 30%. I have only quoted the rates at 29% higher than the two-year old rate, and you should take into account the inflation in the next two-year period till when I am bound to execute this work. Moreover, I am likely to hardly get 75% of the quantities tendered as per my previous experience, but I have to deploy the same quantum of labourers, everyday. We are not coming here to do charity or make losses. I also have to sustain my family and my labourers' families. You also don't pay interest for the 5% Security Deposit that you deduct from our bills. You are not willing to incorporate the Price Variation formula suggested by Sachin. If you do that, I will come down from 29% to 14%. You can also show substantial savings in your negotiation report, for now. Or, alternatively, I can come down to 24%, subject to your ensuring a minimum of full quantities advertised at the closure of contract or payment of same." The rates were finally finalized at an increase of 25%.

To avoid negotiations or getting a raw deal if inescapable, the Contractors starting quoting at lesser rates, duly indicating their own price variation formula in their quote, which made things more justifiable for them, and complicated for the Railways, if they did not integrate it in the General Conditions of Contract.

-‡-‡-‡-

In my obsession to write about the Railways, I forgot to tell my progress on the family front. We were blessed with a son and I distributed lollipops to all in the Shed who took it sportingly with a pleasantly amused smile. My son was very mischievously intelligent. Once at his age of five, when I had brushed my teeth, put out the lights and was about to go to bed where my son and wife had already curled up, I made a 'menacing' giant's sound to scare my son. I said in a gruff voice, "I am very hungry – I want to eat a human – whom shall I eat first – the young boy or his mother?"

Pat came the blunt, fearless reply in the darkness in a child's voice, "You just brushed your teeth, so you can't eat. If you are hungry, you just have to swallow your spit." And in the dark, I could see my proud wife's pearly whites flash beneath. To match his energy and vivacity, we needed his milk supplements more than him.

He liked my stories about the good boy and the bad boy and how the bad boy hurts himself driving rashly, while the good boy drives carefully and reaches his destination safely. The other story he liked was the one I narrated in the presence of my 33-teeth decorated wife. It would never get past the first two sentences and we would all be rolling with laughter. It started with, "Once there was this small girl in a village. During birth itself, she had one fully grown tooth..."

He lived in the real world till the age of 12, after which he got habituated to TV, junk food, computer games, mobile phones etc. and started living in an 'unreal' world which gave him instant gratification without much physical or mental effort. His TV viewing was like doing a Ph.D on Cartoons. I tried reasoning that I wanted him to balance his enjoyment and academics and not be either a total book-worm or a total reveller. But today's gizmos, fast food and ready-made things have the kids addicted to them, as they look for where the next enjoyment comes from, neglecting and avoiding life's basics for a healthy future. Hema also reverted to superstition and elderly advice of "wait and watch – he'll change for the better," instead of taking him to task. Now, he would take us to task, if we didn't cater to his wishes. He was obsessed with Basketball but his approach and off the court attitude and activities were unhealthy.

He was proud of his knowledge of the latest mobiles and all their features which none of us knew much about, but couldn't tie his own shoelaces properly.

Once, he and my cousin went to help four relatives to board the train. My cousin told him to buy the platform tickets and instead of two, he bought six. I am grateful to my cousin who made him go back and sell the excess four.

My wife had once asked if I saw heaven or God or a bright light or anything divine or supernatural, when I was unconscious for three hours in the train accident. To her disappointment, I said I didn't and it was like waking up from a deep sleep with no dreams.

HISTORY OF DIESEL LOCOS, LOST & FOUND!

Meanwhile, I was able to piece together the history of Diesel Locos in India which brought even more admiration and respect for the Diesel Locos and the Shed. So I wrote homage for the WDM2 type Locos from the point of view of one of its founders, Mr. Waltair, who had recently passed away. This revolutionary, but trying phase, warrants awareness. Thus ensued the homage to Mr.Waltair and his Diesel Locos;

Most of us knew Waltair uncle as a philanthropist, a humanist, a protagonist and an advocate for enhancing the quality/longevity/self-esteem of Senior Citizens, the lesser privileged, their children etc. Some of them knew him as a retired Railway Officer. But what most of us don't know was his contribution to India in making its Railways the no.1 employer as well as transporter of billions of passengers and goods, in the most efficient, economical and sustainable manner. Railways - the lifeline of the common man of India.

Starting humbly in Railways, he retired as the Joint Director, RDSO (Research Design and Standards Organization, Lucknow) which comes under the Ministry of Railways. RDSO is the Technical Advisor and Consultant to Railways, as well as several other entities which consider RDSO to be their Bible for standardizing Railway equipment, construction, operation and maintenance and is the proprietor of SAFETY in Railways. He was with the RDSO during the critical transition of the phasing out of Steam Locos to the more effective Diesel Electric Locomotives.

With our Steam Engines having a horse power of around 1200, the hauling and speed of long distance passenger/ goods trains were very limited due to lesser tractive effort, what with well laid out rail l tracks underutilized, and the inability to cater to the burgeoning population and GDP (Gross Domestic Product).

Electric Locomotives with mature technology were available but could not be drafted in for two main reasons. Firstly, it required huge capital investment to set up the infrastructure and two – Electricity Generation was insufficient for the towns itself, forget the villages and hence, there was no question of going in for Electric or AC Locos. It is learnt that the power used for switching on an Electric Loco was equivalent to lighting up 6000 homes and while on higher speeds, it was upto 15,000 homes.

Diesel engines were considered as the next viable alternative as they had better combustion and gave six times more useful power than steam engines. But then there were problems on how to converge on the best composite model.

Diesel Hydraulic Locomotives were first tried, which again had limitations and could be useful only for shunting coaches/wagons and other inferior activities, restricted to a small periphery.

Next, they narrowed down to the now standardized Diesel Electric Locomotives. A diesel-electric transmission system (started with the help of batteries) includes a diesel engine connected to an electric generator that powers electric traction motors which drive the axles to which the wheels are fitted. These engines were 4-stroke and turbo-supercharged. The biggest advantage was that two or more Locomotives of this type could be interconnected, and the leading Loco could utilize the haulage power of all of the trailing Locos with only one Loco's crew.

The first lot of WDM1 (W-Wide or Broad Gauge, D-Diesel, M-Mixed-used for both goods and passenger, 1-signifying Horse Power of 1950) Locos of this type were imported from American Locomotive Company, Canada (ALCO) in 1957-58, but were soon out of favour since they were uni-directional (could be operated in a single direction only, needing the 'turn table' arrangement to change/ reverse direction, just like the Steam Engines).

Then, in the early 1960s, they hit the bullseye with ALCO's WDM2 which had a horse power of 2600, and had the capacity to operate in both directions with the same power, using the principle of reverse polarity. This Loco model was the standard workhorse of Indian Railways and is still used in the 50+ Diesel Loco maintenance Sheds in India, today with over 2700 Locos. After the transfer of technology, India manufactured this type of Locos for Indian as well as other countries' from the late 60s.

During the crucial phase of the inception of this mainstay model Diesel Electric Locomotive, Waltair uncle was involved in the RDSO Directorate of Motive Power which is the advisor/consultant for the Locomotive design, its manufacturing, its functioning in Rail Traffic and its subsequent maintenance by the respective Diesel Sheds where these Locos are allotted.

Today, even after standardization, the logistics involved in operating and maintaining a Locomotive is mind-boggling. Hence, one can imagine how it was when Waltair uncle and his team, at the nascent stage, took up the gargantuan task of designing/drafting the Locomotives, its components, its various maintenance practices, and even indigenizing and identifying sources of supply of these materials including classification/evaluation/development of Vendors for each type of item. The Locomotives had to be customized to suit the Indian terrain and climatic conditions. Days and months of midnight oil were burnt in conducting the trials and tribulations of these Engines and each of its working parts, huddled in a goods train engine, in those days of 1960s/70s when there was little technology for communication and with least preference to movement of Goods Trains which would be kept in a siding for hours. RDSO also had to design the infrastructure for Manufacturing or for maintenance at respective Diesel Sheds or for overhauling/component manufacturing/assembly in Railway Workshops with maintenance instructions along with drawings and specifications for hundreds of Locomotive spares. Mind you, this spadework was done during the late 60s and 70s and the age of B.C – Before Computers! After the anatomy of living beings, I feel the next wonder is the structure and functioning of Diesel Electric Locomotives which require the synchronization of so many moving parts/components to produce the required, variable energy levels incessantly and harness it effectively. Having experience from the grass root level, Waltair Uncle could feel the pulse of the Locomotive, and hence perceive and do away with many future anticipated problems at the inception stage itself, which could never be done by direct recruit Engineers who were more theoretical than practical.

Even more herculean was the ordeal to obtain the necessary approvals, sanctions and funds from various levels (read as Accounts) apart from grappling with your own administrative set up. To be part of this exercise, one had to be obsessed and possessed with the fervour to succeed. Such people can hardly have any family/social life. His aptly named better half, Shanti, stood tall and firm by his side. I heard his free annual travel passes were rarely availed. During my interactions with him, his eyes would light up at the mention of his pet Locos and their progress. He voluntarily retired from Railways on being transferred from his patented department. He said vested interests wanted to push their costly, unworthy products to be fitted on the Locomotives which he defied, but the lobby for his transfer won through means of graft. Now that the Locos were standardized, he suddenly became dispensable.

Though many variants/ value added/ upgraded versions/ digital/ Microprocessor type of Diesel Electric Locos have come in (4500 Horse Power and now 5500 under trials), the basic working principle remains the same. Now, purely Electric or AC Locomotives are considered the most efficient and may be the order of the day in the future (only when there is surplus, pollution-free power supply to this starved Country. But if hydrogen fuel cells take over, Diesel Locos can be converted and Electric Locos will have to be scrapped). But, during the critical formative years of the developing Indian Economy/Reforms, the Diesel Electric Locomotive was the prime mover of not just the trains, but also the Nation.

Waltair uncle's magnanimous service to the Nation was not only during his service or retirement, but also after his demise, as he donated his mortal remains to Science – my first God, and not to Superstition – my last.

24

THE SHED, AS IT BLOSSOMED AROUND!

I was glad to be part of Waltair uncle's legacy of Diesel Locos. These Locos worked effectively and reliably. The hiccups were not in the Locos, the homing Sheds or its maintenance formats, but in the Administrative set up, which, on paper, looked fantastic. However, the execution was very much lacking due to the narrow minded approach and biased policies. Hence, I felt that people like me were required to be there to bridge that gap and thankfully, there were a handful, including officers who helped make the difference, making it corruption-free and supplier-friendly to the extent possible in the Shed.

In the Shed also, there was ill-will among the Electrical and Mechanical maintenance staff, but some supervisors took it on themselves to create an amicable atmosphere and any spark of hatred was doused immediately. The under truck section was the most feared section as any failure could lead to an accident, whereas other sections' failures would only affect the Loco. No one wished to be in that section and those who were there thought that it was a punishment for their sins. But the holistic approach by the section-in-charge had now made it the most sought after section in the Shed. Also, in the Railway Quarters, much infrastructure and facilities came, one by one, from nothing, to an open auditorium, a gym, a clubhouse where one could play badminton, table tennis, chess, carroms, Yoga and even Billiards/snooker. A skating rink, lawn tennis and a levelled cricket ground rounded off the facilities. A Kindergarten school and a Kendriya Vidyalaya School also took shape, thanks to the initiatives of the Sr. DMEs. A tree plantation of over 1500 trees and composting initiatives crowned the Shed. A blood group directory and a Technical Training Center also was possible due to some supervisors who could have easily passed exams and become officers, but preferred to stay put in the Shed. All these were self-made initiatives to motivate the staff. But the basic problems of staff shortage and lack of incentives remained. The new recruits were less patriotic or work-minded. While we were afraid whether we would justify our appointment, these people looked for less work but all the facilities, and took liberties.

We used to 'boost' our Peons and handle them carefully, and they would oblige doing more work, and that too, happily. Once a new, impatient Steno complained to the Sr. DME about the two Peons and repented at leisure since the Peons were wild, and gave her a step-brotherly treatment throughout her tenure.

The Administration outside the Chiroti Shed stayed aloof and did very little for the staff members. Whatever was done was after our creating awareness, with an invitation to inaugurate 'achievements' for Divisional Officers. But Chiroti didn't let the Administration's indifference bog them down or depress them. They took their own initiatives and kept people motivated and active. All these initiatives paid off big time for the staff and residents' recreation in Chiroti. Once, a retiring Engineer was not given a send off. Taking it personally, his fellow supervisors formed a team and now, with the help of Trade Unions, arrange grand send-offs, bringing tears and pride to the retiree's family, which remain immortal in one's memories and life's highlights. In Chiroti, it was not like one lotus in a dirty pond, but the pond itself was cleaned and lotuses bloomed in abundance.

-:-:-:-

Chiroti Loco Shed was also a powerhouse of talent – they could build a house from scratch, from the architecture to the construction, and from the furnishing to the painting, in the most professional manner. They built a lifelike giant dinosaur, among other items, from scrapped empty drums and even made Locomotive replicas with intricate details.

I have to mention about the 'Digitally Inspired' innovative cricket scoreboard made in the Shed. On a rectangular metal sheet, welding was done with metal hinges for digits. Each digit contained seven hinges welded with outside plate painted in white and the rest in black. We just had to open/close the hinge plate to get the desired number. e.g. for '8', all the hinges were closed and for '0', the middle hinge was opened. It was such a pleasure to operate the scoreboard - a long way from the cumbersome traditional or sliding numbered plates.

A special mention has to be made about our UPS (unimaginable power supply) which can probably be conceived and built, only in only Diesel Loco Sheds. That is, several aged Loco batteries (12 Volts, 500 Amps), which are working but not risk-worthy on Locos, are connected together, and with the help of an inverter, are able to light up our whole office building, as well as provide power to our computers, with backup of four hours.

There was also an electronic safety device invented by a technician at a cost of less than Rs.20,000, and an encouraging junior officer personally saw to it that he got an award of Rs.5,000 for that. But, within months and without the knowledge or consent of its inventor, the same device was patented and sold in thousands to the Railways, including us, by a Company at Rs. 2,00,000 a piece!!!

-|-|-|-

Mr Daniels was sitting in our office one Saturday afternoon after all the staff members had just left. The Sr. DME was not in his chamber and the peon was to close the office after half an hour.

In walked a tall, fair and white-haired gentleman in a suit and asked rudely, "Where is the Sr. DME? I've been waiting in his chamber for the last two minutes!"

Mr Daniels shrugged his shoulders without answering, which offended him.

"Do you know who I am?" he thundered to the least bothered Mr Daniels. "I am a retired CWM who introduced the Retirement Railway Pass system here for retirees staying nearby instead of going all the way to the Divisional office."

"Oh good, Sir, we should all be indebted to you then. Please sit," said Daniels, gesturing.

"Good, then," said the ex-CWM, still standing, but pleased at being acknowledged, "I need a pass urgently and you may write it immediately, book my ticket and send it to my bungalow which is five kms away from here."

Mr Daniels raised his voice, "I see; so you are that fellow, who, during service, carried and nurtured your false ceiling of an ego, till and after retirement also, and still behaves like God and orders my Sr. DME around, causing a lot of inconvenience to our staff. If you are like this now, God knows how many liberties you took while in service! You take along with you your ego, more than your own shadow."

The retired CWM went red, "How dare you talk to me like that? Who the hell are you, I say? I will have you dismissed."

"I am a retired Engineer of this Shed whose pass is just ready and am waiting for the peon to give it to me."

"Is this the way to talk to a CWM, you lowly Engineer?"

"Retired CWM," corrected Mr Daniels, "and once retired, you and I are in the same boat. But you want to behave as if you are on a Cruise Ship. You don't want to sit here, afraid that you may catch some infection and turn middle-class. I could have requested somebody from the Shed to come and write a pass for you. But I will not do that. Both your children are settled abroad and I know they didn't stay in any hostel when they were studying. They stayed in Railway Guest houses luxuriously, with the Railway staff and vehicles at their beck and call. You had a CBI case pending for wealth disproportionate to known sources of income, and your retirement settlement was delayed. You fell at the feet of some politician and got your settlement. I know how you got your land and how you used our Railways resources – men and material – during your house construction. At that time, the media was not as strong and hi-tech as they are now and your case got buried in the sands of time."

"You bloody bastard," seethed the ex-CWM, searching for words, "I'll....I'll..."

"You will only shut your mouth and listen, you swine," interrupted Mr Daniels, "Whatever you want to do, you better do it fast, because I am in the last stage of blood cancer and won't be around for long. But I can do a lot to you by getting your cases reopened. My son is a partner in a leading news agency and I can get your pompous ass splattered all over the newspapers and on TV. Now get your dirty, sickening ass off my face before I claw at it and rub more salt and chilli powder into it. Go and lock yourself in the safe confines of the Sr. DME's chamber." As the ex-CWM quietly obeyed and left, Mr. Daniels said, "Thank you Lord - this was something to die for. When I come to you, I will be much happier."

-¦--¦--¦-

I was recommended for the GM's award, and I told my Sr. DME that I didn't expect awards, and not to recommend my name. My Sr. DME asked me whether he should send a donkey's name, instead. He gave me a small lecture and told me to keep quiet and play along. I subsequently figured in the final list of awardees and was to receive the same three days later, and had two more deserving Shed staff for company. While going, our tickets were confirmed at the last minute. At Mangalore, I felt that 150 awardees were too many and would diminish the value or the dignity of the award. Maybe 25 were enough. For our return journey, our tickets were not confirmed and we rushed to the Station Master who said that an AC coach, which had come for GM awardees from Demblur, was being attached back to the train. Though we were relieved, we noticed that none of the awardees knew about it, save one or two. At that moment, we felt that getting a berth for the night journey was much bigger than the GM's award.

The flip side of the award, which is announced through Personnel Branch, is that, instead of automatically making the award entry in our Service Register, they expect us to give an attested photocopy and show the original. This is like an insult and breaches the very spirit of the award.

-:-:-:-

Once, a GM awardee regretted getting it. This was because we had to recommend at least ten names, of which eight or nine would be eliminated. So, he was an average worker and was recommended to make up the numbers. But the English citation was good, and so the deserving one was eliminated and he was selected. After returning with the award of Rs.1,000, he ended up spending over Rs.7,000 towards sweets and a celebration party, apart from the endless wisecracks. Also, during his visit to Chiroti Shed, the GM recalled and asked specifically for him, being the youngest awardee ever, and shook his already shaking hands and announced that he was a 'role model' for the Shed and India, and took him, exhibiting him during whole of GM's tour of Demblur Division.

In the Shed, he was then heckled as 'GM's heir', 'GM's P.A (pet animal)' and also as 'GM's future son-in-law'. He was so stressed that if he had known all this would happen, he said he would have given Rs.10,000 to cancel the award.

25

DELAYS IN WAGE REVISION, PROBLEMS COMPOUND!

One morning in February 2014, the train was abuzz with the news that the Prime Minister had consented to set up a four-member seventh pay commission for Central Govt. Employees. This was a good start since the pay scales were due for revision from January 2016. We reminisced that the sixth pay commission, due from January 2006, was implemented only in August 2008 though with retrospective effect from 1.1.2006. We thought that this was the most delayed pay commission, considering the computers and other hi-tech resources available at their disposal, and innumerable data at fingertips in various required formats. The delay resulted in the Govt. having to revise the pay scales much more than if actually revised in January 2006 due to higher, ever-increasing inflation in 2008. Unnecessary extra work of calculation of arrears in 60% and then 40% gave a wrong signal that the Govt. was short of finances. Most employees ended up paying much higher taxes. Less than 1% of Central Govt. Employees or Pensioners knew or claimed rebate under Section 89(1) of Income Tax Act, in which arrears received in a year for the previous years, could be proportionated to those years and relief claimed for excess tax paid. They paid a good bit of their hard-earned money as excess tax. But we learnt that some people from the Accounts and Personnel branch conveniently claimed and got that relief! My colleague and I had sent the necessary form, 10E, for the same, but it was returned unceremoniously. I lost about Rs. 8,000 in it, along with lakhs of other Govt. employees, whose amount would've run to crores. The perception that the money went into the Govt's coffers, and not into some thug's pocket, was no excuse. The Govt. should have provided awareness and guidance on Section 89(1) of Income Tax, due to its incompetency in implementing the Sixth Pay Commission on time. It should have directed its HR or Personnel Departments and Pensioners' Banks to aid the affected. The Income Tax dept. did that. These wage revision delays affect the tax payment of all – even Public Sector Undertakings and Nationalised Banks. Thousands of pensioners die during the delay period without knowing or experiencing their enhanced pension.

-:-:-:-

On the brighter side, our Accounts Data processing Center developed an internet access for employees to view their profile, salary details etc. Payment details to the staff, suppliers and contractors were incorporated, which crowned the feat and brought great relief to us, as well as our service providers.

-:-:-:-

During the train Journey to office, I was told about how the delay of Sixth Pay commission affected one of our sincere employees, in 2008.

Sakharam was promoted from a Class IV employee to a Class III Technician in November 2005. He stayed in a small Railway Quarters in Demblur. He loved children and had four sons – the last two being twins. His eldest son had tragically died in an accident in September 2006, when he was studying in the eighth standard in the Kendriya Vidyalaya School in the Railway Quarters in Demblur. His second son also was studying there in the fifth standard and the third son – the elder of the twins got admission in same school to Ist standard in June, 2007, on the basis of the demise of his brother. The last son was denied admission as the Principal stated that he had already given admission to two and was not in a position to take the third. As private schools were costly, the last son was kept at home for a year. Sakharam had the DRM's assurance that he would admit him from his quota in June 2008 as he had finished it in 2007. But unfortunately, both – the DRM and the School Principal got transferred soon after, and the new ones were apathetic saying hundreds to thousands were there like him or with more genuine problems and that they cannot cater to everybody.

Sakharam was in financial doldrums. Having put in fifteen years service, he had drawn the maximum permissible amount from his Provident Fund Account. He was a member of two Railway Societies in which loans were given against the surety of two other employees with a monthly deduction from their salary. Three people would form a team and avail the maximum loans with surety by the other two. The meek Sakharam had chosen the wrong two – both drunkards and long absentees. One had passed away and the other was bed-ridden and had exhausted all his leave and finances. As per the Railway Societies' policy, Sakharam's surety was exercised and he ended up paying for all six loans, two of his and four of his friends, from two Societies. To add to his misery, a Life Insurance agent, who used to frequent our Shed, 'scared' and convinced a gullible Sakharam, on the demise of his son, to insure himself and all his family members, and high monthly premiums also were deducted from his salary. Against a gross monthly salary of about 15,000, his take home salary was 3,100. He had borrowed money at 5% interest per month from a lending Railway employee and was paying only the interest amount over the months. His wife started working as a poorly paid domestic help in the Railway Quarters and sold vegetables to make ends meet. His Shed supervisor, on knowing his plight, put him continuously on night emergency standby duty so that he could earn Night Duty Allowance as well as some sleep. Sakharam then worked as a morning coolie in a wholesale goods shop and also as a part-time waiter in a bar in the afternoon.

It was April 2008 and he was keen to get his last son admitted into some decent private school as he had already lost a year in waiting. He had barely gathered about Rs. 22,000 and needed money for the Rs. 30,000 rigid donation asked by the private school towards admission. A friend told him to open an Account in a Nationalized Bank in Tirupattur which was giving upto Rs.1 lakh loan on opening a salary crediting account in the bank. Applying leave, his friend took him to the bank in Tirupattur with the necessary documents and Rs.500 for opening an account. The Bank Manager and staff helped him open an account and gave him the pass book on the same day and took the loan application and told him to come the following month to avail the loan.

"But, Sir," said Sakharam's friend to the Manager, "I got my loan on the same day of opening the account. You only gave it. I have brought my friend saying he will get it today."

"Oh, I see," said the Manager, "You must have opened the account during the special drive for Government employees wherein I was given special powers to sanction loan for a period of one month to all new accounts. Now that drive is over and I have to send this application to our Headquarters for approval which will take time. Moreover, his take home salary is very meager and only a small amount could be sanctioned by our HQ."

"Sir, I need the loan amount today," pleaded Sakharam with folded hands, "I have to pay school donation within three days or my son will not get any admission. Can I get an advance of Rs. 10,000 atleast – that will save my day."

"I am sorry, Mr.Sakharam," sympathized the Manager, "but that is not possible."

To this, the friend lost his cool and said, "What, Sir, whenever we give money, you take it easily but when you have to give money, you are talking sweet honey, like an ever-castrated call center employee. You do not understand his problem."

Now, the Manager lost his cool, "What, Mister Railwayman, some Railway employees from your own Division and Shed have defrauded us earlier by taking loans against forged documents and defaulting later. When I approached your Personnel Branch, they absolved themselves saying that they do not give any undertaking of any sort for Bank Loans. Earlier, your staff used to take a loan against salary credit account, and then change the bank in connivance with your Personnel dept. staff. We have registered police cases but have to run around like fools, as well as get a black mark written in red Ink in our Service Register. Now, at least, your Personnel dept. seeks a no-objection and no-loans pending certificate from the bank before changing it. Some employees have damaged the reputation of all Railway employees, as loan defaulters. And, you are accusing me of being bad. If you want, you are welcome to close your account. We will all get into the Guinness Book of World Records for the shortest Account holding period and maybe, they will give you some money for that!"

Sakharam interrupted with folded hands, "Sir, our pay commission is due and all the arrears will come to this account, kindly consider that, Sir."

"Hah!" said the Manager, "Our pay revision itself is overdue and is not done inspite of striking work and holding the Country to ransom; whereas your Central Government is worse off than us. If I read about timely implementation of any of your pay revisions, it will only be in a dream in one of my wildest dreams or in a work of fiction."

Sakharam and his friend returned on the same day and Sakharam attended Night duty in the Shed. The next morning, his body was found with its head cut off in a Loco maintenance pit line!

The Shed officials and the local police termed it as an accident so that his wife got employment as a Class IV employee on compassionate grounds and full life insurance benefits. Not many or even I knew the exact background leading to Sakharam's death.

This really had me thinking. I had seen every 1st day of the month that on-leave or sick employees and lenders do rounds whenever a cash payment is being made towards employees' salaries. Some approach the cashier in his divisional office or in the train to avoid their lenders. Once payment is received, some absent themselves until the money is spent or hunger is felt. If this was the case for monthly payments alone, I hoped if only the Pay Commissions were on time, lives could be saved and many hand-to-mouth existence problems, like Sakharam's, could have been mitigated, along with some dignity or self-esteem brought into their lives.

-:-:-:-

I had planned to voluntarily retire in 2018 and create awareness about Diesel Sheds and their problems, since our cries wouldn't be heard or could get suppressed at some level. We were also gagged from talking/writing to the Media or Public, irrespective of whether it was good, or otherwise. Writing a letter to the Prime Minister of India was out of question as it would get drowned in the three lakh letters received daily by him. Other alternatives also seemed weak. A book seemed the best option at the moment and for that, I could write with a free mind, only if I was not in service and hence, I tentatively brought forward my plan to voluntarily retire in October 2014, on the completion of exactly 25 years of service.

"MOGRI" – AFFECTIONS & EMOTIONS GO AROUND!

Her greyish green eyes were like Aishwarya Rai's. She had a small, pretty face with an adorable pea-shaped nose. Big sharp ears and a black eye-liner like line ran from both the edges of her eyes to her ears. The long, thin paws rounded off her cuteness. She was tall for her age of about two months. Her body was a mixture of grey and white with a long bushy tail. Her thin, soft mewing made her a sitting duck, for a crushing hug.

Her stray mother had left her with us, carefully choosing the house as we all were cat lovers and had fed her generously when she was carrying.

As the kitten sat on the divan, unafraid and very much wanting us to pet, caress and play with it, we could see the trust, affection and mischief in its eyes. We could not determine its gender and as she seemed to have feminine features, we promptly named her 'Mogri' – the affectionate one. Mogri was very affectionate and loved purring (more like Durring) a lot from day one, which made us wonder whether we had adopted her or she had adopted us.

The next morning, her mother brought a white kitten and left soon after, leaving it also with us. He was handsome and bulky, a clone of his father who too would hang around in the vicinity. Befitting his size, I christened him 'Chhota Bheem'. Together, they gave us some very amusing and delightful moments.

Some days later, with the help of the internet and a magnifying glass, we soon found out that both were tom cats. But we continued referring to Mogri as 'she', because of her delicate features and to differentiate her from her brother. She had a big heart, in the sense that the liberal grey patch on the left side of her body was in the shape of a big heart.

During my mother's early morning walk, both would go and roll in front of her, making it difficult for her to keep her balance. A senior neighbouring tom cat was also a friend of Mogri's and it was astonishing and touching to see the three playing innocently, with Mogri acknowledging our presence when seen or called. After some months, Bheem's priorities changed and he would be out of the house most of the time, and would come only to eat and sleep. Mogri expected us to compensate and play with her, and my son would run around the house with her scuttling after him. I could not match my son's alacrity but she was game enough to get excited by slight jerky movements of my head, and would run, jump up the sofa's back rest, grab hold of our face and brush it against hers. If the brush was not satisfactory, she would grip it with her right paw (duly taking care not to bring out her claws), and rub her cheek against ours, two to three times. Her favourite pastime everyday was to go 'window shopping' for the fishes in our aquarium, trying to 'catch' them in vain, but never stop trying.

Inside the house, her trust was so much that she knew that we wouldn't let her come to any harm. She didn't fear anything except the pressure cooker hissing. She would even let the guests to pet her. She slept soundly with a divine look on her face, unlike her brother whose ears would be sharp and rotationally alert even while asleep, and would react to the slightest unusual sound. As she was mostly eating home food, I was sure she would live for 14 years or more due to her sound health.

Later, she too started going out in the night and but would come back in the wee hours, latest by seven a.m. If she came back hungry, when we were asleep, she would first come to my bed-room and make a very small 'Kurr' sound – just enough to see if we were awake and not to actually wake us. If there was no response, she would go to the room where my mother and son were sleeping and repeat the sequence. If still no response, she would go and quietly curl on the sofa until we woke up and fed her. But if she knew we were awake, she would jump on us and start licking our faces like a dog and lead us, with her bushy tail upright, to her saucer in the kitchen.

But she was a scaredy cat outside the house and being weak, was a target for other cats. She would come running home, and, if attacked, she had a skunk like defensive-technique, clearing her bowels on the face of her chasing adversary (and, yuck, we would have to clean her up later). She was afraid of the sound of the garbage auto rickshaw. Lately, she was afraid of the painters painting the outside of our apartments, and would be in the house most of the time. If we called out to her, she would come with an ebullient spring in her stride. During their first Deepavali experience, both Mogri and Bheem were either hiding under the bed or between our legs, under the blanket, out of fear of the bursting sounds of many a cracker.

One Sunday morning, she didn't turn up at all and late in the morning, my son and I went to the neighbouring buildings, when one of the building's residents said that, early that morning, this greyish-white cat had fallen off their third floor ceiling to the ground, but was alive and struggling. It did not drink the milk they offered and limp-walked for about 12 meters before collapsing (it was heart-wrenching to note that the 12 meters were towards the direction of our house, and seeing the 30 ft. wall, she lost hope). Not knowing the owners, they had called an animal shelter which took her in their van.

We found her in the animal shelter, in a small cage where she sat with eyes closed with no hope of any kind. It was, indeed, Mogri and she could be recognized due to an earlier injury mark on her right foreleg. She was reeking of urine and excreta all over. We then rushed her to a veterinary hospital where intravenous feeding through injection was done, during which the doctor ruled out any external injury and seeing no blood near the rectum, even ruled out any stomach injury. But there were traces of blood near the nose which could be due to a small nose injury or even an internal head injury. It was there she opened her eyes and mewed weakly which was encouraging. Back home, we bathed her in warm water and put her to rest on the bed while my son and I went to thank those residents for their concern and the trouble taken.

On our return, we were pleasantly surprised to see my wife sitting on the ground with Mogri on her lap. She had called out to my wife and wanted to be let down on the floor and she went around the house, walking weakly, but seeming happy about being back in her house. After she got tired, she made my wife sit down so that she could curl herself and sleep. We could feed her only with the help of a syringe without the needle, but she would slowly but sportingly swallow the milk and medicines.

That night, she slept on my right side and my wife on the floor, to my left. When I awoke about 1.a.m to see how she was doing, she was not in her place, and had instead crawled near my face, watching with her eyes open, waiting for me to wake up. The moment she knew I had woken up, she started purring and durring loudly, and walked all over me and also my wife, who too had woken up by then. She seemed greatly relieved and happy to have reunited with us, though it had taken time for it to sink in that it was for real and not a dream.

There was marginal improvement that day and the next. When we took her to the doctor on Tuesday, he was happy to see the improvement and reflexes. Back home, she went around and even played with her favourite string, chasing it with her wobbly, slow motion walk and feebly holding it with her mouth. We were thrilled with her progress. But late in the night, she began showing signs of weakness and difficulty in swallowing milk, not opening her eyes properly. As I would call out to her and caress her, she would purr but not open her eyes. The purring also weakened to a whisper by the morning. She made efforts to get up but would fall.

As the hospital was open 24 hours, we rushed, holding Mogri on our lap instead of in the cage. Just minutes before reaching the hospital, she convulsed and foamed from her mouth which indicated the worst, which was confirmed by the doctor on arrival. She was with us exactly for nine months, and her innocent, playful life was snuffed out in less than a year. And even during her last few days, she kept her basic character intact – that of playfulness, affection and zeal to live, and even the one of not trying to wake us up when she was in hunger or in pain. She died, unable to tell us of her ordeal or discomfort, but the consolation was that she didn't die unceremoniously and was with her family in her last days.

A few days later, Chhota Bheem also came with his paws bleeding, which was diagnosed as due to 'electrocution' and required amputation of his beautiful, bushy tail. He recovered well and has sobered down and is at home at least during the day, with his once bandaged paws now healed. He now purrs and 'Kurrmeows', which is no match to that of Mogri's, which still echoes in our ears, making it difficult for us to get over the throes.

-:-:-:-

Sometime later, my college-mate and tennis ball cricket captain, for over five years before my accident, died suddenly due to a heart attack. I too had some sicknesses due to the sleepless nights during Bheem's recuperation, and signs of old illnesses, like pain in the operated portion of my hip, wheezing, positional vertigo, stomach upsets and the like. That was when I decided, told my unconvinced family on 1st May 2014 and applied for Voluntary Retirement the next morning, from 1st November 2014. My colleagues and the Shed staff were in shock, as also my relatives and well-wishers. I had completed 25 years and had 12 more in service. My officer too initially objected, but later relented and forwarded it to the Personnel Branch.

I told everyone that the timing was important since there was a restructuring exercise, due to which there were six people excess in our Cadre, and that two years later, many would retire above me and my conscience may not allow me to apply. I wanted to write my dream book while I was alive, in good health and a proper frame of mind. In my work front also, there was no significant improvement in our Cadre though I still enjoyed my work. Ten years back we were working hard and smart, now we're working harder and smarter. No new recruitment was made and only peons were promoted as clerks who could do minimal work – no drafting skills or computer usage. If I retired, four employees, down the line, could get promotions.

I felt I could serve the Shed better by writing a book and creating awareness, and hope that things went well for the Shed in the future. I wanted to be the change to make the change for the better – a great gamble, no doubt.

Everyday thereafter, there were signs as if to emphasize that my decision seemed justified, like our train was late and more crowded in the mornings and evenings. The morning train was also advanced by 35 minutes but would still reach late. Coming to work by my bike in the heavy, unruly traffic and pollution was out of question, and by bus, it took more time, and would nauseate and cure us of seeking alternatives to the train. Whenever we felt bad about the train journey, we would think of other more affected daily train travelers who would travel much further. One Rural Bank lady worker had to go by the 8.a.m train and return by the 7.p.m one. Another few colleagues of mine, to avoid the higher living cost in Demblur, would reach home at Hindupur at 11:30 p.m and start again at 03:30 a.m. They knew the true value of a holiday or leave. This thought of we being more privileged, comparatively, was our pacifier.

Colleagues fell sick and we had to do their work at the cost of ours. My vehicle parking attendant asked me about my early retirement, for which I joked that he had increased the monthly parking fee by Rs.10 and that's why.

But the most important sign was that the General Election results were out and I had hoped for any one party to win with majority, and so it happened with the bonus of the Railway Minister being from our constituency. While all of Chiroti Shed was happy about the Railway Minister being from Demblur, the Divisional Office higher-ups were groaning that the frequenting of the Minister meant protocol and other arrangements like escorting him from/ to Airport, Railway Stations, apart from the execution of works. But this Minister, being aware, told the DRM and GM not to follow Railway protocol, and focus on their routine since, as an MP, he was entitled to security and escorts which would suffice. The Railways did not need to lose manpower, money and sleep unnecessarily. That sent a welcome and positive signal to all.

-:-:-:-

After a few days, my wife and mother started cribbing about my retirement, due to others' concern, comments and pressures. I took cognizance of that and sat them down and told them, "Look, I understand your problem. But stop living for others' thoughts or taunts about you or your family members. Start living for your opinion about yourself, your self belief in you and your family members. Encourage right, discourage wrong. In this case, keep your trust in me because what I am doing is not for myself, but for all. I know there are risks involved and in the worst case, we may have to sell our house and go and stay far, far away. But then, it is a well calculated risk which may pay off. It is an Arithmetic of Life and not just plain Math. Please understand my attempt, effort and purpose. There is no going back on my retirement now. With you cribbing or bickering, I will lose focus and make things only worse for ourselves. So please wait and watch." This explanation helped, to a great extent, to quieten and calm them down.

-:-:-:-

Our previous Sr. DME, now in Kerala, was visiting our Sr. DME and I met him in his chamber, in the presence of all officers. He heard me out and wished me all the best on my retirement. He turned to the other officers and told them, "You and I are all going to face problems in the future. The old efficient workers, on retirement, are either not replaced or the new recruits lack proper attitude. There will be no clerks and we have to manage somehow like how some Sheds and HQ are utilizing highly qualified Engineers to do clerical jobs. There are so many compassionate appointments as technicians. I wonder how they fail the clerk's aptitude exam and pass the technician's – that too mostly ladies. I have 81 ladies, and as on date, 43 of them are on Child Care Leave (CCL), wherein the Central Government has offered up to two years of paid staggered leave to mothers of children upto age 18, for two eldest children. When my CME asked me how I granted CCL to so many of them, I told him that I had to, at some point. I could not keep refusing. I also received a call from a Member of Parliament (MP) as to why I was asking a Class IV helper to clean toilets and do other menial jobs, when she was a double graduate and capable of doing better things. I told him that I give the work according to the designation, and not qualification. The girl in question was regularly absent and couldn't be risked being put in a Section. The MP threatened to transfer me to which I said that my suitcase was always packed and I was ready to go anywhere. I also told him that you fellows spoil the atmosphere in the Railways by transferring efficient officers for silly, unjustified reasons, while no Minister resigns or no officer is suspended when a major accident takes place, killing and injuring several people.

However, a high ranking Railway official was transferred because a Railway Minister, who arrived late, found his food was cold. Another was transferred, and an Engineer suspended, because somebody had left the Railway Minister's coupe's wash basin tap open, and all the water had drained out. I said I will see to it that she continues doing what she's doing. The MP threatened to remove me from service to which I told him that only the President of India has the powers to do that and the MP can only transfer me, at the most. These things left a bad taste in the mouth when we were already struggling to run the Shed with limited resources. In the Railways, at all levels, a donkey can be made a King and a King can be made a donkey. Some of these politicians use Railways like a prostitute to meet their selfish, populist ends."

When he came to know about the theme of the book, he said, "Good good! I heard about a writer who didn't want to be remembered; he wanted to be missed. I want your book to cause all dirty officers to get pissed, and their pretentious asses kicked – to the optimum that it should keep echoing in their bum."

He also said that we uniquely called ourselves as Human Beings, but now-a-days, we are less 'human' and more just 'being'.

27

MYSELF, HOMEBOUND!

Against a mandatory notice period of three months for Voluntary retirement (VR), I had given it six months in advance, anticipating delays of inefficiency from the administration. I found that my application was kept aside in the Personnel Department for more than three months and processed only after I complained to our Vigilance Department. A Personnel or HR Department is meant to serve staff and I hold them in high esteem, on par with noble professions, like Doctors and Teachers. But this Personnel Branch behaved as if the staff were meant to serve it and, save a few dedicated ones, worked at their own will and convenience, as if they were doing some great favour to the staff. I then sought details vide the Right to Information (RTI) Act and, hey presto, within two days of my application reaching them, I got the VR acceptance from the administration on 21st October without which, I would have retired anyway on 1st November, but unceremoniously.

I have to mention here that when I wanted to pay money towards the RTI application and get a receipt from Chiroti Railway Station's ticket counter, the Station Master said it was not possible since many people came, asking for tickets. I told him the purpose and told him not to give the receipt if he had no complaints about the Personnel

Branch. He immediately stopped the issual of tickets, gave me the receipt and even asked me to join him for tea, which I politely refused.

-|-|-|-

As an honour, my cricket wards arranged a farewell cricket tournament in which I played well and my team won in the semi-finals. Some IT train friends also joined us in the finals. In the finals, as an honour to myself, I gave the idea and opened the batting for both the sides, which was liked by all. That way, I ensured I was on the winning side and also that, in case I failed in one innings, I had another chance. I did well in both the innings and when I got out in the second, for my last innings on that ground, I could not hold back my tears, having played the maximum matches by anyone in that ground and having contributed immensely for the Shed cricket's well-being. The best part was being able to catch the 6.05 p.m train by the skin of our teeth along with my IT friends.

-|-|-|-

The retirement send-off in the Shed was a grand occasion and I was one of the beneficiaries of the reinvented send-offs. I was busy even on the last day, unable to prepare for my speech and had to deliver it extempore. Hema and Malini, along with my mother and a cousin attended the send-off, which was done in the presence of hundreds of Shed staff, with a proper stage and acoustics. Apart from 21 garlands and 17 shawls, I got a Locomotive model, a gold ring put by my wife thanks to the gracious gesture of my Sr. DME who normally does the honours. And I got a lot of kitchen items at which I joked whether I had retired or my wife, or whether they wanted me to step into the kitchen after retirement. When my turn came to give the speech, I huffed, puffed and managed to deliver one as follows, extempore;

"Respected dignitaries on the dais, dear colleagues and friends and, of course, my family members and relatives. I will ensure that you all catch the 4.00 p.m train after giving a few messages. From childhood, I wanted to be in the Defence Services as I thought you could serve the country best from there. Also, I wanted to be a soldier, not a commanding officer, so as to be where the action is.

I had passed an Airman Technical Trade's exam, but failed in the physical examination which preceded an obstacle course test. The evaluator told me that everything was right but for my height, due to which my chest was not in proportion. I told him that my body constitution was like that, and that I was an athlete having stamina and could prove myself in the obstacle course, for which he said he was sorry as he had to follow the minimum requirements, without any compromise. He told me that it could be probably that, if I looked like a tall, scrawny scarecrow, the enemy would become confident. I was disheartened and demoralized. I knew that my future Defence entry expeditions would also meet with the same fate. I lost interest in coming up in life.

Next, I passed the Staff Selection Examination for Clerks in various Govt. Ministries and incidentally, my posting was in the Ministry of Defence at Delhi. I was very happy that at least I was joining the Defence in civil dress, if not in uniform. But I was involved in this accident while going to join, and came here, with my first posting in that dungeon of a Store. I was depressed. I had even missed a bank interview on the verge of my second operation. But as days went by, I found that I really enjoyed myself here, as it was challenging and all my knowledge and skills could be put into good use. I felt like a soldier. After I went to the Sr. DME's office, I was thankful that I was first posted to the Shed so as to gain respect for the Shed and feel its pulse & pain, and was able to process its requirements with gusto.

Over the years, I experienced that the material mobilization in Diesel Sheds is one of the most difficult industrial activities in the whole world. In fact, later when I again compared Shed to the Defence, I found that you can serve the Country much better here. There, one can serve only if there is a war; otherwise you have to indulge in proxy wars, drill and exercises whereas, in the Shed, it is a daily war, to maintain the Locos and meet the deadlines. In the office, my main intention was to make our sister departments do away with unwanted misconceptions and help and root for our Shed. In this journey, I have to thank the patience and co-operation of first, my mother, and then, my wife who I involved in my dedicated service of the Shed. My son is playing Basketball nearby and hence couldn't come here. I was kind to work but cruel to myself and my family. Also, if I have hurt anybody with my talk during my service or now, I am not sorry in most cases, since I would have done it in the interest of the Shed or his or her personal development. Some of you cannot climb a Loco but there are enough works available without the need of going near a Locomotive. Don't think you are working for the Sr. DME or for your salary. Think that you are working for your Country. If you really want to serve the Country, this is your best chance! Compete with yourself, your own evaluation, not for others' attention. Also, don't think I am like a soldier who has deserted midway. I will be serving the Shed in a different, better way and you will all know it one day. I thank you all and the organizers for everything. For me, Chiroti Shed was a Celebration of Life

– like a second coming and another chance at Life! Thank you!" I looked skywards.

-|--|--|-

As a tradition, two or three retirees would pool together and sponsor lunch for all those who were available in the Shed. I wanted to change that tradition, and along with another like-minded retiree, gave coffee mugs stickered with our names which went down very well with the staff. I was particular that the 750 coffee mugs were purchased from a Jain businessman, for sentimental reasons.

-|--|--|-

On my retirement day, I was busy till the last minute, even after the function. My family had left in my cousin's vehicle and I went by train. As I was about to leave my office the last time, I went to the urinal where my bachelor friend gathered my colleagues and gave me a standing ovation as it was my last pee in service. Someone suggested even taking a photo when, while in action, I took a bow. As I finished and came out, I commented, "Ah! That felt good, now there are no dues left whatsoever. All over!"

I also recalled that in the 25 years of daily journeys by train, my greatest achievement was that I never had to use the train toilet even once!

Before boarding our train, I thanked my IT friends who wished me, and one girl by mistake said "Congratulations," and appeared embarrassed, to which I said that she was not out of context as her wish had complimented my having received official communication of the acceptance of my retirement, before my retirement date. Hence, I could retire with dignity and honour. However, I wanted them to alight from the train just like climbing down a ladder while facing it, as they were dangerously doing it in the opposite direction, and where there was no platform.

That evening, after I reached home, I felt very tired and sleepy – as if some huge burden of 25 years was off my back. The first sms I received read "Happy Independence Day." Only at 2.00 a.m when I woke up, the feeling sunk in and I was in tears. The feeling of fatigue continued for another two days, wherein I took sufficient rest and then started writing my book. I followed an office lifestyle at home – work on the book from Monday to Friday, take Saturday as weekly off, and Sunday was reserved for Tennis Ball Cricket. My wife also took it in her stride and even joked that she would pack lunch on my working days and send it to my work table. Sometimes our cat, Bheem, would give me company, sleeping peacefully on the side of my table.

-!-!-!-

Knowing some of the thick-skinned staff in Government offices, I had not yet got my retirement settlements, nor was the excess Income Tax deduction refunded. One thing about some apathetic staff or officials – there was no bias and all employees – whether hardworking or insincere, serving or retired - all got third class treatment at one time or another. Bank Interest rates were also about to reduce. Being desperate to avoid losing interest amount in the long run, I approached the considerate ADRM Madam, who gave instructions to the concerned and got the settlement payment made in the nick of time, thanks to a promotee Accounts officer, dealer and Budget-in-charge who went out the way and dealt it as a special case. The pension was to start after seven months!

-!-!-!-

Earlier, when in service, whenever technicians or engineers were sent to outstation firms to inspect/collect items, they used to ask me to speak to the firm, asking about the location etc. But now, after my retirement, they talked on their own. During one of my visits, I overheard them talking to one such firm, "What Sir, you are only telling us timings and location? Your only other competitor, when we went there for the same product, provided us transport, food and accommodation. We would prefer to buy their items in future." After the conversation, the technician winked at me and said, "When we arrive at their station, a red carpet treatment will be there in position. Did I do ok, Sir?" I replied, brimming with pride, "You couldn't have done better. But when did you go the place of their competitor?" He replied with a broad grin, "As far as I can remember, Sir, never!"

28

THE BOOK, THE IDEAS ABOUND!

The book progressed quite well. It was categorized as a fictional biography. I knew what to title it with an illustration on the cover, and also how to start and end it. But the real challenge was to sequence the other events in-between, keeping some humour as succor to serious proceedings. I had to keep it crisp even if crude, with my limitations, and combine two or more incidents/problems into one. While writing, I got more and more ideas and had to hold back and keep some in the reserves. I finished my first draft after a couple of months and then looked at all the points I had noted down while in Service, to see if they were incorporated. Then, I read it, incident by incident, from a layman's point of view, one who knows a bit of English, and made a final draft.

Then came my big plans of publishing. After exploring and weighing many options, I finally decided to go in for self publishing and recalled my journalist friend who had suggested Notion Press even before I'd retired. So I revisited their website and a few others but found them most suited for my purpose and convenience.

In their website NotionPress.com, I read the basic traits of the young and dynamic trio who headed the Self Publishing Company. My book's contents and mission quite matched their attributes. If one was a poet, another was a humor monger and the third used to get riled up by the social, political and cricket issues in India. It was love at first site.

So I registered for an appointment and insisted on meeting them all in their Chennai office itself, and gave a presentation;

"Guys, I'm Sachin Khanauji. I am a voluntarily retired Office Superintendent from the Railways, appointed there thanks to a train accident, and having to forego my Defence job. I worked for 25 years in a Diesel Locomotives maintenance Shed in Chiroti in Demblur and have outlined many of my life's experiences in this book."

As I kept a copy of my final draft on the desk, I briefed them about the significance of the cover, the title, the illustration and the book. "Through this book, I have brought forth many problems faced in Govt. offices and how Diesel Loco Sheds are affected the most. The book has a fairy tale type climax with an "all is well that ends well" conclusion, but with realistically possible solutions for many problems, along with some social messages. The mild suspense and the feel-good factors are the many goodies that befall the Diesel Loco Sheds, hard working Government Employees as well as the society, in the end. I want you to read the book and you have to play your part here because, until now, it is like an believable biography, and from now onwards, it is fiction, speculation and a series of dreams which can become true, one by one, starting with Notion Press. Whatever you feel about the writing, I am sure you will appreciate my gritty effort and the indomitable spirit. My SOUL is in that book and you have to bring life to your role in the book."

When they asked how the book could be a bestseller, I told them that it has a universal appeal. It's a heart-warming, heart-rending and a heart-winning story for all. I then told about the USP (unique selling point) of the book and the target audience or the readers. This book should start a movement and the readers will root for the protagonist and the purpose for which the book stands for. In the end, the book brings and spreads cheer. We should be able to generate enough media interest and create hype. "Once you read it guys, you'll see that the book has the potential to be the bestest seller and, if so, could even appeal to readers in and outside India, and be translated into many languages. But then the world's unpredictable. The book can create hysteria or history or become history."

In another few minutes, I was able to convince them and of my expectations from them, and they shook her hands with me and said, "It's a deal, Mr Sachin, which, subject to our reading the book and convincing ourselves, we'll seal." I thanked them and left, feeling positive about the whole proceedings.

-:-:-:-

The book was published in the second half of 2015, and being a new kid on the block, I was nervous. After a few days, luckily and thankfully, it did well and went viral on the net also. The reasonable pricing really had it going for it and its contents through word of mouth. Notion Press's end to end logistics and our campaigning also helped. It became a best seller in a very short time. The media literally had some food for thought and went gaga over the book, and started interviewing me as well as debating it with the Government spokespersons and Ministers. The opposition parties also threw their hat into the ring and the media had a gala time. I had my day in the sun and knew that all things – good or bad – are short-lived. So I made hay when the sun shone. The Jains were pleased about the way they were portrayed in the book and contributed in its sales. Libraries also lapped up the book in good numbers. Critics were also positive.

My 50-year old bachelor colleague was feeling disappointed that he didn't find a mention though he loved the book. I told him that there was more than enough content and I had to edit out his part. Moreover, he was a sincere worker and a boring, unmarried bachelor but for being the butt of all jokes – mostly dirty, perverted and insulting. I did a favour to him and the readers by not penning them down. I didn't need salacious content to sell, I had many other ingredients. I had even left out a hilarious situation exposing sex for favour.

Everyone was obsessed with the climax of the book, especially about the contents I had written in the book as to what happened after a few months of the book's publishing, apart from the media glare, hype etc. The book's climax had thrown an open challenge to the Government to become efficient and show to the world that they would remove the cobwebs of delays, inefficiency, corruption, outdated policies, misuse/abuse of power, ego trips etc. in their own backyard before giving confidence to outsiders to "Come to India" or "Make in India" or "Invest in India." The compliance of the key factor in the book was the Government's litmus test to show that they would actually do what they have been saying so far – that they would walk the talk and not just balk and squawk.

During a TV Interview in September 2015, I was asked;

Q - Do you think this Government will do it?

A - I trust this Government and I think they'll do it. It'll make History. It is not about the Govt. investing or spending money – it's about pulling up its socks and optimizing its efficiency.

Q - What if they don't?

A - They have themselves to blame and will need to hang their heads in shame. This book should whip their backsides. But if their backside is made of steel, or their heart is made of stone, I can't help it. I've not tried to get it done by hook or crook; I've visualized and proposed directly through a book.

Q - Where does that leave you? You have written and said that it's done.

A - It is just a speculation. If it happens, all the better, or I will be bitter. To make the book a reality or a fantasy is in the hands of the Govt.

Q - Don't you think you've bitten off more than you can chew?

A - Time will tell and you'll change your point of view.

Q- You already made an indication of the key feature of the climax during the outburst by a Bank Manager in the middle of the book.

A - Yes, I dropped a hint there. But first I should thank you as this question indicates that you have read the book properly, and in its context and view, and didn't make this a casual, just for the heck of it, interview.

Q - What does your gut feeling say?

A - I think Santa Claus will work overtime this Christmas, in the form of our Prime Minister and he will start announcing and giving goodies from the 1st of January 2016, till the Budget in February.

Q – So the Book and its mission is your target for the year 2015-16.

A – The book is my soul and its purpose is my Life's goal.

Q - What will you tell the viewers who have not read the book about the climax - to read the book?

A - No, I will tell the climax now itself. They'll read the book to cross-check the facts leading to the climax, out of curiosity.

Q - And what is the climax?

A – Here goes - the climax brings a lot of goodies, but the key feature will not come in the beginning of the climax; it will spring up quietly but suddenly in-between.

29

THE GOODIES, A MERRY-GO-ROUND!

Here goes the climax of the book! It is months after the book is published and is a hit. The goodies start pouring in, one by one, in the not so near, not so far future, from the Society initially, then the Industry and finally, the Government.

-|--|--|-

For the ensuing Diwali, Sachin involved the local MLA and Corporator to reduce/stop pollution and alleviate the torture to morning sweepers and the poor animals scared out of their wits at the sound and light of crackers.

It was to gently dissuade residents from bursting crackers and instead, collect Rs.50 (per ticket) from each house and arrange for a display of fancy crackers on three evenings in the big playground, where seating and safety arrangements were to be made and all house inhabitants (maximum four per ticket) would be invited in one ticket for any one day, which had safety instructions. During the daytime, till 6.00 p.m it was a carnival with stalls of games and food. Ambulances and fire tenders were also on standby. A live TV broadcast of the event was also arranged. Companies came forward as sponsors and advertised or gave samples of their products to all ticket holders. As money came through the sponsors, the MLA arranged for cakes, sweet and savouries for each ticket and a raffle was arranged with companies sponsoring prizes. Local film actors also came and entertained. As an extended part of the raffle, the actors also drew the winners and posed with them for exclusive selfies.

Budding local rock bands and orchestras also performed free. People got goodies much more than their ticket's worth. Everyone went home dazed, and with hope that this would be emulated in all constituencies. The fire cracker sellers, who used to be given temporary licenses, were given licenses to put up food/game stalls and/or seat vending with strict spot quality check, and they made more money in the three days, than selling crackers over ten days.

-¦--¦--¦-

Water purifier companies made a special drive to check their water purifiers for any UV light diode mischief and rectified them. They also acceded to the idea of no claim reduction of Rs.100 to Rs.200 from the next AMC charges wherever they didn't have to exceed the mandatory two visits and renewal within due date. This way, silly or crank calls, due to machine not plugged in or no electricity or water supply problem, stopped, with customers checking these before calling. The customer also felt good about renewing the AMC at a discounted cost. Also, while fitting and commissioning new purifiers or washing machines, without the knowledge of the manufacturer, the franchisees would 'fool' the customer into buying a Rs.2000 'water thinner'. This was also stopped through indications in bold letters in the operating manual front cover which showed genuine concern for the customer.

-¦--¦--¦-

My suggestions for making Indian Premier League Cricket more entertaining, and a win-win situation for players, spectators, viewers, broadcasters, franchisees, organizers, sponsors and Indian team selectors, were also accepted and became a grand success. I had felt that, in the second innings of a match, both teams could replace upto three players, to beef up their bowling or batting, respectively. During the toss, only eight players should be announced and the other three just after the toss, while being interviewed on the ground itself. Of the three changes in the second half, only two can be foreign players and replacing two foreign players mandatorily. By this, there would be an element of suspense as well as excitement, and even the bench strength utilised, and upto 14 players can be played in a side. Even those warming the bench, who were being paid fully, got a chance and franchisees got value for money. Batsmen could play more freely and high scores meant more entertainment and more viewing. At the same time, two out of five bowlers have to play while batting also, which means some Indian players will target those two all-rounder spots and strive for it, as India needs all-rounders in their national side. Others will target the specialist batsmen or bowlers' spot and not try to be all-rounders. Earlier, in one team abounding with foreign stars, one foreigner was not getting enough chances since only four were allowed per match. When he switched sides next year and played all matches, he became a legend in the first three matches itself because of his lusty hitting. Similarly, specialist bowlers also got chances and the scores, as well as the matches, became even more competitive. Power plays were for first four overs with the batting side deciding the other two, till the last over, so that strategies were changed in-between an innings, bringing in more unpredictability for either side. DRS or Decision Review System was also introduced, to add to the suspense.

The level of entertainment led to such a frenzy that the barely tested waters of USA also became T20 cricket crazy.

-:-:-:-

The FM Radio stations also acceded to my request. Many a song's starting jingle laid a beautiful foundation for the song and the Radio Jockeys used to blabber away during the jingle, played feebly in the background, till the start of the vocals. They stopped a second before the jingle now.

-:-:-:-

The AADHAR card, having received a lot of criticism, was upgraded as an all-in-one, one stop card for identification and transparency. Explicit details of the card holder were diligently and securely incorporated and linked at all possible levels – a person's identity, address location, bank and balance, income, expenditure, IT PAN card, marriage registration, family details, Passport, Visa, Assets and Liabilities, Healthcare, Employment Exchange registration with e-mail alerts for jobs, job counselling, jobs history for employers' and general monitoring, criminal records and rating, etc until death, but with confidentiality and regulation of details with limited, paid access and data updating only to concerned. Initially, there were problems with the black money lobby criticizing, finding loopholes. But later, it became a benchmark to reduce wrongdoings and clean up the society and system. Even the card holders could access a lot of information to learn and also see where they stood – both in terms of finance and credibility. The AADHAR card also became a major amalgamation to "Swachh Bharat."

-:-:-:-

For all landline and wireless/mobile phones, the STD or the roaming terms were dropped and all of India was made into one.

-:-:-:-

And now cometh the key factor of the Book – the implementation of the seventh pay commission for Government employees.

The delay in implementing the sixth pay commission in 2008 had brought in a lot of flak about the Government machinery. Now, merger of Dearness Allowance, to be done after it reaches 50%, was not done even after it reached 113%. It was told that the Government offices were a reflection of the Government in Delhi. And in this hi-tech age, if a critical decision to be made once in ten years is not done in time, it mirrors the image of India to the world that is looking for key indicators of proper governance. Any delay would indicate poor finances, tardiness and inefficiency, which was the last thing a Government needed, while reforming, motivating and building India, its image, and seeking foreign investment. It would show India as slow and unsteady. In trying to woo investors, delays in internal decisions would boo and shoo them away. The World was watching since this book also had made inroads there. Before setting about reforms, you should show how the Government performs. The newly setup National Institute for Transforming India Commission (NITI Aayog), which was to do away with slow and tardy implementation of policies, also took cognizance of this, and made the timely implementation of the Seventh Pay Commission as its flagship foundation to show the world that it meant business.

As per the deadline given by the Prime Minister, the Seventh Pay Commission's recommendations for the work and pay structure of Central Government Employees were placed before the Government in September 2015. This was taken up for discussion in the Winter Session of the Parliament on a priority basis, and finally, on the eve of 1st January 2016, the Prime Minister addressed the nation, announcing the acceptance and implementation of the new pay revision for lakhs of Government Employees and Pensioners, with immediate effect. This was a landmark decision which made history. All details were published on various Governments' websites for early and easy access to all. The Govt. took the bull by its horns this time. This sowed the seeds for a Confident, Credible India!

-|--|--|-

Ratnakar, an aged Government Pensioner, now counting his days, and his wife, were elated. The increased numbers in his pension brought him some dignity and financial independence. He felt he could die happy. His son, also a Government employee, was overjoyed as he could now afford to grant his son's wish to join the new school hostel which encouraged inherent sports' talents, balancing it with academics. Their maid servant was also happy and expected increased remuneration. Their landlord was the happiest, as he could raise the rent now itself and not wait for three years.

-|--|--|-

The Personnel Departments were also relieved that they didn't have to make calculations, miscalculations, misinterpretations and multiple work later to compute the arrears, as done in earlier delays. Employees wouldn't face income tax losses like in the previous occasions. Confusions/anomalies of retired employees' settlements, commutation of pension in the intervening period, due to delay, were done away with.

-|-|-|-

But this Pay Commission and Government also demanded its pound of flesh in terms of work optimization, and also termed that egotism, delays, inefficiency or the indifference to it, are also forms of corruption.

-|-|-|-

The irrational and biased downsizings/deployment of staff was done away with and rational downsizing was done with proper work study and representation from the grass root levels also. The work study also revealed that 70% of inefficiency was avoidable.

-|-|-|-

The Prime Minister also announced that the Pay Revision periods of Central Govt., Banks and Public Sector Undertakings differed and hence, there was a need for standardizing it and the disparity would be dealt with during the budget presentation in February.

-|-|-|-

Incentives were given and measures also taken to encourage small, joint families.

-|-|-|-

The Dearness allowance due for revision on the 1st of January and July every year, was always announced/given three months later based on the consumer price index for industrial workers for the preceding six months, that is July to December for January 1st. Instead, the calculation was advanced by three months, i.e. April to September, to facilitate timely payment and the DA %age was announced for January in the first week of January itself and likewise in July, to avoid arrears, supplementary bills and confusing income tax calculations, later.

-!- -!- -!-

Some State Govts. also adopted all of the above and benefitted.

-!- -!- -!-

The Railway Minister visited Chiroti Diesel Shed, held a lunch meeting and encouraged representations and discussions from all levels – not just the officer or Trade Union level. I was also invited to the meeting.

In the Railways Budget in February, the passenger fare subsidies were made more rational than populist. Focus was on increasing the efficiency of the Railways, not on fancy announcements. Cleanliness and Hygiene problems in stations and trains due to toilet discharges were addressed, seeking public suggestions, and prizes were given to the best solutions. The Loco driving crew/Train Guard vacancies were to be filled up to avoid harassing and overtaxing the existing, which could lead to accidents.

During railway accidents, the staff with supervising officers would be deputed to be with injured, shocked victims and take care of their basic needs until relatives or proper, manageable help arrived.

The e-reforms would be initiated and the Railways would be made e-Railway and paperless to the extent possible. All departments would be inter-connected and e-proposals processed with proper security and authentication, optimizing the Railway connectivity already available through RailNet.

-!- -!- -!-

The Productivity Linked Bonus base, which was a meager 3500, was done away with, giving room for higher revision as per the existing wages.

-|-|-|-

Due to the advent of Mobile Phones, Faxes and Internet, the works of stenographers were reduced and hence, volunteers were made to do clerical work also on computers and paid an extra allowance of 20% of their salary but with at least an average of four hours of clerical work per day, duly monitored and certified by the Office-in-charge. Similarly, the office staff who used computers effectively for more than four hours, thereby reducing the need for manual working clerks, were paid 12% of their Salary as computer allowance. Again, if they were on leave for more than 10 days, they wouldn't be paid that extra allowance that whole month.

-|-|-|-

The Railway Minister stated that from next year, the Railway budget would be merged with the General Budget since, when compared to the Defence budget, which is part of the General Budget, the Railways budget was a fraction. However, the Railway Minister would announce the highlights of the Railway's portion in the budget after the Finance Minister's presentation.

-|-|-|-

Once Black Money was traced and taken in, instead of budgeting in February, the exercise of Budget presentation was done on April 30th with tax payments by April 25th to get a correct picture and not revise or speculate, as being done at present. But interim Govt. related budget was announced on March 15th to avoid delay in Govt. payments till main budget.

-:-:-:-

A plan was also afoot to do away with Zonal Railways nomenclature and call it Indian Railways with one Schedule of Powers governing it.

-:-:-:-

The provident fund interest of all Railway employees in the old scheme was kept on par or higher than other Central Government offices. As the Railways were short of funds for projects and based on suggestions by Trade Unions, the Provident Fund and money from Serving and Retired Railway Employees were invited optionally as fixed deposits, with an annual interest of 10.5% paid monthly to retired employees, and quarterly to serving employees. The Government stood guarantee for the Principal amount and timely payment of interests.

-:-:-:-

Railway Recruitment Exams for similar non-gazetted posts would be called simultaneously at all Zonal levels and selected candidates would be strategically appointed, absorbed/swapped, so as to keep them in or near their hometown for taking less leave and improving efficiency. However, consistently inefficient employees would be transferred to their inconvenience.

-:-:-:-

Voluntarily Retiring employee should be counselled by a medical doctor or a personnel branch officer, duly evaluating the mental make-up and also the reasons behind it, in case the applicant is having some medical condition or harassment or work-related problem and if possibly, right the wrong.

-:-:-:-

Tax holiday was given for supplies/services made to the Railways since subsidies in passenger fares warranted that – especially in the tax/duty/levy structure in HSD oil. The Railways were given Defence-like status and privileges.

The Defence Canteen Stores Department-like facilities were also to be extended to serving and retired Railway employees by building them on Railways land with its women's welfare organization running it, as well as having a women's section where their products from art to apparel to food items were sold. But no Liquor was to be sold, neither in its original nor surrogate forms, like music CDs, mineral water etc.

-:-:-:-

Medical facilities to the Retired and Serving Railway Employees would be streamlined by reducing procedural bottlenecks to make the sickness and recuperation periods less painful, with barely any money spent by the patient or his family. Now, many more area-wise, reputed private referral hospitals, including all CGHS (Central Government Health Scheme) hospitals, would be available for direct hospitalization, with a single medical card, usable in all the hospitals. Earlier, nearby reputed hospitals were de-recognized accusing them over-billing, whereas those hospitals denied it. In fact, they said that they short-closed or didn't want to extend the Agreement with the Railways as their bills were not paid for months citing scrutiny and what not. The Railways countered that by saying that the bills were not raised regularly, but after many months by the hospitals, sending a truck-load of bills which had to be verified. These issues, which were scuttled at the higher level earlier, were now taken up on a war-footing and settled rationally with long-term sustainment of both parties. The Railway websites would educate all the medical related facilities and latest developments. Medical reimbursements were also to be scrutinized and settled within a strict time frame of 20 days.

-:--:--:-

Since TVs and monitors were now costing less, in major Railway Stations, in place of one, two monitor displays were kept side by side – one for entertainment/advertisement alone and the other for scrolling the train timings and other official announcements.

-:--:--:-

The Railway Minister announced that Incentives would be given to Diesel and Electric Loco Sheds from April 2016 by monetising the actual Loco outages against the monthly target, as well as the average salary of the number of vacant posts, duly subtracting any surplus. Incentives would not be given to employees for that month who were not on duty for any 10 days in that month or in the subsequent month, if a 10 day leave at a stretch staggered to that month. This would make staff think twice about taking and wasting leave.

-:--:--:-

Production units supplying material were to give traceability and other required details to the consignees for proper accountal of material and money. Production Units had less approval or funding problems, as they had every department, including the GM, in the same compound, whereas the problems were compounded for Sheds with corresponding departments and HQ being far away. So special and more powers were given in the Schedule of Powers to all Sr. DMEs considering their urgency, distance, technical complexities and processing problems. Emergency expenditure of upto Rs 3 lakhs per annum were empowered with Sr DMEs, and upto 10 lakhs per annum with DRMs for Diesel Sheds only, subject to a specified process, accountal and subsequent ratification.

Diesel Loco Sheds having 500 or more regular employees, irrespective of department, were given Canteen Subsidy.

A flexible formula for Stocking Locomotive Spares was introduced to mitigate the Materials management problems.

The General Conditions of Contract for Works Contracts were also customized to suit even awkward situations in Mechanical and other departments and made more friendly for Contractors' participation.

-:-:-:-

All signatures and initials in letters were to be made in blue or grey ink only and never in black or green. Ditto with rubber stamps!

-:-:-:-

A long standing Nemesis of HSD oil (High Speed Diesel oil) accountal and issues were solved in a beautiful manner with the intervention of the Railway Minister along with the Railway Board and the Public Sector Undertaking (PSU) supplying the oil, lubricants. HSD oil was received in Tank wagons or Lorry tankers and there were always quantity shortages measured due to temperature variation at loading and receiving point, pilferages and other 'factors' and while decanting to storage tanks for subsequent issuals. There were demands for a flowmeter at the time of decanting, which was never looked into. Instead, in one stroke, almost all the problems were solved in a better way.

The Railways were looking for downsizing and Govt. wanted to create employment in other sectors. So the whole issue of oil and lubricant receiving, decanting and issual was privatized diligently. Just like the PSU franchisees, a petrol bunk type arrangement was made and fuel/Lube oil issued to Locomotives. The Railways provided land and existing storage tanks and assets to the franchisee who employed his own workers with safety and security. The Lab testing of the properties of the oil and certain security aspects only were done by the Railways. The existing Railway staff members of the Fuel section were deployed for other core Railway activities.

-:--:--:-

Over the years, the big fat white elephant and the black sheep of the Indian economy became a winning horse.

-:--:--:-

Various Govt. organizations/Trade Unions wanted to felicitate me. I excused myself saying the main credit goes to the Govt. who I was confident about. So, work hard and sincerely for the Country to show your appreciation. I am honoured that you all read the book and helped take it to its ultimate objective. The Govt. was planning to do it anyway; the book and you only ensured there was no delay.

30

THE SWANSONG – WITH FULL LIGHTS & SURROUND SOUND!

As I was coming to the end of a TV interview, the host put forth his last flurry of questions...

Q – What was the best thing that could've happened to you in Life, in the Railways?

A – Almost everything – the accident survival and recuperation gave me a lot of mental strength. My sports' fitness and fighting spirit helped me recover early and positively. My employment in the Diesel Loco Shed was the best thing that could've happened to me. The accident survival was like a second coming and the Shed was like a CELEBRATION OF LIFE – all the ups and downs in it. I could be myself and, whatever I learnt or came across in life before the accident, everything complimented and complemented my work. It was also not about making money or searching for fame or looking smart or hard selling a product which was lame. I could be in India and contribute towards the Nation. Being a vital link in the all-important stores chain, the teamwork and role play learnt in cricket, came in very handy in setting up a proper foundation, making it smoother for the others to follow. The Shed's unity led from one thing to another, and now we have so many recreational, learning and skill-honing facilities. We are a benchmark for other Sheds in many aspects. I experienced all types of emotions and didn't require living on borrowed jokes or plastic smiles. In the rugged atmosphere, there was room for so many situational jokes, classy, cruel or corny and the laughing was natural and profound. I used to sleep so well; it was like I was dead in the night and then reborn in the morn. I felt blessed. Of course, the dedication meant having less time for me, my family, friends and I became a social outcaste. I used to introduce myself as 'a friendly guy who doesn't go around making friends'.

Q – So you feel you've achieved your dream?

A – My dream was to write a book, create awareness and hope for the best. Many a seed I have sown for India's progress to be shown. So far things have gone well. The purpose has got a good foundation but the job is still half done. The future looks positive. My wife may not leave me, now that my Voluntary Retirement doesn't look bad, when earlier she took me for mad. From being my better half, she'd become a bitter half, and now she is the brighter half.

Q – Any regrets?

A – Still love the Shed. Used to help many staff members on their Income tax. I used to drop Emergency Quota applications of all in the Shed in the box at Demblur. Miss doing that.

Q – Do you think the Railways can reform for the better? Is it now or never?

A - The Railways is the Soul of India. If only a token or superficial attempt is made, not removing the cobwebs of egotism and inefficiency, allowing the hitherto uncontrolled, unchecked hierarchy to remain, and permitting things to drift aimlessly again, instead of purifying the Soul, they can turn this celebrated Soul into a mocked Asshole. The Railways is an ocean, no doubt. But India is a bigger ocean. When progress can be achieved in India, can the Railways be left behind? Rather than now or never, at sometime or the other, the things will get much better.

Q – So you left no stone unturned for the purpose?

A – I have left some stones, but hope I didn't leave any bum unturned! The big bums matter more than the stones, you know! I hope I have picked on all the asses, of all grades, all classes, all shapes, all sizes, at all levels and whether fresh or pickled or rotten or even the forgotten. I would like to read out a sort of humorous poem about a retired Railway dignitary who thought he had escaped, his dirty deeds forgotten.

A KICK-ASS STORY.

Curious to see if his bad ass was pricked,
anxiously, one by one, pages he flicked.
He saw that all others' asses were ticked.
Some got away, just nicked or snicked,
while others got it bloody-royally kicked.
Just when he thought his was not picked,
he had not been, instead, he had tricked,
so far his was not smeared or lipsticked,
was ready to champagne and get rollicked.
But near the end, what he saw he panicked.
His was carefully and specially handpicked.
It was bashed, pulped, and grandly hoicked,
See how it'll be ripped, if in future, mimicked.

Q – What next?

A – Never thought beyond the book. Let me bask and savour my endeavour, and then I will think it over. First, I will take a long rest which will include a visit to my in-laws' coastal place. Then, translation to other languages or inspiring a film will be my next grace. Also wish that the Diesel Sheds' vagaries make it to sensible TV shows, in the next phase.

Q – Any more wishes in life?

A – Yes, with the book, I have to meet my Orthopaedic Doctor and the Physiotherapist who brought life to my life! But I have more wishes in my afterlife. If I had the option of meeting someone who has predeceased me, it would first be to reconcile with all my cats. I want to ask them what led to their premature deaths, and what could've been done to prevent them. They would've surely said, "Some human kindness, care and consideration would've stood us in good stead, then. Did you know that we cats are the vehicle of Goddess Shasti - believed to bestow children and assist during childbirth? And in India, instead, among domestic animals, we are the most unwanted and neglected." Looks like clerks and cats are meant only to be subtracted.

Q – And if you were reborn – would you want to work in a Diesel Shed?

A – Yes, but I would prefer to work in a Shed with Diesel Locomotives converted and upgraded to Hydrogen cell powered Locomotives.

Q – Satisfied with life?

A – I couldn't have asked for more, I couldn't have asked for more, because, if I had it easy in life, these moments I could not savour. It was a life worth living the encore.

Q – Any famous last words?

A – Yes, of course and here it goes – **AND SO I LIVED… AND SO I LIVED!!!**

GLOSSARY OF ABBREVIATIONS

ACP - Assistant Commissioner of Police.

ADME - Assistant Divisional Mechanical Engineer - Sub-ordinate officer in Shed. The junior most post among officers – Reports to Sr. DME

ADRM - Additional Divisional Railway Manager – Assists & Reports to DRM.

AMC - Annual Maintenance Contract of Machines/ Equipment.

CAG - Comptroller Auditor General – the Apex Auditor in India.

CEO - Chief Executive Officer

Ch.OS - Chief Office Superintendent – Office-in-charge of all OSes & Clerks

CME - Chief Mechanical Engineer – Principal Head of Department (Technical head for all Mechanical activities in a Zone). Sits in Zonal HQ & Reports to GM.

CMPE - Chief Motive Power Engineer – Technical Head of Department for Diesel Loco Shed activities only. Assists & Reports to CME.

CTI - Chiroti – Railway Station code.

CWM - Chief Workshop Manager – Head of a Railway Workshop but reports to CME of the zone where workshop is located.

DBRC - Demblur City – Railway Station Code.

DSL - Diesel

DME - Divisional Mechanical Engineer – Sub-ordinate officer in Shed

Dy.CMM - Deputy Chief Materials Manager – Stores officer in Headquarters

DRM - Divisional Railway Manager – The Head of a Railway Division under whom all Branch Officers of other Departments operate. DRM reports directly to the GM

GCC - General Conditions of Contract – governs all Works contracts.

GM - General Manager - Head of a Railway Zone which has Divisions.

HQ - HEADQUARTERS or the Zonal Office Headquarters.

HSD - High Speed Diesel oil used as fuel in Locomotives.

IPF - Inspector of Railway Police Force.

JE - Junior Engineer – Technical Supervisor one grade below SSE.

LF - Loco Foreman of the Shed – same redesignated as SSE.

MIO - Material Inspecting Official – Nodal point of Material Management in Sheds, monitors, arranges all the Shed's requirements, repairs. Later redesignated a SSE/Stores

MNC - Multi National Company.

MP - Member of Parliament.

NS - Non-stocked items being procured on need basis. Stocked items or regular items are procured and monitored by Stores Department.

OEM - Original Equipment Manufacturer.

OS - Office Superintendent – Supervisor of Clerks.

POH - Periodic Overhauling of Locomotives done in specific Workshops.

RC - Rate Contracts - wherein specified items/ AMCs could be purchased/ exercised by all departments instead of multiple tenders

RDSO - Research Design and Standards Organization – Technical & Safety consultant and Advisor of all Departments of Indian Railways.

RPF - Railway Protection Force – Railway police.

RH/PER - Railway Hospital at Perambur – full fledged hospital.

SIPF - Sub Inspector in RPF

SMM - Senior Materials Manager – own office head in Diesel Sheds to maintain the Diesel Stores Depot (DSD) which handles, monitors and procures Locomotive spares (mainly Stocked items).

Sr.DFM - Senior Divisional Finance Manager– Divisional Accounts head who verifies/ approves Shed and all other Division's proposals.

Sr.DME - Senior Divisional Mechanical Engineer - the overall-in-charge of a Diesel Loco Shed coming under Mechanical Branch, Diesel wing. Also called a Branch Officer. Another Sr.DME is also in Division for other Mechanical Branch activities. Both report directly to DRM in Division but to CME, the technical head in Zonal Headquarters.

Sr.DPO - Senior Divisional Personnel Officer – Head of all staff matters in the Division. Reports to DRM.

SO - Section Officers in Accounts who scrutinize our proposals, bills.

SOP - Schedule of Powers delegated by the GM to all his sub-ordinates. SOP governs all the activities in a Division or Workshop or any Zonal Railway entity.

SSEs - Senior Section Engineers in Diesel Shed with one SSE/Genl. having an office and being overall-in-charge for staff and maintenance activities in Shed. Other SSEs are in-charges of Sections.

SWCR - South West Coast Railway abbreviation.

TC - Ticket Checker

TTE - Train Ticket Examiner